# OREGON STATEHOOD

## (EZEKIEL'S JOURNEY BOOK III)

## JOHNNY GUNN

**WOLFPACK PUBLISHING**
— EST 2013 —

**Oregon Statehood**
**(Ezekiel's Journey Book III)**

Johnny Gunn

Paperback Edition
© Copyright 2018 Johnny Gunn

Wolfpack Publishing
6032 Wheat Penny Avenue
Las Vegas, NV 89122

ISBN: 978-1-64119-039-8

I

---

# BOOK TEN: ONE PROBLEM AFTER ANOTHER

"THEY TOLD ME TO COME TO OREGON TERRITORY because of the good water." Zeke Hawthorne shook his fist at the downpour. "The last time I saw this much water was when I crossed the Mississippi River." Spring thaw also brought spring rains with enough water to wash the Willamette Valley into the Columbia River. "How are those dikes holding up, Hiram?"

"They're holding, Papa. I've got everybody out with shovels and those diversion ditches are working, too. Sure, glad we emptied those ponds before the thaw."

"Were you able to get up to see Silas Williams last week?" Zeke had been in Salem City on legislative business and asked his son to make the thirty-mile ride to Williams' ranch.

"I spent a day with him, Papa. He can sure tell stories. Did you know he fought Santa Ana? Anyway, as you thought, there have been outlaw problems north of us along the River Road. He thinks it will get worse when the springtime immigrant wagon trains start coming through."

"I found out about outlaw trouble brewing south of Eugene, also," Zeke said. "These roads through the valley, the roads along the coast, carry so much merchandise. They are economic drivers for the territory, but now they have become magnets for those that have no use for the law."

"Mr. Williams said almost the same thing, Papa. He said something about those that break the law go where there is no law."

"Makes sense to me," Zeke said. "I can't keep up with you and that shovel of yours, old man. Too much time being an assemblyman and not enough time being a farmer."

"You're still bigger and stronger than I am, Papa," Hi laughed, piling mud and more mud on top of a dike.

Hiram had joined the family in 1852 just as they were leaving Fort Bridger for the long wagon trip to the Willamette Valley in Oregon Territory. He was twelve, as near as anyone could tell at the time, the son of an old trapper and his Shoshone wife. Zeke and Sarah adopted the boy and he had thrived over the years.

Hiram was skinny, had little education up to that point, and hadn't been trained into any kind of work. With Ezekiel's background in farming, cabinetmaking, and metal working, the boy blossomed and now was all but running the large farm. The Hawthorne farm, grown from its first quarter section to a full section, six hundred forty acres. They operated the properties as one unit.

"We've had a good winter, son. Lots of snow up in those mountains and good rain down here. It's just that sometimes old Mama nature overdoes herself. I've seen hundreds of young deer and elk so far this spring."

"Those mules have become fine ditch diggers, Papa, and the Saunders brothers haven't taken a break in days." They hadn't seen the sun all day but assumed it was close to sunset just because it got a little darker than it had been. "Mama said she's roasting an entire shoulder of pork and I'm worried that you and the twins might not get any," Hiram laughed, ducking a swat from Zeke.

"Aren't you glad the legislature broke up in time for all this springtime work?" Hiram and Zeke spent a great deal of time joshing with each other. Ezekiel Hawthorne was serving as one of the Willamette Valley members of the territorial legislature and missed a lot of time on the farm due to political and territorial duties.

This last session began in December 1856 and had ended in February1857, and Zeke felt he could reach out and touch statehood; that it was finally going to happen. It had been a huge fight and he knew it wasn't going to be a waltz in the door, but could sense people throughout the territory anticipating statehood.

"Don't you worry your head about that, old son. I've got a lot of years left in me and just one more session of the legislature to worry about. Then, you'll be wishing I was off on some political adventure instead of being Boss of the Farm."

They were laughing and joking, peeling out of rain-wear, pulling muddy boots off on the weather porch, and walking into a warm kitchen. "That smells good," Zeke said. He gave wife Sarah a big hug and stuck his head over her shoulder to smell what was in a large cast iron Dutch oven.

FOUR MEN WERE HUDDLED around an open fire burning in what was left of a trapper's cabin, built sometime around 1830. "Might as well not even be a roof on this fine castle of ours," Hank Jenkins griped. The dirt floor was slowly becoming a quagmire, but at least the fire kept them warm.

"We'll be good here, but when the weather breaks some we got to get down into that broad valley, boys. They ain't no law along the Willamette River from Salem City north, according to some fellers I talked to."

One-Eyed Frizell added a couple of logs to the fire. "Hank, when I started up the trail earlier today, I spotted a ranch that we hadn't seen before when we were scoutin' out this country.

"Saw a man and woman out near a barn. They couldn't see me, and I watched 'em for a few minutes. She was a looker, Hank, and I didn't see no kids or other people around."

"What are you thinkin', One Eye?" Jenkins and the others were most interested in that comment about a fine-looking woman at a ranch near-by. "Besides the woman, you see anything else we might want?"

"Ranch house isn't new, so they been there for a while. Probably got stuff. Got food for sure. When the rain quits we could ride over nice and friendly like and take what we want."

"Why wait?" Jenkins looked around at the other three and got nods from all. "Let's just go be neighborly, boys, and bring some good food back with us."

"And something warm, too," Ornery Smith cackled, doing a little Texas two-step across the muddy floor.

Joshua Peterson walked out on the porch when his wife Edith pointed out riders coming up the lane. "Howdy," he said. "Kinda wet to be out for a springtime ride, boys. Come on in and get dry."

"Don't mind if we do, friend," Hank Jenkins said, stepping off his horse. He and the three outlaws tied off and walked up on the porch. Peterson held out his big hand to shake and was clubbed unconscious with the butt end of a rifle, swung by One-Eyed Frizell.

Edith Peterson screamed when she saw her husband's head smashed, and made a fast dash to the fireplace where the couple kept their weapons. She was reaching for a shotgun when that same rifle butt knocked her to the floor.

Jenkins and Smith dragged Joshua's limp body in and tied him to a chair while Lefty Thompson and One-Eyed Frizell made plans for Edith.

"Later," Jenkins growled. "Let's see what we can claim first."

They were riding up to their old cabin within the hour, each man carrying a large sack of food and there were sacks filled with jewelry and some gold and silver coins. "We've done better," Ornery Smith said. "Damn woman scratched the hell out of me. But I showed her who was boss."

"Sure did," Lefty Thompson laughed. "You might have broke her nose and split her lip, but you ain't gonna stand up straight for a long time."

Ornery Smith stepped off his horse, his big, right hand hovering close to his belted knife. "Want to take that one more a little bit?" he snarled, slipping the blade free, daring Thompson.

"That's enough," Jenkins said. "We all had some fun, we got some good grub and a little money, and nobody got hurt. Let's get that fire up. Looks like we might even have some sunshine later."

"Shoulda brought that wildcat with us," One-Eyed Frizell said. "She was a looker."

THE KITCHEN at the Hawthorne farm was long and wide, and was headquarters for meals, for political conferences, for family gatherings, and was usually more than chaotic, with twin girls, Susanna and Joanna scampering around, the youngest of the brood- a boy named Travis- on his hands and knees, and housekeeper Rebecca Williams trying to herd the menagerie.

The farm had four fulltime employees, Skinny and Sam Saunders, and Toby and Brian Stockbridge. During spring planting and fall harvest, Zeke often hired many others. Wheat, corn, beans, rye, and hops were the main crops, and an apple orchard had been plotted out and planted two years earlier. Hiram raised hogs and lambs both for the family and commercially, and Sarah had a large kitchen garden as well.

The kitchen table was groaning under the weight of two massive Dutch ovens and platters of potatoes, vegetables, and baskets of steaming biscuits. Generally, the Saunders and Stockbridge boys cooked their own suppers in the bunkhouse, but during stormy weather, Sarah liked to make sure they were fed proper and had them in the family kitchen.

Weather dominated most of the conversation. "When will we be able to get the corn and beans in?" Sam Saunders asked.

"Even when the rains stop, it will be some time before the ground is dry enough to plow," Zeke said. "If all these ditches keep working and the dikes keep holding, it will speed up the process. We won't run out of work, gentlemen," he chuckled.

"I'm more worried about the spring salmon and steelhead runs," Hiram said. "The creek across our place is so high they won't be able to spawn. The Willamette River is almost over its banks, too." Almost to emphasize what he just said, there was a massive bolt of lightning and thunder shook the large farmhouse, scaring the little kids.

"Maybe we ought to not worry about the ditches and start building an ark." Hiram chuckled as another lightning bolt flashed across the sky. "I'm just glad we terraced those hills for the wheat and beans. Those hillsides wouldn't be there if we hadn't."


"THOSE PEOPLE ARE GOING to be working all spring and summer to promote the statehood platform, George, and we have to see to it that our program is not left out." Peter Flowers was a cattle rancher along the Willamette River north of Salem City and a strong believer in Oregon becoming a slave state. He was having a late supper with territorial assemblyman George Belknap at Belknap's farmhouse, near Eugene.

Belknap had lost his wife a few years ago and the old

home had changed considerably from when Maryanne held sway. Paintings didn't always hang level anymore, nor were they dusted regularly. In fact, cleaning was not done on any kind of schedule. Belknap had not bothered to hire a housekeeper and he didn't really give a hoot about the way the place looked.

A member of the landed gentry where he grew up in Virginia, Belknap came west and while he was a successful rancher, his dignified ways stayed in the east. Friends accepted him as the slob he was, and with his quick temper, few ever mentioned his less than adequate table manners or manner of dress. His high level of arrogance was always present.

"Because of idiots like Clive Newton and Bud Best, I almost lost my seat in the assembly, Pete." Newton and Best were members of Oregon Firsters, and were responsible for the death of assemblyman, Nate Bishop. "Whatever we come up with, we have got to shy as far away from those fools as possible. And, before you say anything, I'm well aware that publicly denounced Newton, Best, and the Firsters is what led to the big ruckus! We won't make that mistake again, either."

George Belknap had gone to the press denouncing the Oregon Firsters and several members by name after giving the Firsters the impression that he was backing them. It was probably a Firster who'd assassinated Assemblyman Nate Bishop with a gunshot to the back as he entered the legislative building two years earlier. Sheriff Fred Sharp was never able to make an arrest in that matter, or any other atrocity that took place during that legislative session.

The question of how Oregon would stand on the

subject of slavery was being discussed throughout the territory, sometimes at extreme levels. Many knives had become part of discussions, many friendships had ended because of the question, and the possibility of statehood was somewhat in doubt because of it.

The country was divided on the question of slavery, with most of the southern states fully behind the proposal while northern states were mostly against it. It was the newer frontier territories wishing to come into the union that might change the balance, and it wasn't fully known how the congress and the president would react if Oregon wished to be a pro-slavery state.

The territory had a black exclusion law dating to 1844 that banned free blacks from coming to Oregon. There were many that demanded the exclusion law be contained in any constitution written for the State of Oregon. Besides the exclusion law, there were also many that were demanding Oregon be a slave-owning state.

Belknap had arrived in Oregon from his family home in Virginia. He believed strongly in slave ownership and supported the exclusion law. Some of his followers were far more criminal than political and he was aware that he had little control over their actions.

Belknap continued, "I think our plan should be to work on members of the legislature to get their support rather than try to sway public opinion." He sat back in a large leather chair and took a long drink of bourbon. "The public won't have an opportunity to vote until the legislature creates the constitution after the constitutional convention is called. We need to work for the support that will really count, in the legislature."

Flowers was standing in front of the fireplace, drink in

hand, thinking about what George Belknap had just said. "Going to the various members of the legislature makes sense, George, even though I would prefer using strength on some of those soft-hearted fools. I wonder if some of your legislative friends might be swayed should certain incentives be included in our arguments?"

"Incentives?" Belknap sat a little straighter in the chair. "Are you suggesting bribery or buying a vote or two? I'm not sure I could support that, Flowers."

He had a sneer on his face and in his words as he said this, and poured himself another drink.

Flowers shrugged. "Outright bribery? No, that would come back and bite us, for sure. Someone like Hawthorne would trumpet that up and down the river. I'm thinking more along political lines, George. Tit for tat and all that. We'll support this if they'll support that, and maybe throw a little business their way as well. Make it well worth their effort to support our platform."

"I suppose helping one of our fellow legislators in their business ventures wouldn't be classified as a bribe," Belknap murmured. "Trading votes happens all the time, but the idea of seeing to it that certain members' businesses are taken care of might help sway a vote or two."

His thoughts immediately turned the other way, but he did not bring this up in their continuing conversations. *If their businesses, homes, or families are threatened... not by a fellow legislator, but by an outsider, it might have about the same affect.* Belknap had a nasty smirk on his face as he thought about who might be available to begin such an effort.

It was those same thoughts that backfired two years earlier but the man had not learned his lesson.

"I think you might be right, Flowers. I'll work up a list of those who might be against our program and see what kind of businesses they're in. We can then work toward making their lives a bit nicer if they should swing their support our way." *And maybe a bit ugly if they don't.*

The meeting broke up without Belknap ever offering his guest anything other than a warm fire and a glass of bourbon. It never entered his mind to suggest a light supper or a platter of meats and cheeses. Bourbon would be his supper and Flowers was on his own.

Belknap had the rest of the spring, summer, and fall to build that support. Many believed that the legislative session of 1857-58 would make the call for a constitutional convention, and would have a state constitution drawn up and ready. This session would be their last stand to bring Oregon into the union as a slave owning state.

Belknap mused, *If we could sway votes by way of offering business help, we could offer more if we were very careful of who we offered it to. I can name several members right off the top of my head that could use a bit of financial help. And I know there are others that might flinch over the suggestion of problems cropping up in their cozy little lives.*

THE ORIGINAL TERRITORY of Oregon was huge; extending from the Pacific Ocean all the way to the continental divide in the Rocky Mountains, from near the Canadian border south to the Utah Territory, with Washington Territory making up the northwest quadrant. Those east of the Snake River, wanted to break away and become Idaho Territory, and that happened in an interesting way.

The area simply became the Unorganized Idaho Territory, and part of that then became the Unorganized Wyoming Territory. There were no legal treaties, it was simply accepted as fact. Oregon Territory then extended south from Washington Territory to California and Utah Territory, and east from the Pacific Ocean to the Snake River. There were four distinct geographic areas in the territory. There was coastal Oregon, the Willamette Valley Oregon, the Columbia River Oregon, and the Eastern Great Basin Oregon.

Each had distinct climate, political, and economic bases. The question of slavery was argued vehemently in all areas. Many of those coming to Oregon in the 1830s and 1840s were from Missouri, Virginia, and the Carolinas, and were well aware of the slave owning concept of economics. Farms of vast size were always worked by slaves. Those coming from the northern states and territories were more familiar with smaller, family worked farms.

As Oregon developed, the farms and ranches that succeeded were not the southern plantation size, rather more like the Pennsylvania family-farm size. The only black people in the territory were slaves brought by southern emigrants. The territorial constitution allowed for slaves to be brought in, but slaves were not to be bought or sold. Free blacks were not welcome.

Many of the questions facing the citizens of Oregon Territory in 1857 had already been discussed and answered in California, almost ten years earlier. Many of those same questions would be faced in Utah Territory, and other sections of the west.

Along with statehood, the citizens were also plagued

with problems relating to the huge numbers of immigrants moving into and through the territory. Questions dealing with native populations, water rights, property ownership, education, and transportation were rampant at every meeting of two or more people. The Indian population along the Snake River was incensed over how the immigrants with the wagon trains were killing game and the fact that their stock was eating grasses the native's stock needed.

Western Shoshone, Bannock, and Northern Paiute tribes were fighting back; killing immigrants, stealing stock, and burning wagons. The call for the army to come to the rescue was heard regularly. Oregon volunteer companies were formed, companies of California volunteers were called upon, and regular forces from Utah Territory were also on the march often along the Snake River. Thousands of wagons filled the Oregon Trail from spring to first snow.

## 2

HELLO, MR. O'BRIEN," Hiram said. He took the lead rope from Michael O'Brien's horse as the big cattle rancher stepped off.

"Papa's in the blacksmith shop. Should I put your horse in the corral or just tie him off?"

"Corral would be good, Hiram. I might be here for a while."

O'Brien raised beef for meat and hides and was one of the Hawthorne's good customers for corn and wheat. The O'Brien ranch was less than five miles north of Hawthorne's and the two families had been close since Ezekiel's arrival in the territory.

The man stood a full six feet plus and weighed well over two hundred pounds. He was just as strong and burly as he looked, and Hiram watched him stride toward the ironwork shop wondering just how powerful the man might be. Hiram had helped at a branding the spring before and remembered seeing O'Brien lift a large steer clear off the ground.

"Morning, Zeke," O'Brien said. "Got time for some talk?"

"Always have time for you, Mike. Is there a problem?"

"Maybe," the rancher said. "I lost three fine steers last night, and they didn't just wander off. It's the second time in two weeks that some of my prime beeves have been rustled. I've heard that people traveling along the River Road have been robbed. Even Johnson's wagons have been robbed!" Mike sighed.

"There's a band of outlaws working this territory, Zeke," he continued. "What have you heard from Sheriff Sharp? I've lost a lot of money."

"You're not alone, Mike. Hiram and I were talking about that at supper last night. It seems that a man named Henry Jenkins has put together a group of criminals into an organized gang. Most of the men have drifted in from California and some from New Mexico and Texas. I'm not sure that Fred Sharp is even aware of any of this. His business is strictly inside Salem City, and I don't think his chief deputy, Simpson, has ever even been this far north."

"Something needs to be done, Zeke, that's why I'm here this morning. You're an assemblyman, a leader, and you can get things done. I'm just an old cowman. I can talk to you all day about cattle, but I don't know what to do about this problem we're facing. Those immigrants on the highway are being robbed and threatened, my cattle are being stolen, and I've heard that some farmers have been accosted right in their homes.

"What can we do?"

"Mr. Peterson and his wife were attacked last week," Hiram said. He had come in and heard O'Brien talking. "They took a lot of gold and silver from Mr. Peterson."

Hiram sat down on one of the benches. "Mr. Peterson was hurt pretty bad and the men also attacked Mrs. Peterson. Joshua Peterson is one of the nicest men I know."

"I didn't know that," O'Brien said. He took in a deep gulp of air. "Those bastards break in and frighten my wife- they'll die on the spot. This has gone far enough." The fury was evident in the burly man and the muscles in his jaw, along his neck, and in his massive shoulders that were tensed for battle.

"Fred Sharp's job is Salem City Sheriff, and as far as I know, we don't have any actual sheriff or marshal along the Willamette River or the valley area. The county commission has never created such an office," Zeke said. "I can suggest it to the commission, but even if they agree that we need a marshal, it would be some time before that happened."

"I can't wait for that," O'Brien said. "No, we need something right now."

"I know we do." Zeke walked over to the potbelly stove and grabbed the coffee pot and poured coffee for the three of them. His mind was working hard as he distributed the cups and found a flask to add some taste to the coffee. If he put a little rum in the coffee it might calm the big Irisher down some.

"Hiram, you ride out and spread word up and down the valley that there will be a general meeting of all the farmers and ranchers here at our farm, in five days. The purpose of the meeting is to form a Willamette Valley Farm Protective Association and end the criminal activity. Can you do that?"

"I'm on my way, Papa," he said, walking out toward the barn. "I'll bring everyone I can find."

"That's a fine idea, Zeke. Then what?" O'Brien had his Irish up and wanted more than what he'd just heard. Zeke knew it might take a bit of time, but O'Brien wanted action this very minute.

Zeke refreshed their coffee and rum and walked out toward some benches that were set up under wide cotton-wood trees. "Let's bounce this around some, Michael," he said.

\* \* \*

HANK JENKINS PACED around a small fire, watching some of his riders come up the long trail from the River Road. The camp was nestled in a heavily forested area that was several hundred feet above the big river that split the valley. From the River Road, the camp could not be seen and Jenkins demanded that fires be small and smokeless. "Now that the rain's quit, this is a much nicer place than that foul cabin. Keep that fire low, boys. We don't need nobody knowin' we're here."

The trail made several looping horseshoe bends and turns and gave the impression that it really didn't go anywhere. There was no indication that it had been used by horsemen or wagons for some time. Standing orders for his men were to not use the trail that led off from the River Road, but to come in cross country until they were far enough off the main road that their prints wouldn't be seen. Most of the gang members followed his orders, but not all of them.

The camp was at the head of the alluvial plain and in big rocks and boulders that screened them from anyone's view. It was almost a perfect outlaw's hideout and Jenkins was pleased with himself in finding it.

Jenkins had learned the art of stealing cattle during a two-year spree in Texas, being chased through New Mexico and ending up serving time in a miserable prison near the Mexican border. It was there that he met the men he now rode with, including one he called Ornery. Jacob Smith was ornery to a fault and Jenkins was taken by his obnoxious behavior.

"Did you really smack that little girl?" Jenkins listened as a couple of his gang described robbing a wagon coming up the River Road that morning.

"Little bugger tried to bite me," Smith said. "Yeah, I knocked her on her kazoo. Taught her a thing or two."

Laughter spread around the fire when One-Eyed Frizzell asked if she drew blood or whiskey from the bite. Even Smith had to laugh. One-Eyed Frizzel was wanted in Texas and Louisiana for cattle rustling, and there were always rumors that followed the man with the black patch about dead men on his back- trail. He carried an old flint-lock pistol that probably hadn't been fired in years.

His weapons of choice were a wide bladed, long knife and a short, thin-bladed dagger he could pull from his boot. Frizzel spent hours each week keeping those knives razor sharp. Hank Jenkins was also a knife man, and considered most of the handguns available, inferior in a fight.

Tom Peabody led Teddy Jewel and Irish Jack Wellington into the deep forest and rock-strewn camp. "Got a group of three wagons coming up the road, Hank. They be about two hours out from here. Only one outrider and he's carrying an old flintlock rifle. Should be easy pickins."

Peabody was another Texas cattle thief with a price on his head. When Jenkins and One-Eyed Frizell broke out of that miserable jail along the Mexican border, and brought Ornery Smith with them, it was Peabody who'd shot the two deputies guarding them with their own pistols as they slept. "Me and Irish Jack drove the cattle into Portland and got a good price for 'em."

He stepped off his pony and handed a leather pouch to Jenkins. "That's got a good heavy feel to it," Hank Jenkins smiled. "Three wagons, eh? That would probably mean no less than four men, what with the outrider and all. I prefer just one or two wagons, but with three, there would be more gold." He was joined by the others in an ugly chuckle.


MOST OF THE families coming into Oregon Territory came with all their worldly possessions; including silverware, jewelry, and money, usually in the form of gold and silver coins. Those in the east might have a liking for paper money, but not on the frontier. It was hard metal or nothing. Spanish and Mexican coins were far more trusted than paper money.

For many, it had taken years to accumulate enough gold and silver to make the great adventure into the frontier and they hoped they had enough money on hand to buy good land and live for at least one, maybe two seasons before their farm or ranch started paying back.

With at least three families in this train, there could very well be many hundreds of dollars in Double Eagles,

Spanish Reals, and silver dollars. "I don't suppose you talked a bit with that outrider, did you, Mr. Peabody?"

"I most certainly did, Hank. I told him about a very nice little spot a bit off the River Road where they could spend a comfortable evening, have plenty of grass for their animals, and sweet water to boot."

"Okay, then. Gentlemen, we'll ride out to that little pasture in about an hour and see for ourselves just how much money these pilgrims wish to deposit with the Hank Jenkins trust fund."

HIRAM HAWTHORNE PUT his horse into a strong trot riding north on the River Road trying to remember where each of the ranches and farms were along the lush valley. He knew there would be at least five stops before he ran out of daylight and then four or five more the next day. His first stop was going to be Joshua Peterson's place.

"I know you think you're about the toughest man in the valley, old son," Zeke said as Hiram was saddling up, "but there are criminals operating up and down that road. You go armed, young man."

Hiram didn't need to be told twice and put his Hawkins cap-lock rifle in a saddle scabbard, grabbed his favorite bow and lashed a quiver of arrows across his back. "Don't worry, Papa, although, if Moose was with me I'd feel better." Hiram had been learning the art of metalworking from Zeke for several years and strapped his favorite knife on. It was Damascus steel that he had worked up into a piece of art. Honed, razor-sharp art.

The blade shone with all the brilliance and color of that fine steel, the edge was as sharp as a scalpel, and the handle was elk horn that fit his hand like a kidskin glove. "I could start a war, Papa, but I won't. I'll hurry back."

Peterson had been farming in the Willamette Valley since the territory came into existence, back in forty-eight. He met his wife on a visit he made to Fort Vancouver one spring to sell furs he had trapped during the long winter. Edith Peterson was tall and thin with flaming red hair she kept long and braided. Peterson said she was his protection, and then ducked when she took a poke at him.

Their marriage was warm, loving and filled with humor. The only sadness was from their inability to have children. Edith worked right alongside Joshua on the farm and they raised corn and wheat, supplementing their income by smoking salmon during the runs, and winter trapping. It was a marriage made of frontier life.

Hi made the turn off River Road onto the Peterson trail and back through two small hills before reaching the main ranch. The farm was a full three miles back from the River. *Maybe that's why the gang attacked Peterson. Can't be seen from the road, and no neighbors even slightly close.*

When Hiram rode over the top of the second little hill and looked down on the Peterson farmhouse, he saw Joshua come out onto the porch, a long rifle in his hands. *Bit once and he ain't gonna let it happen twice,* Hi chuckled. He waved and rode slowly up to the fence in front of the house.

"Howdy, Mr. Peterson," he yelled from a hundred feet out. "It's Hiram Hawthorne. I need to talk to you."

"Ride on in, Hiram. It's good to see you. My goodness, you've grown a foot since I last put eyes to you, boy. Step down, let's talk." Peterson let the rifle come down from the ready position and opened the gate for Hiram after the strapping boy tied his horse off.

It was about half an hour later that Hi rode back to the main road and took the turn north. *He's a good man. It was a shame that he just walked out on the porch and welcomed those men to his home. He'll kill that Jenkins fellow if he ever sees him again. Probably sell his skin,* and he laughed, kicking his horse into a strong trot. *I might even let him use my good knife.*

He spoke with cattle rancher Amos Johnstone, then Silas Williams, and figured he would not make it to the Whitman ranch before sunset. *I'll have just three places to see tomorrow and then I can ride straight home. I like old Silas Williams. I bet he was hell on leather when he was younger.*

Williams was straight out of Texas, rode with the Texians when they whipped old Santa Ana, and carried scars from frontier fights dating back to the twenties. "Oh, Hiram, I hope your papa has some good answers for what's going on along this here valley. Those are some bad men, and I know what I'm talking about.

"You tell that fine father of yours that I'll be there. I might be fifty years old, maybe more, I don't know, but you tell him there's still some whuppin' left in my bones. What they did to Joshua and Edith ain't gonna be forgot. We didn't forget the Alamo, by damn, and we ain't forgettin' Joshua and Edith."

The day was fast coming to an end, and Hiram watched fleecy spring clouds drift across a sky so blue it almost hurt the eye. A light breeze was drifting down the wide Willamette River, and the soft noises of the water were muted. Spring along that valley proved what happened when ample rainfall was joined by considerable warm sunshine. The intensity of the various shades of green coupled with explosions of wildflowers, overwhelmed the senses.

Hiram was still chuckling at Silas William's comments when he spotted three wagons about half a mile in front of him, making a turn into a lane that he knew led into a fine grassy meadow split by a cold stream. He was planning to make that turn himself to make up a quick camp for the night.

He rode toward them with the idea of giving them news of the gang that was terrorizing the River Road, and then making his own camp another mile or so north. Each of the wagons was driven by a man and there was one outrider who led them through some trees and back toward the meadow.

*I don't recognize the outrider. I wonder how they knew this little meadow and creek were right here. They aren't trailing any cattle or extra horses. There aren't any children that I can see, either.* He rode slowly, several hundred yards behind the wagons and they were turned in a half circle by the time he rode up.

"Howdy," he said, sitting straight in the saddle. "Which one of you is the wagon boss?"

## 3

"NAME'S CLAPPER, JOHNNY CLAPPER." HE FONDLED the old flintlock rifle but didn't pull the hammer back or drop the striker, Hiram rode closer, keeping a close eye on the other men as they scrambled off their wagons.

"My name's Hawthorne. We have a farm several miles south of here. There's been trouble along the River Road recently and I thought I'd better let you know about it." He kept both hands in plain sight and didn't attempt to step off his horse until invited.

"What kind of trouble?" Clapper was a tall, thin man of about thirty years, wore a beard and his hair hung long and blond over his shoulders. He wore denim britches, a wool shirt, and had a slicker tied to the back of his saddle.

"A gang of outlaws has been troubling many of the wagons on the River Road and some of the ranches as well. How did you know about this little pasture and stream tucked away back here?"

Clapper took a step toward Hiram, thinking hard on what he had just heard. "Maybe you better step off that horse and talk to us, son." The men were unhitching their teams and walking them down to water before hobbling them in the deep grass. Hi and John Clapper walked over to one of the wagons and Clapper helped a woman out from the back.

"We're from the Church of Eternal Peace back in Ohio country, coming west to establish our own little village where we can practice our religion in peace. Some people don't appreciate how we think and what we do. Hope you ain't one of them." He put a couple of boxes on the ground to sit on and several people were moving about making ready for supper fires.

"Don't think I've heard of your church, Mr. Clapper, but I think we need to talk and the sooner the better. These outlaws have been very active, and you moving back off the road into this meadow worries me."

"Earlier this afternoon we met a couple of men who told us about this place, that there was good grass and sweet water. I guess he knew what he was talking about," Clapper said, motioning with his hands at the grass and stream. "Seemed to be nice fellows."

Hiram didn't think that a couple of men were just being nice and welcoming folks to Oregon. He was sure this little wagon train was sent here to be robbed. "I would suggest that you make yourselves ready to fend off these outlaws, Mr. Clapper. Get your guns out and make them ready, because when that sun goes down, Jenkins and his gang are going to pay you a visit."

"We don't believe much in guns and violence, Mr. Hawthorne. We're the Church of Eternal Peace. We don't have much of anything anyone would want to steal."

*You have women-folk, horses and mules, and I would bet a*

*little strongbox tucked away somewhere with enough gold to keep you alive until your crops come in. How can people be so stupid?* "Mr. Clapper, these men are vicious killers and thieves. They won't care much about your church of peace, they'll be more likely to care about the fact you have women, horses, and more than likely some money."

"We'll manage, Hawthorne," Clapper said. His demeanor turned sour at once when Hiram mentioned the women and money. "I think you would be best to move on." Several of the men returned from staking out the animals and stood with grim faces around Johnny Clapper.

"Very well," Hiram said. He walked to his horse, mounted, and rode back toward the River Road. *Fools. I know what I'll find in the morning and there isn't a single thing I can do to prevent it. They have made the trip all the way from Ohio and learned nothing about the frontier. How have they managed to stay alive this long?*

The only conclusion that Hiram could come up with was that they must have been part of a much larger group of immigrants. They simply travelled with a large group, did what they were told to do, and never questioned why, thereby learning nothing about protection from those aiming to hurt, steal, or kill.

He rode about two miles upriver and found a nice copse of trees to settle in for the night. He hobbled the horse, made the smallest of fires and cooked a pan full of side meat along with a pot of coffee.

*Everything I know tells me I should ride back there and demand that those folks prepare for that gang, but I know they would force me to leave. What would Papa do?* He gazed at his small fire, wrapped in a buffalo robe, using his saddle for a pillow, while his mind worked over and over the question of what Ezekiel Hawthorne would do in this situation.

It was late in the evening now. Fighting sleep wasn't working, he was worrying too much about what to do when it came to him. He knew what 'Papa would do.' *They will die if I don't do something, and that's what Papa would do. Something.*

Hiram took the Hawken out and checked the load, slipped his bow out of its buckskin scabbard and slipped the quiver of arrows around his shoulders. He strapped the big knife back in place, and started walking cross-country toward the Church of Eternal Peace campsite. *I hope I'm in time. I've got something Papa wouldn't have, and that's my arrows.* He was smiling and wishing that Moose was walking alongside him.

Walking cross country through heavy forest after sunset can be difficult at best and Hiram could very easily gotten himself turned around, walked in circles as so many have, but he'd spent too many hours of his young life in wild country. *That camp of theirs should be over there, maybe a mile or so, and I can use that big star right up there as my guide. I just hope I get there in time.*

He walked for fifteen minutes and spotted their fire. *My God, look at that. Why not hire somebody to send up a clarion call? Here we are, look, we've lit a huge fire to lead you in. That fellow, Clapper, is one stupid man.* He chuckled, mumbling, "I know what Papa would do. Whack that fool across the side of the head."


"JUST LOOK at the size of that fire," Tom Peabody said. The

gang was strung out single file threading their way through heavy timber, led by Peabody. Jenkins was right behind him, then One-Eyed Frizell, Ornery Smith, and Irish Jack Wellington. Teddy Jewel was standing back with the horses and would bring them up when signaled. "We don't need no moon to guide us tonight, Hank. That fire could be seen in Salem."

"Quiet now, Tom. Don't want them to know we're here. Not just yet, anyway." Hank Jenkins turned and gave the signal to those following to be quiet, and followed Peabody.

The trees, a mess of aspen, pine, spruce, hemlock, and fir made a good screen and they got to within about twenty-five yards or so of the meadow and camp. The horses were so busy eating and far enough removed that even they didn't know the murderous gang was close.


BUT, even if they had made any noise would Clapper know what it meant? To his relief, they were now in Oregon Territory, and no longer under threat of Indian attack out on the Prairie. In addition, they were no longer under the kind of threat they had been as they passed through the Rocky Mountains, and made their way through even more Indian country along the great Snake River. They were in Oregon Territory, safe at last, on their way to their new home south of Salem City.

Johnny Clapper didn't understand what that young Mr. Hawthorne was talking about. An outlaw gang out to attack their little group? Nonsense. On the trip across the continent his little group had not participated in the general security arrangements that the large wagon train prepared each night.

*We believe in peace and offer only friendship and peace to those around us.* Clapper remembered telling that wagon master that his group would not carry arms, and it was the wagon master's job to keep them safe from harm.


Jenkins used hand signs and brought everyone up close, then spread them out so there were at least five yards or so between each man. The members of the Church of Eternal Peace were sitting around the large bonfire singing a hymn of some kind. Johnny Clapper stood up when the singing ended and looked around at the group. Everyone was there, and the first thing Hiram Hawthorne would have asked was, "Where is your night guard?"

Clapper was single but the others were all married. Hubert J. Law, II, and his wife, Gloria, sat across the fire from Clapper. Next to them were Gerald Tobin and Samantha, then Sammy Sinclair and Judith, and wrapping around to Clapper's other side, Earl Sorenson and Wilma. Most of the men were in their thirties and Gloria Law was the youngest of the women, just seventeen years old.

"I'll lead us in one last prayer," Clapper said, "and then we better turn in. It'll be a long ride to Salem tomorrow. We can resupply there and then make the trek on to Eugene and our property. We should make lists of what we need for at least the first several weeks. We know there's plenty available in Salem, but don't know much about Eugene."

That prayer seemed to last half the night, according to Jenkins who was just about ready to pull the rope and sound the bell for his charge. Clapper looked up from his prayer, about to say amen when he saw Hank Jenkins striding into his little camp, a big knife in one hand and a cap lock rifle, cocked, in the other.

"Nice talkin', preacher. Now, sit down and keep your trap shut! One of you fools move, you're dead." Peabody, Frizell, Ornery Smith, and Willington walked into camp from the various angles and stood behind each of the couples. Gloria Law screamed when she saw One-Eyed Frizell come up behind her husband.

Frizell simply bashed her across the head with his rifle butt, knocking her ten feet toward the roaring fire. She was bleeding heavily and tried to scramble to her feet. She was dazed and unable to get her feet under her. Her skirts were showing far too much of her long teen-age legs, and Hank Jenkins decided at that moment, that she was his.

"Sit down, woman, and shut up," Frizell said. He smashed Hubert J. Law, II in the back of the head with the rifle butt, too, sending the man sprawling, almost into the fire.

"Where's the money, preacher?" Jenkins walked over to Clapper, the heavy knife just inches from the man's throat.

"There's no need for violence," Clapper said. He was visibly shaking, looking from outlaw to outlaw, and down at Gloria, who lay in the dirt bleeding. "We have little money, little of anything valuable! We're God-fearing folk. We'll give you anything we have."

"Damn right you will, preacher," Jenkins said. "Might take a couple of them women, too," he said.

"Might take 'em all," Ornery Smith said. "Looks like a couple of 'em might just be a little fun." He was going to say something else when an arrow pierced his back, coming all the way through his chest, the bloody steel arrow head still aimed at Clapper. Smith coughed twice, grabbing the point of the arrow sticking out of his chest, and collapsed to the ground.

The attack came so fast, so quietly. No one even heard the swish of the bowstring, never heard footsteps creeping closer and closer. Jenkins stood, knife poised near Clapper's throat, looking about wildly, waiting for the screaming assault by whatever Indian tribe was attacking.

A second arrow whistled through Irish Jack Wellington's chest, killing him, and just as Jenkins was about to grab Clapper as a shield, he saw Peabody go down. Jenkins turned and ran as hard as he could back toward the horses, and heard footsteps pounding behind him.

He turned to shoot his pursuer and found One-Eyed Frizell gaining on him. "Hurry Hank, I think the whole damned Injun tribe is after us. Run, man," he said, passing the gang leader. They reached the horses, and led by Teddy Jewel, raced out of the forest back toward their camp, looking behind them every five seconds or so.

"Where did the damn Injuns come from? How many were there? Jesus," Hank Jenkins said, "let's move." Through the pitch dark of late night, the three outlaws drove their horses through scrub brush, ravines, rock piles, and into their little camp. All the horses were worse for the wear, bleeding and bruised from the wild ride. Jenkins jumped off his horse, and rifle in hand dove behind some rocks, prepared to shoot whatever might have followed.

"Can you hear anything?" he whispered at Frizell. "ust

have been a hunnert of 'em. Them women are gonna be ruined."

Frizell was thinking back on the attack. "I never heard nothin, Hank. No Indian screaming like they always do. Never saw nothin either. Maybe we shoulda stayed and put up a fight, and kept them women for ourselves." Jenkins didn't say anything, only remembered that he and One-Eyed Frizell had turned and ran as hard as they could from the attack.

"Maybe just a couple of drunken bucks out for trouble, Hank."

Frizell was quiet after that.

THERE WAS chaos in the immigrant camp as Hiram Hawthorne strode in, an arrow knocked and ready, his rifle slung across broad shoulders. Ornery Smith, the arrow sticking out of his chest was taking his last few breaths and tried to swing a knife toward Hiram, who simply kicked it out of his hands.

Wellington's arrow had pierced his backbone, killing him all but instantly, and Thomas Peabody had bled out by the time Hiram checked him. "Anyone besides the girl hurt, Mr. Clapper? Come on, man, there'll be time for praying after we make sure everyone is safe. Get yourself put together." Hiram slapped him, not too hard, and straightened him up.

"You folks that have weapons, get them out now. Anyone that's been hurt, you women take care of them. Anyone of you men that don't have weapons, gather those animals in close and start hitching them to the wagons. Move, damn it, your lives are in danger."

Clapper was in a daze, not responding to anything and Hubert Law was tending to his young wife. It was Samantha Tobin who seemed to take charge. "This man just saved our lives, we best be listening to him. Mr. Law, we'll take care of Gloria, you go get them animals."

She added, "Mr. Sorenson, go get those rifles of yours, and Mr. Sinclair, you help Mr. Law with the animals. What's your name, mister? We owe you our lives."

It was Clapper that answered. "You were right, Mr. Hawthorne. You were right. I feel like a fool, putting all these people's lives on the line. I should have listened to you."

"Only harm done is to the outlaws, I think. Hope that girl is going to be all right." Turning towards Clapper, Hi said, "You come out here to the frontier and somebody tries to help, you better start listening, Mr. Clapper. If I hadn't felt sure those men were going to attack and simply gone to sleep you men would be dead and your women would be in hell."

"Let's get this little wagon train hitched up and moved into a safe spot."

A couple of hours later, Hiram had the Church of Eternal Peace bedded down near his camp and he was laying under that buffalo robe watching the stars wink their goodnight at him. Sleep was far off. *I sure wish Moose was here right now.*

*I just killed three men. Those were living human beings and now they are dead. Could I have saved all those people without having to take lives? Was I doing the right thing in even trying to help? Is this how Papa would have handled the situation?* He couldn't get the thought of three dead men out of his head.

They were outlaws, he knew that, and they were in the process of doing wrong- of trying to hurt or kill the Clapper group. He wondered if the men had and family and then justified again, doing what he did. *They were outlaws and those women would have become their playthings. The men would have been killed, and everything the group owned would have been stolen or burned. I did what had to be done, just as Papa would have.*

He watched as the sky lightened, a morning breeze causing the grasses to do their ballet, and heard the morning songs of the birds fluttering their way through the trees and bushes. Another glorious morning along the Willamette Valley. But, Hiram's thoughts were still anchored in the deaths of three men. He heard noises from the immigrant camp and knew what he had done was right. *They aren't very smart but they are alive.*

Morning found the pilgrims almost walking in a daze. "I don't think I slept a wink," Samantha Tobin said. "I saw those ugly men in my dreams all night. Thank you, again, Mr. Hawthorne."

Hiram stuck his nose into the Hubert Law wagon to check on Gloria. "That was a nasty bash, Mrs. Law. I'm sure you'll be okay but it's gonna hurt for a few days. How's your husband's head? He took a pretty good hit, too."

Gloria Law gave Hiram a grand smile. "Thank you, brave man. You saved all our lives. I'll be fine, just sore, and so will Hubert, but he'll let me know how much he hurts."

"Where will you folks be making up your little village?" Hiram didn't fully understand everything that Clapper and Mrs. Tobin had tried to explain.

"We've got some property south of Salem City. It's on the road to Eugene. Will you come visit? We owe you so much."

"No, you don't owe me anything. I'm just glad I was able to help. I need to continue my ride this morning and then head back south to our farm. I'd like to see you folks again, so after you get set up, maybe I'll swing by."

*That girl is as pretty as Barbara and just about my age. I wonder why she's married to that old man? He's fat and weak and sure does like himself. I shouldn't have these feelings, and I'm sure glad they're moving out, cuz I might just get into some kind of trouble.*

Hiram spent two hours burying the dead men, trying his best to find identification on them, worrying about whether the rest of the gang would show up before he was through. He took all their possessions and made a cache so they could be recovered, and headed off to finish his ride. *Other than the other gang members, will anyone even care that these men are dead and buried? I'll never be an outlaw.*

## 4

JEREMIAH TRAVIS WAS THE TRADER AT FORT BRIDGER
when Ezekiel had arrived in 1851, and he now ran the
Salem City Trading Post in Salem, Oregon's capital. His
partner in the trading post, Hector Snyder, was kept more
than busy as Travis was constantly adding on, bringing in
new merchandise, and having, as he put it, "the time of
my life."

The trading post had been expanded twice in the last
three years, and was jammed, floor to ceiling, wall to wall,
with anything and everything a person might want or
need to live the good life in Oregon Territory. Bear traps,
snowshoes, buffalo robe coats, cast iron pots and pans,
sewing needles, thread, and farm fresh eggs were available, if you just took the time to look around some.

Travis spent his early years, first as a trapper and then
operating trading posts during the fur trade years. He and
Jim Bridger had been friends for many years and Old
Gabe, as Bridger was commonly called, depended on him
when he opened his fort along the Green River. Travis

married a lovely Shoshone girl named Elaine and they had three children, two daughters and a son. The eldest daughter, Sarah, trained in the east as a schoolteacher and had married Zeke after a whirlwind romance.

The middle child, known as Moose Travis, was almost as large as his huge father, and was a partner in the Donaldson Lumber Mill near Salem City. A second mill operated near Oregon City, and old man Donaldson ran that one. The youngest of the children was Barbara Travis, now married to Angus Whitell. Barbara was tiny, mainly stemming from childhood illnesses. She was also a fine seamstress and operated a women's dress-making shop in Salem. She was so full of energy that Whitell had started calling her his own little tornado.

Along with the trading post, Travis was also a partner in a large warehouse and transportation company head-quartered in the bustling harbor city known as Portland. The business began in Oregon City but had moved to the deep-water port when that mud hole became a viable port for ocean going vessels. His partner, Rutherford Johnson, a teamster, ran a busy operation.

Along with moving wagons back and forth between California's Central Valley and cities in Oregon Territory, Johnson ran a distribution warehouse in Portland, bringing in merchandise from around the world to Portland's deepwater docks. He and Travis had started their business with two wagons and four mules. Like any good teamster, he liked to say, he was loud, boisterous, and somewhat naughty with his language.

"I'LL TELL you what's next, Travis, but I don't know how

we're gonna get it done. We need a railroad like they're building back east. They's using the same kind of steam engines that Moose has up at the mill. Big and strong... we could move tons of merchandise from and to California and Washington every day of the week."

"I've read about 'em in the east coast papers, but it seems that none of them gets built without government money. I think that's gonna be a long ways down the line, Johnson.

"To change the subject, did you invest in those coastal steamers we talked about? I think that's where we need to put some of our money. From Seattle to San Francisco, even down to Los Angeles."

"There's two companies working their boats right now, Travis, and I'm talking with one of them. California has a lot of product we need up here, and we have a lot of product they need, so if I can swing it, we'll be partners in a coastal steamship company before long.

"Got a problem with that gang of thieves south of here. I had two shipments held up last week, I guess you heard. We were moving gold from the San Francisco Mint to Sinclair's bank here in Salem when they hit us. It's the second time we've been held up, and our contract might be in jeopardy if we can't keep their gold safe."

"Fred Sharp told me about that. He's a good local sheriff, Johnson, but he ain't much for going after a gang like that. I think we'd be better off if we do lose that contract. It costs us a lot of money for security, for special wagons, and we're not really in that business. I assume the bank or the mint had that shipment insured."

"Oh, yeah," Johnson said. "It's still our responsibility to get the shipments through. We're gonna need to hire more armed guards, Travis. That's the only way. They just rode down, guns a-blazin', and stole everything. Two of our people died, and four had to walk in the last seven miles. I don't think Sheriff Sharp has the slightest clue where those bastards are."

TRAVIS WALKED Johnson out through the trading post to see him off. He'd spend tonight with Hawthorne and then on toward Portland tomorrow. "You give old Zeke a good back pounding from me, Johnson."

As Johnson mounted and rode off down Mill Creek Road, Travis watched three wagons thread their way toward the trading post. *More immigrants. They are coming in by the thousands.* Seeing a young, ill-looking girl he wondered, *what happened to that little girl? Man, somebody doesn't much like her.*

"Howdy," Johnny Clapper said, tying off his horse. "Glad you're open. We're just about out of everything. Name's Johnny Clapper and we're homesteading near Eugene, south of here. We're the Church of Eternal Peace."

"We got plenty of peace but you're welcome to add some more," Travis said. "Bring your list in and we'll get your wagons filled up. That little girl needs some medical help? We got a good doc right down the road."

"We ran into some outlaws up the road a piece. Lucky for us a young man, said he was half- injun, chased 'em off after killing two of 'em."

"Didn't get a name, did ya?" Travis already knew- felt that he knew, anyway.

"I believe he said his name was Hiram Hawthorne. He

used a bow and arrows to kill the bandits even though he carried a big rifle."

"He killed three of 'em, Mr. Clapper," one of the women hollered from a wagon. Clapper just scowled.

Travis's smile could have lit the west. "That's my grandson what saved your skin, preacher. Now, about that girl. Should I send for the doc? She doesn't look too good."

"Be a good idea. Our women folk did what they could but she got hit mighty hard. Her husband got hit, too."

Travis hollered for Heck Snyder to run down and get the doc and invited everyone into the store. "Why don't you come back here with me, Mrs. Law. You'll be more comfortable in my office when old Doc Spears gets here."

He helped her make her way through the clogged aisles, around stacked merchandise, and carefully near bear traps.

"Did I hear you say that man that saved us was your grandson? He was so brave, so big and strong." Her eyes were wide and she tried to smile through her bruises, scrapes, and cuts.

"Yup," Travis said. "My daughter is married to Zeke Hawthorne and they adopted Hi several years ago, when we all moved here from Fort Bridger."

He got the young lady settled, found a clean cup and filled it with coffee. "Don't have tea, ma'am, hope you like good, strong coffee."

He poured himself a cup and laced it with some rum and settled behind his desk. "What's this Church of Eternal Peace? We got Methodists and Catholics and a few others. I hope you're not like the Mormons. They burnt us out at Bridger."

"Johnny Clapper and my husband are all excited about it. I really don't understand what's so different from when I went to church growing up. My husband sold our farm and gave most of the money to Mr. Clapper so we could come here to Oregon. I miss my family and our farm."

Travis felt he was hearing things he probably shouldn't be hearing and was trying to figure out just what this preacher Clapper was up to. At the same time, he knew he didn't want to get involved. *We got immigrants of all kinds, colors, and shapes comin' in. I don't want to judge these people, but her story would put a good man to thinkin'.*

"Here you are, doc." Snyder said ushering Doc Spears into the small office. Doc Spears spent some time with the army in California before coming north to Oregon and wasn't always gentle with his patients. The sight of a pretty girl softened the old fellow.

"Hello Miss. My, that's a nasty little mess there, but we'll get you fixed up. You boys get out of here so I can do my work."

Heck Snyder and Travis looked at each other and smiled slightly, knowing they had never heard Spears talk so soft and sweet to anyone. Ever.

IT WAS several hours later that Travis stood on the trading post porch and watched the wagons move on down toward the Willamette River for their trip south. "That preacher's got something going more than just religion, Heck. That feller Gerald Tobin said that he chased Hiram off when Hiram rode up to warn them about the outlaw problem on the road.

"The little girl, she's still just a kid and married to that old guy. She said that Clapper isn't always nice to the women. He's the only one that isn't married, too. Well, not my problem, eh? They paid us with good coin, and they're safe because of Hiram. Something about them that's gonna bother me for a bit, though."

They walked back into the large outlet and closed the double doors. "Long day, Heck. I think I'm going to ride up to Zeke's place in the morning if you don't need me around here for a day."

"You do that, Travis, and give that grandkid of yours a good whop on the back from me. Sounded like he ran off that whole Jenkins gang singlehanded. That young girl had mooneyes when she talked about him. That isn't good for a marriage."

"You saw that too, did you? Well, if they set up their homestead ten miles south of here and Hawthorne's place is twenty miles north, maybe nothing will come of this, but you sure are right about what you said. She said she was seventeen and Hiram's eighteen, and she's pretty as a picture married to a crybaby rich old man. He whimpered more than a sick calf when the doc cleaned up his face."

Snyder was laughing when he said goodnight. "Don't tell Hiram what you just told me, or that boy will be riding south at a full gallop."

## 5

ANOTHER WET WEATHER SYSTEM HAD FINALLY moved out of the vast Willamette Valley and warm sun and blue skies were on the day's menu when Hiram saw the first guest riding up the long lane. Josh Peterson was the first of the ranchers to arrive, and Hiram hurried to greet him. "I'm glad you're here, Mr. Peterson. Papa's in the kitchen with Mr. O'Brien. I'll take care of your horse."

Peterson handed Hiram the lead rope as he stepped down. "You must have left early."

"Did that, Hiram. I heard a story from Whitman about you. About the Jenkins' gang. Was it true?"

"Yup. Hank Jenkins' gang tried to rob a wagon train, but I ruined their play. Bunch of religious fools that were too dumb to take a warning. Jenkins is short-handed right now but I doubt he's out of business."

Hi trotted off with Peterson's horse and Joshua headed to the big house, shaking his head.

"That boy of yours is something, Zeke." Peterson shook hands with the big farmer and gave Sarah a warm smile. "He was a skinny little kid when you folks hit this valley, and now, here he is taking on the Jenkins' gang as if he did this sort of thing every day of his life."

"I think that little boy we brought with us is a full-fledged man now, Josh. How's Edith holding up?"

"She's a tough lady, Zeke. Those foul men tried to best her and they couldn't. God help any of them that Hiram left alive if either Edith or I find them." There was anger from the attack and hurt that came from Peterson's feeling that he let his wife down. "I walked right out the door with a glad hand, Zeke, and they attacked my wife."

"They are vile people, Josh," O'Brien said. "But what can we do, really?"

"We're growing up, Michael," Zeke said. "The county never considered law enforcement for those of us living out here like we do. They allowed for a sheriff or marshal in the townships, but why would *we* need one?

"The fact is, it's the criminal mind that saw the opportunity and now we have to close that door. As I mentioned the other day, Mike, I have been working on a plan and when everyone gets here, I'll explain it."

Zeke, like the others, felt let down by the county while, on the other hand, he realized that until the criminals recognized the lack of police or marshals, there really hadn't been a need.

"Looks like the others are turning into the lane, Zeke," Sarah said. "I'll keep the sweet rolls and coffee coming. Are you going to be using the kitchen?"

"No, I think we'll have our little discussion out under the cottonwood trees, pretty girl. You can have your kitchen back," he chuckled. He and Josh Peterson walked out the kitchen door in time to welcome Amos Johnstone and Silas Williams.

"Glad you were able to come, gentlemen. Hiram and Skinny will take your horses. Looks like another couple of riders coming up, too," he said. Two riders could be seen a couple of hundred yards from the farmhouse. "By golly, that's Travis. He picked the perfect time to ride up here."

Travis rode up with K.C. Whitman, one of the ranchers that Hiram had visited on his trip north. The two just happened to arrive at the Hawthorne lane at the same time. "Mornin' Zeke," Travis bellowed from thirty yards out. "What kind of party have you got planned that I wasn't invited to?"

"I wish it was a party, Travis. I'm glad you're here. Good morning to you, K.C. Was the trip good?"

Hiram had all the horses taken care of, helped Zeke get the chairs and tables set up and started to head back to the barn. "Hold up there, young man," Zeke said. "You're a big part of this conversation. Have you got the crew set for this morning?"

Hi gave him an affirmative nod. "Good, then set yourself and let's talk about Hank Jenkins and what's left of his gang."

Sarah had two platters of warm sweet rolls and a large pot of coffee out for the men. "Just holler when you need more coffee," she said. "I'll keep the twins with me."

Zeke cleared his throat and began, "I guess what we're facing is part of the growing up process that Oregon Territory is dealing with." He produced his bottle of rum and let it make its way around the table, lacing the cups of coffee. "With more and more people coming into the territory, and more and more actually settling, it's an invitation to the criminal element. The immigrants carry money and possessions, and those that are already settled have possessions the criminals want."

"It's been more than just money and possessions, Zeke," Josh Peterson said. "It's the women folk they're wanting, too. I can vouch for that, and Hiram, you said those men specifically threatened those women on the wagons."

"They did," Hi answered. "They were lewd and demanding. Those women were in serious danger."

"That boy needs to be honored, Zeke," Silas Williams said. "Why, back in Texas, he'd be made a captain in the rangers cuz a what he done. Boy's a winner, Zeke."

"He is," Zeke said. He had a smile smeared across his face, thinking how fate had offered this little boy to him and Sarah just a few years ago, and look at what they had now. He had to force himself to let those wonderful thoughts go and concentrate on what they were doing today.

"What I'm suggesting here today is that we form what I'm calling the Willamette Valley and Farm Protection Association. The towns and villages of the territory have localized protection by way of a sheriff or marshal, but for areas like where we all live, there are no lawmen. We need to form a district and create an office for a lawman position."

"The problem we have is *right now*, Zeke. What you're suggesting would take months through the county commission, or years through the legislature." Williams was chuckling slightly, giving a little goad at Zeke, but deadly serious too.

"It would," Zeke said. "So how do we do this and make

it happen today?" He sat back and looked around the table. Hiram stood up and grabbed the coffee pot, pouring each man's cup full.

"We simply do it," Zeke said. He stopped and let the comment sink in. "Yes. We make it operational, and give it to the commission as a done deal."

The men were slightly taken aback by this suggestion coming from a member of the territorial legislature. "You're thinking we create this office and then tell the county what we've done after we done it?" Mike O'Brien sat back with a broad smile slowly spreading across his face. "They're elected to do those kinds of things. We would be usurping their authority, Zeke."

"Okay," Peterson said. "We say we have this protective association, but what do we do about the protective part of that? I think you have this already put together, don't you, Mr. Hawthorne?" Peterson was almost laughing and the others joined him.

"Zeke's been working on this from the moment he heard about the raid on your place, Joshua," Mike O'Brien said. "When I complained to him about losing cattle he laid some of it out for me. Keep going, Zeke."

The enthusiasm was contagious and the bottle of rum made another pass around the table. "This is just the rough idea," Zeke said. Knowing looks were passed around the table, with a couple of hearty chuckles thrown in. If Zeke Hawthorne was going to call it a rough idea, that meant it was fully written, almost in stone. All questions answered, all ideas thought out to the last word.

Zeke smiled and continued as if not seeing or hearing any of it. "We will make changes as they are needed, and for it to work, we all have to agree and be a part of it. The sticky part is simply this; it isn't going to be free. We need lawmen in our district. It is illegal to rob and steal from the wagons moving through the valley," he nodded toward Hiram. "It is illegal to rustle cattle," he looked into O'Brien's bright eyes. "And it is illegal to raid a ranch or farm and threaten those living there." He pointed a finger at Josh Peterson.

"We all agree with that, but how do we stop that from happening? We will have to create the office of Willamette Valley Marshal, and that person will have to have at least one person working with him. That, gentlemen, costs money and that's why this must be done just as legally as possible. We will write the articles of incorporation for our association and they will include a tax that will pay for all this."

"All these things you mentioned, Zeke, the robbing and terrorizing, are illegal but why hasn't this county, or the other territorial counties, created the lawman position?" Travis had been thinking about the problem and the solution. "Why isn't Fred Sharp the county sheriff, not just Salem's lawman?"

"Salem has grown considerably since the position of sheriff was created, Travis," Zeke said. "The township needs its own lawman. It has even become the territorial capitol. Now, our farming and ranching district has grown as well, and we have the added burden of the wagons moving through filled with immigrants. We're now a rich little target for these criminal gangs. We need this Willamette Valley Marshal.

"It will be accomplished and operating before it is even presented to the county commission. They, hopefully, will be pleased that they won't have to do anything except accept our association and take over the collection of the tax and continue the office of W.V. Marshal.

"Now, who wants to start this discussion?"

"I guess I do," Silas Williams said. "As you know, I was with the Texas Rangers many years ago. I'm an old man now, hell, I'm half crippled, bald, can't hear, and don't see everything a whipper-snapper like Hiram here, does, but I still know what it will take to keep this valley safe.

"Your idea of a marshal and a deputy is only a start, Zeke. I think it would take a marshal and at least two deputies to patrol this long valley... and territory is important. Where would our marshal's territory end and Sheriff Sharp's begin on our south? And the same for the north?"

"I really like the idea," Josh Peterson said. "Edith and I don't have much. Our little property feeds us, and what little actual money that comes in comes from our trapping during the winter. I'm worried about this tax. I know a marshal and deputies have to be paid, but shouldn't that come from the tax we already pay?"

"I know how a new cost can have a big effect on a family," Zeke said. "We'll keep this tax as low as possible, but without some kind of monetary return, nobody would take the job of Willamette Valley Marshal and face the Jenkins' gang. I can't think of another possible way of getting this done."

"I'm in, Zeke, that's not what I was saying," Peterson said. "I'm just worried that this tax will become as burdensome as the damn outlaws."

THE MEN TOOK a break for a wonderful mid-day dinner of

boiled brisket in a rich chili sauce, sopped up with hard rolls. The meal ended with bowls of fresh ice cream. "I'd much rather take a nap right now than listen to more word mongering," K.C. said, rubbing his ample belly. "That was a fine meal, Mrs. Hawthorne. Fine indeed."

It was several hours later that Zeke called it a day. "We've just done what couldn't be done, gentlemen. We have our compact, we have voted ourselves a tax that will be collected, and there is but one thing left. How do we go about finding the man for the position of Marshal?"

"My first thought would be Hiram Hawthorne," Silas Williams piped up. "But, I suppose work on the farm here would override my idea." He nodded to Hiram with a smile. Hiram was vigorously shaking his head.

"There's a man lives in Oregon City who rode for one of the Texas cattle ranches that would surely fit the bill. The ranches hired their own lawmen sometimes, the Rangers always being short-handed with empty pockets, and old Slim Hastings knew how to deal with rustlers and criminals."

"What brought him to Oregon, Silas?" KC asked. "Not running from anything, is he?"

"No," Williams chuckled. "Well, maybe a pretty girl or two down in the Pecos area." He laughed and continued. "He grew up cowboying, knows beef inside and out, but wanted to be a farmer. Turns out he don't know Jack about farmin', but just about everything about lawing."

It was decided that Williams would make the offer to Hastings and the new association would interview the man and hire him if he was what they wanted. The pay would be twenty dollars a month, a place to live that would include a jail, and each of the farms and ranches would also provide food. "I think I might want that job," Travis laughed as the meeting finally broke up.

TRAVIS SPENT two days at the farm, taking Hiram fishing one day, and having a picnic with Sarah. The twins, Suzanne and Joanne, and baby Travis, joined in the fun. Finally saddled up on the third morning for the trip back to Salem City and the trading post, he felt like he just got there. "By golly, I like this grandpa stuff, Sarah. I think I might mention it to Barbara."

"That grizzled old fur trader is getting soft," Zeke said. They stood on the porch watching the big man with his long, braided hair swinging with the horse's gait ride down the lane. "I bet the grizzly bears feared him when he was younger."

"Are you getting just a bit soft, Sharp Knife?" Sarah jabbed him in the ribs, dancing away as he feigned a swat at her behind. "I don't think that will ever happen to Papa or to you. You are the most righteous and strongest men I've ever known."

Just as Travis reached the River Road, he turned in the saddle, toward the north, and waved at someone. Within moments that person turned up the lane toward the Hawthorne farmhouse. "I think that's John Bradley ridin' in," Zeke said.

"I'll get the coffee cooking," Sarah said slipping back in the house. "Is there ever going to be a time that won't be having visitors? I'm married to a visitor magnet," she said, laughing and dancing away from another swat aimed at her behind.

Bradley was one of the legislative leaders and had

supported statehood from the beginning. He worked long hours with Zeke and the late Nate Bishop, served on some of the same committees with them, and detested the thought of slavery. "Good morning to you, Mr. Hawthorne," he said, stepping off his horse and tying it to the hitch rail. "No rain for a week now, and the river's going down some too."

"It's a beautiful morning, Mr. Bradley. What brings you to our humble abode?"

"I think I've discovered what Belknap and his people might be up to. Can we talk?"

Zeke showed him into the kitchen and offered a chair, a cup of coffee, and a little added incentive from his ever-present bottle of rum. "Mr. Belknap has made my life miserable for several years, John. He won his seat back, and I'm sure the votes were manipulated some. That man is bound to disrupt our move toward statehood."

"He may be moving away from violence, though," John Bradley said. "When his supporters shot Nate Bishop in the back, he lost many followers as did their campaign for Oregon to enter the union as a slave state.

"Belknap still supports the idea of statehood, but his way, as we know. Let me tell you what happened to me just two days ago. I was sitting in my law office when Pete Flowers came in."

"The rancher? He runs cattle upriver from here and I think he has property somewhere along the Snake River, too," Zeke said. "I remember he campaigned against me during my first election. He owns some slaves, and has one of the quickest tempers of any man I know. He can be dangerous, Mr. Bradley. If you're going to be doing any kind of business, be aware of those dangers."

"That's the man. He's a Belknap supporter from the first. He suggested that my law practice would be very much enhanced if I threw my support to Belknap and his pro slavery position. He came right out and said it."

"And, of course, it was just the two of you in the room," Zeke said. "A blatant bribery attempt and not one witness. If they would attempt such a thing with you... my God man, you're dead against slavery and they know it, they might very well swing some votes from those on the fence.

"Have you discussed this with anyone else? This Mr. Flowers is underhanded in his dealings with other stockmen and the buyers in Portland and Oregon City. We've got to make some moves fast to curb their attack."

"That's why I'm here, Zeke. You're the man to lead this. I've talked with Harold Meir and he agrees. You have the ear of the reporters in Salem, Oregon City, and Portland, and the public needs to know what Belknap is up to."

"We're right in the middle of spring planting, we're fighting an armed gang of thieves, and now Belknap strikes. Good timing, eh? Of course, I'll take this challenge, John. Who else have you talked with?"

"I'm on my way to Salem, Zeke, but I'm not sure who to talk with." John Bradley's law offices were in Oregon City along the Columbia River, the district he represents in the legislature.

"Your first visit should be with the governor, John. He'll be most pleased to learn of this. I think I'll ride to Salem in the morning and have a visit with Virgil Brown, the district judge, and Ted Chapman."

"Chapman? I don't know him," Bradley said.

"New in the territory. His east coast insurance

company just opened offices in the territory. He's a natural leader, John, and already has some excellent contacts here. He and his company are strongly anti-slavery. He and Paul Pritchett have become good friends too."

Zeke didn't mention that his brother-in-law, Moose Travis, was engaged to Chapman's daughter, or that Zeke was going to support Chapman's run for the office of State Treasurer, once the constitutional convention was called. "Thaddeus Chapman will spread the word on this business quickly, John."

## 6

"THAT DOESN'T SURPRISE ME IN THE LEAST, ZEKE." District Judge Virgil Brown's white moustache was bristling as he shook his large head. The man was ancient in most people's eyes, but his energy level was that of a forty-year-old. Brown let his snow-white hair grow long and it hung in great waves and curls around his neck and deep into his back.

Brown came west as a young man, and became active in the fur trade during its early years. He left the mountains to study law and returned to help the traders in their fights with the British and French, and then with the formation of the Oregon Territory. He'd been a district judge for eight years but still felt like a mountain man and explorer. His language was often considered colorful.

Those of a less than generous nature suggested that his language could best be considered crude while others cringed at his use of profanity in the courtroom. "If a man acts like a rotten bastard then it shouldn't surprise anyone that I would call him such," had been heard more than once. Judge Virgil Brown was well acquainted with John Barleycorn and had put more than one attorney under the table.

There had been a movement, an undercurrent of thought, that Brown should have been appointed Territorial Governor. His opinion on the matter had never been made public, which, in itself, indicated how he felt.

The man always wore a coal black wool suit, white shirt and collar, and a black silk scarf tied vaquero style. "George Belknap has very little use for the law unless it favors him or his ideas. He's from Virginia, you know," Brown said, as if that answered all questions. "Truth be known, his family sent him west before he ruined their good name." He chuckled at his own little joke, a rumbling, deep-throated, forcefully ironic chuckle that could rattle windows.

Zeke understood no charges could be filed against Pete Flowers and his bribe offer, simply because there was no witness. "It's John Bradley's word against Flowers', and that wouldn't be accepted by any judge. What do you suggest, Judge Brown?"

"Make it public but don't name names. Name Bradley, of course, but not who made the attempt. You won't have to. Let those wolves who call themselves journalists make the connection. They will, you know, and you'll be forced to defer. You watch, the *Oregon Statesman* will have many editorials demanding that heads roll." He was chuckling again, his hair doing a little dance across broad shoulders, gleaming in the noon sun streaming through his office windows.

"I think I'll go visit those offices right now," Zeke said. "That newspaper has always been fair with me, and they have asked for an interview. Thank you, Judge. John Bradley also made that suggestion."

The *Oregon Statesman* had offices in the same block as the Bank of Oregon, and Zeke stopped to say hello to the bank manager, Obediah Sinclair. "Good morning, OB. Looks like things are trying to dry out."

"It's a beautiful spring, Zeke. Come in, come in. After the winter we went through, this is pure pleasure." He was standing outside the heavy doors of the bank enjoying the sunshine. "Just look at that sky. I wonder if maybe your friend Roland Sullivan might call that Oregon Blue." He laughed and ushered Zeke inside. "I just had a visit from John Bradley and he told me a fantastic story."

"Every word's the truth, too. Our mutual friend, George Belknap, is up to his tricks early this session. I'm on my way to see Clarence at the newspaper right now. Both Bradley and Judge Brown suggest I be the one to release the information. Damn shame that John was alone when Flowers made his offer."

"It won't take old Clarence Parson two minutes to figure out where the offer came from," Sinclair laughed. "Since I brought up his name, what's going on with Roland Sullivan? Haven't seen much of him lately."

"Thousands of new people coming into the territory has our land commissioner tied to his office desk, OB. Doesn't even have time to visit his own brewery. I hope to meet with him later today if he can break out. Spread the word about the bribery attempt and maybe we can shut these fools down. It's months before the legislature convenes and none of us has the time to fight this kind of fight."

"That's their plan, Zeke."


"TELL me what old man Parson said. I want to know." Sullivan was sitting across the table from Zeke at the Willamette Valley Brewery, puffing on a cigar. Zeke had to threaten the man with physical violence to break him out of his land commission office. "It seems that even though we call ourselves a sophisticated and modern society, we're surrounded by intellectual dwarfs, Zeke.

"George Belknap must understand that he is responsible for old Nate Bishop's death, and that Henry Foote and Phil Mason are in prison because of his shenanigans. Now, he is behind an effort to bribe a member of the territorial legislature? Man's a fool."

"No one's arguing with you, Sullivan," Zeke laughed. "Judge Brown said it would take Clarence Parson two minutes to pin the bribe on Belknap. It took less than one. I had to say I didn't know where the offer came from." There was gentle laughter from both men at that comment.

"Do you expect the offer of bribes to continue? Belknap's platform needs a considerable number of votes. Will he be buying those votes all summer?"

"That would be my guess, Sullivan. Belknap is devious at best, and I would be willing to put some money on the table that he would turn to threats of violence if the bribes don't work. As if we don't already have enough violence in our territory."

Zeke and Sullivan spent another couple of hours

enjoying a few cold draughts of beer and conversation. The idea of the Willamette Valley Farm and Protective Association was fully discussed. "I like the idea of a marshal in that district, Zeke. You're talking the northern valley, say from Salem City north. What about that long area from Salem City south to Eugene? Many immigrants are moving into that rich little area."

"It isn't a little area, Sullivan. Not small at all, but that would be up to those living there. I think our organized association may spawn others, I hope it does, but it would be up to those people to decide." Zeke took a breath, and a goodly draught of beer. "Maybe we should include in our constitution, when we write it, that each county has an elected sheriff to maintain law and order in areas outside towns and villages."

"I think it's past time for you to start thinking about the state constitution, and one thing that might be included would be that. That way, the people living as the farmers and ranchers do, well outside population areas, would have protection from real lawmen.

"But you're right, Zeke, Eugene is growing from the mud hole it was. There's good land still available, but they have that same problem you're facing and it may even be the same gang of outlaws. Johnson's wagons were hit recently and he may lose his contract to ship gold and silver coins from the San Francisco mint because of it. I've heard rumors that it was the Jenkins gang."

"Jenkins is short-handed right now, Sully. My son Hiram took the whole bunch of 'em on, singlehanded. That boy's got spunk, I'll tell you."

"What do you know about this Slim Hastings?" Sullivan asked. He had a twinkle in his eye and continued,

"If he's like Silas Williams, he'll be a real character. Can we handle another Texan around here?" Sullivan was cackling.

"He'll be at the farm next week, Sully. I'm looking forward to spending a few days with him. Most of the association members will be coming out to meet the man, as well. I'll sure feel better knowing we have a lawman to call on in our valley. Texans are different, Sully, I'll give you that, but they're honest as the day, tough as iron, and you'll never find a better friend."

"Have you ever been to Texas, Papa?" Hiram and Zeke were riding in from the north wheat fields for mid-day dinner and to welcome Slim Hastings when he arrived from Oregon City. "I love listening to Mr. Williams tell his stories."

"The people of Texas formed their own country years ago, but that vast area is one of the states of our union now. Texas was a state before Oregon became a territory, son. Tall tales of Texas is what Silas Williams is all about, Hi, and I think most of his stories probably have a basis in truth." He was laughing at the thought as they undressed their horses and led them into a corral.

"I like to listen to his stories," Hi said. "He's got a way about him. Mama's told me stories about you, but you don't tell them yourself. Your stories are better than Mr. Williams's. At least I think so."

Zeke was embarrassed and flustered and took an extra moment before answering. "Don't believe a man should talk much about himself, son. Proud talk is vain talk, Hiram, and you know I'm not vain."

Hiram understood instantly that he had just been slightly reprimanded by his father, because he had been just a bit boastful with the Saunders boys about how he stopped the Jenkins gang of outlaws from robbing the Clapper wagons. "I understand," he said and Zeke heard more than just the words, he heard the full meaning of the word *understand*.

"You boys look tired and hungry," Sarah said when they came into her kitchen. "Are we waiting dinner for Mr. Hastings?"

"No," Zeke said. "Rebecca took a full load of food to the boys in the field and we need to eat. The little ones must be hungry, too. If Hastings comes during dinner he'll be welcome to sit with us but we shouldn't wait. He's not on any kind of schedule that I know of."

"What is Judge Brown going to do about that bribe?" Sarah brought a platter of pork chops and a bowl of bean soup to the table. "Biscuits coming up."

"Not much he can do," Zeke said. "Old Flowers was pretty smart offering the bribe when no witnesses were around. His word against John's. I'm going to take a ride around the territory as soon as the planting's done and talk to everyone I know about the bribe offer. The more people that know about it, the better.

"It's really sad when a man can get his way only by paying for it. When his argument is so lacking in truth or benefit that agreement must be purchased, it's more than wrong, it's an indictment. The problem is made larger when the bribe is accepted by those equally weak-minded.

"We're elected to represent those that live and work in our districts and there's supposed to be a level of trust that goes along with the vote. When that trust is violated, society, as a whole, is the victim. The intolerance that Belknap represents is something I'll fight until my dying breath, and his violation of the trust put in our hands by the voters is something I will make that man pay for."

That was a level of anger that rarely made it to the surface, and Zeke coughed gently, regretting that he had vented his rage at the dinner table. At the same time, he knew his anger was justified and he had no intentions of apologizing for what he said, despite the fact he felt bad about saying it at the table.

The meal was a quiet one. It seemed to Hiram that even the twins were busy absorbing their father's words. *It's interesting to think that Papa was elected because people trust him, and yet, this Mr. Belknap was also elected. Is he trusted by those that voted for him? Maybe those bribes Papa talks about go to more than other legislators.*

The dinner table had been cleared and the children were put down for their mid-day naps. Hiram rode back out to the cornfields and Zeke was working at the forge when Slim Hastings rode up the long lane from the River Road. Zeke saw a tall thin man, probably in his forties with long grayish hair, a thin moustache, and eyes that seemed to be looking in several directions all at the same time. He was curious, inquisitive, searching for something- or maybe everything.

Zeke walked out and hailed the man who turned his horse toward the shops. "Hello," he said. "You be Mr. Hawthorne?' There was no question in Zeke's mind. This man was , from Texas.

"I am. Are you Mr. Hastings?"

"Yup, just call me Slim," he said. He stepped off his blue roan stallion and stuck a long arm out to Zeke. "Nice place, sir." He said, looking all around. "I like this Oregon country." His Texas drawl had a musical lilt to it that Zeke liked and ushered the man into the barn.

"Let's tie that fine horse of yours off and have a chat, shall we? Did Mr. Williams give you an idea of what we're up against here?"

"Shorley did. Renegades from society is what these outlaws are. Can't make an honest living. Find it easier to suck hind tit off those that can. Yup, old Silas, he told me about this Jenkins gang. Told me your son whupped on 'em pretty bad, too. He's half injun is he?"

"He is, as is my wife. I hope you don't have a problem with that."

"Me? My God, man, I'm half Cheyenne myself. I was raised by a couple of old Mexican priests down in El Paso when whoever bore me out into this miserable world left me under a mesquite bush."

Zeke's mouth opened but he didn't say a word. *There's a revelation I didn't see coming. I like this man, and I think I like his ways, as well. About as honest as one can get, and seems to demand without saying so that those around him be honest as well.*

Zeke and Slim Hastings sat at the tables under the cottonwood trees and Sarah came out with hot coffee, cups, and a fresh bottle of rum. "Slim Hastings, please meet my wife Sarah. Sweetheart, this is Slim Hastings, hopefully our Willamette Valley Marshal."

"Mr. Hastings," she said, extending a hand. "Welcome to our home."

"It's my pleasure, Ma'am," he said. "I just told Mr. Hawthorne what a beautiful place you have. It's so green, nice and clean, and I feel like I've been wanting to be here for a long time."

"I'll have some smoked meat and bread coming out shortly, Zeke." Sarah smiled at the two and hustled back to her kitchen. *He sounds like honey tastes. He'll be noticed by all the women in this valley.* She was chuckling lightly walking back to the kitchen.

Now," Zeke said, splashing some rum into their coffees, "let's talk about the Jenkins gang and the Willamette Valley. Williams tells me you have some background as a lawman."

"There was a lot more Texas than there were rangers, Mr. Hawthorne, and many of the big spreads hired their own protection. I rode for a couple of them ranches during a period when stealin' a man's cattle was getting' popular. I'd be proud to give you names and addresses if you want.

"I'm not one of those varmints feels that a criminal needs to die just cuz he is a criminal, but there are good reasons for some of them to go away permanent like. It's kinda fun to bring 'em before a mean old judge and watch 'em squirm, knowin' they was gonna be poundin' rocks for a spell."

Zeke tried but couldn't control a chuckle listening to Slim Hastings. "We've got a judge in Salem City that you just might cotton right up to, Mr. Hastings. I think you and Judge Virgil Brown just might find yourselves spinning a few yarns. How would you go about protecting these farms and ranches?"

"Mr. Williams said you folks were thinking that you would want a marshal and two deputies, and I pretty much agree with that. What keeps folks on the straight and narrow more often than not is the fear of being caught. A lot of very law-abiding folk are that way from that fear, not from being almighty law abiding." Zeke laughed out loud at that comment and nodded his head vigorously.

Slim Hastings continued. "I would want me and my deputies to be seen out and about all the time. I would want folks to not be surprised when one of us just happens to show up. We would want to find this Jenkins if he's still in the territory, but it is best to deter a criminal than to have to catch one after the fact."

"That's a good philosophy, Mr. Hastings. How would you go about hiring these deputies that would work for you?"

"That's a two-bit question, Mr. Hawthorne. I think I would want to meet this Judge Brown you mentioned, and the Salem sheriff, and possibly ask some of the ranchers around the valley too. Get a couple of young, honest men with good backgrounds that way."

The men spent the rest of the afternoon discussing how to make the Willamette Valley a safe place to live and work. They rode their horses all over the farm, Zeke showing the effects of his and Hiram's efforts over the last several years. They found Hiram and his crews just finishing planting corn.

"Hi, meet Slim Hastings. Mr. Hastings, my son, Hiram."

"Well now, I've heard stories about you, young Mr. Hawthorne. It's a pleasure, sir." He stuck his hand out and felt a firm grip back from Hiram.

"I'm pleased to meet you, Mr. Hastings. Mr. Williams has said some fine things about you, sir."

"Are you finished with this field? Send the crew back and we'll ride back to the house together," Zeke said. "Tomorrow, I want to take Hastings on a tour of the farms and ranches and you should ride with us, Hi."

"That will be my pleasure."

II

BOOK ELEVEN: LIFE MUST
GO ON DESPITE CHAOS

## 7

"YOU SEE TO IT THAT DAMN FOOL PAYS FOR WHAT HE said. You whip that man but don't kill him." Belknap was shaking, his beet-red face covered in angry sweat, as he pounded his fist into an open palm. "I want that Clarence Parson to understand that if he ever prints lies about me again, he will pay dearly for them."

Steve Mastos was known around Salem's criminal element as an enforcer of sorts. He wasn't smart enough to create his own crimes, to perpetrate a crime; in fact, the man was almost not smart enough to follow simple orders. But, what George Belknap was discussing was simple enough for Mastos to understand.

"Why not just kill him? I'll whup him good if that's what you want, but it would be easier to just kill the man."

Belknap thought about telling him how much more important a beating would be than a killing, how a beating would not only make Parson think twice before printing lies about Belknap, but how the threat of beatings would put fear in others that might contemplate going up against the Virginian. He simply said, "No, Steve, killing is too good for that man. I want him hurt."

Mastos came to Oregon as a runaway from somewhere. Every story he'd ever told had been different; as if the first story was a lie and then he could never remember the lie, was afraid of the truth, and so he just told another lie. He cowered at loud noises, shied from aggression shown by others, yet was vicious when he was in a rage, which usually came on after he took three good solid shots of whiskey.

He carried a stout length of oak that he had carved into an ugly-mean cudgel and always had a broad bladed knife in his belt. Mastos stood about five feet, eight inches and weighed over two hundred pounds. Massive shoulders and chest topped heavy legs, and his short arms ended in broad hands with long fingers that could squeeze the life out of anything they held.

A man who does what he's told without giving any thought to why, a man who had never had an original thought of his own, a man with no discernable personal morals or ethics, and one with incredible strength, could be described as the most dangerous animal another man could face.

Steve Mastos left George Belknap with just one simple thought, beat the hell out of Clarence Parson.

Mastos didn't look good sitting a horse, his stubby, thick legs didn't hang right in the saddle skirts, he slumped in the saddle, and bounced when riding. No one ever laughed but many were seen to turn aside and give a snicker or two. He came up Mill Street from the river and jerked his horse to a stop near the newspaper office, dismounted and strode down the boardwalk.

He was trying to remember what Belknap had told him. "Tell him you're upset about the lies printed about the assemblyman.

*"Yes, I can remember, and how I should be angry about lies being told about my good friend.* He was muttering as he walked and almost went right past the *Oregon Statesman* offices. He looked around to make sure nobody noticed, and walked into the building.

"Parson, you dirty sumbitch, you wrote lies about my friend," he said. The office was rather simple with two desks facing each other with an aisle way between them that led to the composing room in the back. Parson was sitting in the desk to the left as you entered the building. There was a banister across the room separating the front areas from the desks, and a swinging gate at the aisle way.

"What are you talking about, Mastos? Are you drunk? Get out of here." Parson wasn't a large man, hadn't been in a fight since he was a kid, and probably couldn't defend himself with fists, feet, or teeth. But, in the second drawer down on the right side of the desk was a fine little cap-lock, thirty-six caliber, pistol.

Mastos didn't hesitate, he'd come to beat the hell out of Parson and that was what he would do. He wrenched the gate open and moved quickly toward the desk. "You lied about what you said about George Belknap, my very good friend, and I'm going to make you sorry you did that."

Parson didn't think twice. The drawer opened and his hand fished the weapon out, had the hammer back, and fire flashed from the muzzle. Mastos stood straight up when the lead ball slammed into the middle of his chest, staggered a step or two backward, looked down at the

75

stream of blood pouring from the hole in his wool shirt, howled a vile obscenity, and lunged at Parson.

It was just Parson's luck that Mastos ran out of blood half a step from the editor's desk, and the squat, heavy man fell onto the desk, his hands reaching for Parson. The gunshot brought Parson's compositor, Gilly, running from the backroom and two gawkers in from the boardwalk.

"Go get the sheriff, Gilly. Hurry." He looked at the two visitors and shooed them back out the door, closed it and put the closed sign in the window. He went to a side cabinet, found a bottle of whiskey and a glass, and found he couldn't control his shaking. He spilled as much as he got in the glass.

He stood, holding the glass with both hands. The glass was almost full of Kentucky's best, brought in a barrel all the way across the continent, and he drank it down.

"Whew," he gasped. He couldn't look at the body, couldn't look out the front windows, just stood there, staring into an open cabinet. He poured a second glass full, found there weren't quite the severe shakes, and drank it down all at once, also. The fire in his belly was lit and the shakes slowly went away. Parson was numb and frightened, not the least bit sure of what he should do next.

It was the rattling at the front door that got the editor moving. "Sheriff, thank God. I killed him, Fred. He's dead. I've never killed anything, and I killed him." He was shaking again, uncontrolled, and Fred Sharp helped him into a chair behind the other desk.

"Take it easy, Clarence. Calm down and tell me what happened." Sharp eased Mastos' body off the desk and onto the floor and saw the hole in the shirt, mid chest, and the great amount of blood on the floor and desk. *Good shooting for a man who doesn't hunt.* "Did Mastos threaten you, Parson? Why did you shoot him?"

It took the better part of an hour, another glass of whiskey, and some gentle talk to get the story out of the editor. "He had that knife in his hand, Fred, almost ripped our little gate off its hinges, and was going to kill me. He was screaming that I lied about George Belknap. Called him his best friend. I'm sure Belknap put him up to it, Fred. I wrote that story about John Bradley being offered a bribe and insinuated that Belknap was behind it. There won't be any insinuating on the next edition of this newspaper. I'll put it on the front page." The whiskey was not calming Parson down, it was getting him angry and he was ready for retribution.

Fred Sharp had a smile on his face, listening to the tirade. *Belknap misjudged this little play if he thought he could frighten Parson. The man might be a wreck right now, but he's an angry wreck. I just wish that I could walk up to that arrogant Virginia fool and arrest him. He has others break the law and we can't pin these things straight to him.*

"HERE'S A PAIR TO DRAW TO," Travis thundered from his back office at the Salem Trading Post as his son Moose and Ted Chapman walked in. "I hope you've got good news. We need some in this old town. Come in."

"Hello, Papa," Moose said, fighting his way through the store. Even the aisles seemed to be filled with merchandise. "Good news is what we have."

Travis found two cups and filled them with half coffee,

half rum, and invited the men to sit down. "Have you read the latest from the *Oregon Statesman*? Mr. Belknap may have finally gone too far in his efforts to make Oregon a slave state. What's your good news?"

Ted Chapman smiled at Moose, then at Travis, and simply said, "They finally set a date."

Travis jumped to his feet, spilling coffee and rum about, and grabbed his son. "When?" he stormed. "You two should have been married a year ago. I've got the party all planned. We'll go to Zeke's, and invite the whole Willamette Valley."

"No, Papa," Moose said, quickly, but quietly. "Clemmie and I are going to have as close to a traditional Shoshone wedding as possible. You and Mama and Ted will be there. That's all. Mama will burn sage and you will bless us as you did Zeke and Sarah. I will give Ted three horses and a fine knife, and Clemmie and I will go into the mountains, to a place I have, and we will raise a lodge, and be there for two weeks."

"That's fine," Travis said. Moose expected him to fight him to the death over not being able to have a huge party, but all he said was, "That's fine," a second time. Travis had a large smile on his face, refilled his spilled coffee and rum, and continued. "Then, when you come back, we will all go to Zeke's and we'll have a party. You bring the elk, Hiram will bring the deer and salmon.

"Ted, you bring the turkey. Sarah and Elaine will make the pies and bread. It will be a two-day party. When, Moose? When will you and Clemmie have your ceremony?"

Moose and Ted Chapman were laughing too hard to talk and it was a couple of minutes before Moose could say, "We want to get married this coming weekend, Papa. We will all come to your big house on Saturday morning at ten."

"Good. And then two Saturdays after that, we will be at Zeke's. Don't be late," he said. "Now, you better run along, I have much to do. I'll leave for Zeke's as soon as I tell Elaine the good news. Good for you, Moose. Ted, welcome to my family."

"You were right, Moose," Ted smiled. They were walking out of the trading post, "You said he would have his party despite your feelings on the matter. He's as good a politician as Zeke, I think. You got your way and he got his and you're both happy with the outcome."

"He's the best friend a man will ever have," Moose whispered.

THE SUN WAS ALMOST DOWN on this late spring evening as Zeke, Hiram, and Slim Hastings turned off River Road for the short trip up to the Hawthorne home. "Long day, Hastings, but we covered a considerable amount of this valley. As you heard, everyone we talked with agrees that you should be our valley marshal. It's up to you, now."

"I met some very fine people today, Mr. Hawthorne, and I would be proud to be your marshal. I will need some kind of official recognition in order to bring someone before a judge. I understand there will a jail and office provided."

"We'll take a ride into Salem City and see Judge Brown. You'll get your recognition, and Mike O'Brien has set a small piece of land aside near the main road for your office-jail. You'll have living space included. We'll need to put the word out that you're looking for a couple of deputies, too."

"I feel like I'm home, Mr. Hawthorne," Hastings said.

"Looks like Mama has company," Hiram said. "Is that grandpa's horse tied to the rail?" Hiram nudged his horse into a gentle lope for the last hundred yards or so, jumping from the saddle, tying off quickly, and racing to the house.

"He's still a little kid in some ways," Zeke laughed. "He and his grandpa are like ten-year-old's' when they get together, and when his Uncle Moose is in the mix, it can almost get dangerous."

"You seem to be very comfortable being married to an Indian," Hastings said.

"I was raised in the Ohio Valley during the times that all Indians were referred to as savages, Mr. Hastings. My family came to America in the sixteen-hundreds and by the mid seventeen hundreds were settled in what today is called Kentucky. It was Virginia back then and very much on the frontier. It wasn't until I spent almost a year at Fort Bridger that I came to know and understand, as much as a white man might, the mind of the Shoshone.

"You're half Cheyenne, you said. Have you spent time with the Cheyenne?"

"The priests made it clear the Cheyenne were savages as I grew up and it wasn't until I was a man that I even met one. I'm afraid I don't understand the mind of the Cheyenne, nor do they understand mine. Those I've become friends with tolerate my white mind and I tolerate their Indian mind.

"I really don't believe I could marry and live with one, though. On the other hand, I've met your wife and the

Shoshone must be vastly different from the Cheyenne. Your son must understand the Shoshone way as I don't understand the Cheyenne way."

They walked into the kitchen, a scene of complete chaos on this lovely evening. The twin girls were sitting on Travis's lap and little Travis was up there as well. "Have I got some good news for you, Mr. Assemblyman, Sharp Knife, Hawthorne, sir," Travis said through loud laughter.

"Who's that with you?"

"Travis, I want you to meet our new Willamette Valley Marshal, Slim Hastings. Slim, this is the former fur trapper and former Fort Bridger trader, Jeremiah Travis, my father-in-law."

Travis didn't try to unwind himself from all the children and simply stuck his large paw out for Slim, who shook it with a smile. "I'm glad to know you, Mr. Travis. I've certainly heard much about you."

"Skip the mister stuff, Slim. Nice to meet you. Understand you're gonna bring peace to our little valley. My wagons have been hit twice now by that foul Jenkins bunch, so you've got my backing on wiping 'em off the face of the map. Don't have much truck with outlaws, Slim."

"All right, now, Travis, what's all this good news you were ballyhooing?" Zeke said.

"Moose and Clementine are going to be married this Saturday at my house." Everyone started talking at once and Travis raised his hands to shush them. "It's going to be a simple traditional Shoshone affair with just the two of them, me and Elaine, and Ted Chapman."

"I'm so glad for him," Sarah said. "Will they live at the lumber mill?"

"I'm not through," Travis said, and spent the next five minutes outlining the part that he would provide for the couple two weeks after the marriage. "I'm running out of time on this old earth of ours, and I want Moose to have the best party yet."

"You've got eons left in you, Travis," Zeke said.

"Maybe, maybe not. I came out here from Pennsylvania back in 1828, Zeke and I ran a good trap line for the company for two years. When I met Elaine, my trapping days were over and old Bridger set me up with the trading post. Here it is 1857, I'm something over fifty, don't know exactly, but I can feel an awful lot of those fifty some years. The last big fight I had was when those Crow came down on us and you saved my butt, Zeke. Wouldn't be here right now if it wasn't for you. I want to do right by Moose, and this party will be part of that. Will you do it?"

Zeke whopped Travis across his shoulders and said "Yes, Travis, we'll have us a grand party. I was going to leave next week to ride the territory, but it can wait. This is family.

"Speaking of family, it's late, we've been on the road since sunrise, and it's time to eat. Looks like we've got a full table for you, Sarah."

"Mike O'Brien brought a tenderloin of beef over just after you left this morning, Zeke, and I've roasted it. Everyone clean up and Rebecca and I will serve up some fine victuals."

## 8

"WHAT DID YOU FIND OUT, LEFTY?" HANK JENKINS was pacing around a small fire deep in a rock canyon south of Salem City. He, One-Eyed Frizell, and Teddy Jewel travelled south the day after the aborted hijack of the wagon train to an area they used when hijacking commercial transport wagons on the road between Eugene and California. Many of those wagons were hauling freight from California. Some, like Johnson's, were hauling gold and silver for the banks.

Lefty Thompson joined the gang after they set up their new camp. Jenkins sent him north to find out which Indian tribe had attacked his gang. "Weren't no Indian tribe, Hank. Was one boy," he said with an almost smug grin on his face. "It were a half-breed belonging to one of the farmers near there. Name's Hawthorne. Some kind of territorial big shot."

"A boy? A half-breed boy whupped us? That boy just signed himself a death warrant. A boy killed Tom

Peabody, Ornery Smith, and Irish Jack? That boy's one dead little half-breed.

"What else you find out? These roads is fine pickins and we've got a long summer of wagons moving down the River Road, of merchandise coming north from California, and we ain't gonna let no half-breed kid stop us." Jenkins was in a fury, but also remembered that he's run like a yellow dog when those arrows started flying and now to find out he ran from a boy...

"There's more, Hank," Lefty Thompson said with that nasty little snicker of his. He took a bottle offered by Teddy Jewell and drank long from it. "They hired themselves a marshal to protect the farmers and the wagon traffic north of Salem City."

"Who'd they hire, that half-breed boy?" One-Eyed Frizell was chuckling, and jerked the bottle away from Lefty for a drink. "Hired a marshal? What's this territory coming to?" He was doing his best to make fun of the whole thing, but also remembered that he, too, had ran like a coward when those arrows started killing people.

"Marshal's name is Slim Hastings," Thompson said.

"From Texas?" Jenkins said. "There was a Slim Hastings was a Texas Ranger or somethin' that I heard of down there. Can't be the same one. Doesn't matter. Boys, what we've got to do is establish ourselves up there, hit a farm or two, take down a wagon or two, and put fear in those peoples' dinner plates. I think we should move out now, and after we get camp set up, we take this Hawthorne big shot and wipe him out. Kill that half-breed boy and burn the bastards out. We do this for Ornery Smith and the boys what died because of that boy."

Whiskey strength and rot-gut courage uttered loud was always a motivator, and the gang got their gear together for the long move north. The ride was difficult since they couldn't very well use the main roads and trails, instead they travelling cross-country, usually through heavy timber and steep mountainsides.

"MISTER CHAPMAN? I'm Paul Pritchett, the barber at the Salem Hotel. Can you spare a moment?"

"Mr. Pritchett, come in. We've not met, but I've heard your name mentioned a time or two. What can I do for you?" Ted Chapman was expecting an answer dealing with his insurance business and was surprised by what he heard.

"There are stories circulating in the newspapers and at my barber chair, that bribes are being offered to some of the members of the legislature to ensure a vote for slavery. I also understand that you are opposed to that very thing."

"I am indeed, adamantly opposed to slavery in any sense of the word. Come in, Mr. Pritchett and sit down. Can I get you a cup of coffee?"

"I'd like that, thank you," They walked into Chapman's living room that doubled as his insurance office and settled into large leather armchairs. Chapman's new housekeeper brought a pot of fresh coffee along with a tray of cups and saucers.

"I'm baking sweet rolls, sir," she said. "Would you like a couple when they come out of the oven?"

"That would be very nice, thank you. Pritchett, this is my new housekeeper, Olivia. My daughter Clementine married Moose Travis two weeks ago." He was still wearing the smile following that wedding ceremony at Travis's home.

"Now, Mr. Pritchett, about these bribe attempts."

"I hear things in my barbershop when men are talking among themselves, oblivious to the fact that I'm standing right there. This man George Belknap is the one offering the bribes, just like the newspaper conjectured, but I think he's going to do more than that. I think there are going to be threats made against some of the lawmakers that won't take the bribe."

"That's very interesting, Pritchett, but why are you coming to me with this? I'm an insurance agent."

"I know, sir, but your daughter married into the Travis family which means you probably have direct access to Zeke Hawthorne. I've met that man, helped get him elected, and I trust him very much. He's honest, truthful, and courageous. If Oregon is going to be admitted to the union, it must be as a free state, and Hawthorne is the one to make that happen.

"He needs to know this information, needs to be able to fight these men that want to bring slavery to Oregon. Will you pass on what I've just told you? I'll tell you every-thing I've heard and who I've heard it from. I can't go to the newspaper, that kind of information would destroy my business. They'd burn me out in a minute. Or worse. Look what they tried to do to Clarence Parson?"

Parson evaded the beating that was aimed at him by killing the attacker, and that was the biggest topic of conversation in Salem even after all this time. Parson didn't let the attack slow him down, and his front-page editorials slamming the bribery attempts and the slavery question had been lively and pointed. Many had been expecting a second attack on the editor, but it hadn't happened yet.

"I will, Pritchett. I'm spending this weekend at the Hawthorne farm, as a matter of fact. Give me everything you've heard, even if it's just a rumor. Zeke needs to know these things. When the wedding festivities are over, he plans on travelling around the territory and speaking on statehood and anti-slavery."

"I'm glad to hear that, Mr. Chapman. I've been to one of those parties at that farm. You're in for a fun time, sir."

It was a full pot of coffee and a platter of sweet rolls later that Paul Pritchett left the Chapman home, a broad smile on his face. *We might win this fight yet. So, the whole Travis clan will be at the farm this weekend. Sure, wish I could be there, I like those people.*

TRAVIS AND ELAINE arrived Friday afternoon and Elaine and Sarah started working on their baking projects immediately. Travis made his way to the barns and shop to find Zeke and Hiram. "How are you two coming with the meats?" he said.

"Some people have been known to say, 'Hello, how are you today?' but not my father-in-law," Zeke laughed, grabbing the huge Travis in a bear hug. "I'm fine, Travis, and we do have meat smoking right now. Elk and deer, there's salmon filets, and some ducks as well. We decided not to slaughter a hog, instead, Hiram shot us a fine-looking bear that we'll roast.

"Just how many people did you invite to this little party of yours?"

Travis didn't answer the question, and instead started talking about Oregon and some of the things that had been happening recently. "I'm seeing more crime than when we arrived here, Zeke. More like frontier times when anarchy seemed to be the order of the day. What happened to ordered civilization?"

"I don't think there's more crime, as such, Travis, but there has been a lack of this civilized order you talk about. The towns, villages, and cities have police protection, and until just recently the concept of law and order hasn't been questioned in the outlying and remote areas.

"With this influx of people filling in some of the rural areas, the criminals see an opportunity. There are at least two types of criminals operating in our area right now," Zeke said. "The outlaw is one type. He robs and steals, threatens and hurts his victims. The other is the one who works in illegal ways to change the way we live."

"You're talking about men like this George Belknap and his bribery attempts," Travis said.

"That's right. He wants to make Oregon into a little Virginia, with vast land holdings and slavery. Where moneyed landlords are the privileged class, and make the rules. He feels it's his right to work toward that end with or without the law on his side. That's what killed my friend, Nate Bishop. No, Travis, I don't see more crime, but I do see an insidious effort to change the way we live, and an outlaw element that is taking advantage of a lack of lawmen on duty. I think we've changed part of that picture with the hiring of Slim Hastings. I like that man."

"I hope he's going to be here for the party." Travis said. "Where's that eldest grandson of mine?"

"He has two crews out working the fields, Travis. He'll

be in for dinner, but these are busy times on our little farm. Along with corn, wheat, barley, hops, beans, and peas, we've now added a large twenty-acre plot for potatoes, and we've got an orchard that needs lots of attention. With many new families here in the valley, the towns have grown considerably, as well. We'll be helping to feed Eugene, Salem, Oregon City, and Portland.

"When do you expect Moose and Clemmie to get here? Or have you even heard from them?"

"Nary a word, Zeke," he laughed. "The last I saw of them, Moose was giving her big moon eyes and she was returning them. He told me he built a small log cabin on some property that he found, in the forest about two miles from the mill, and that's where they would be. He is one independent young man."

"Seems to be very much like his father before him," Zeke said. As they were walking out of the shop Hiram rode up and jumped from his horse, running to greet Travis.

"I knew you'd be here today," he said. "Didn't I tell you that he'd be here this morning, Papa?" He didn't wait for an answer. "When is Moose coming? I've never even met Clemmie."

"I doubt they'll be here before morning, Hi," Travis said. "But, I have been known to be wrong." He pushed Hiram back a step to give him a good look. "You're as big as your father, Hiram. You'll be catching up with me and old Moose here, shortly, I do believe."

"He may be about my size, Travis, but he's twice as strong as I am. That boy lifts and moves things I can't budge."

The three large men walked toward the big house

looking forward to a midday meal and more family talk. It would be the last time they would have the chance as the farm yards would be filled with wedding party guests all weekend.

"EVERYONE TELLS me how much like Papa I am, but he loves these parties that he throws, loves the singing and dancing, the telling of tall tales, and between us, Clemmie, it wouldn't bother me if we didn't go to this shindig of his." Moose was stretched out on a buffalo robe laid across the bed in their cozy log cabin.

"I'm not the most social person you've ever met, Mr. Moose Travis," she said. "It is important for us to be there. I don't think there's any kind of rule that says we have to stay for the entire weekend, though." They laughed, and an immediate conspiracy was born. "We would be the wicked ones, eh?"

"The thing is, after everyone says hello to us and congratulations and all that, they won't know if we're there or not. They won't even care or miss us," he laughed. He reached out and pulled her down to the bed and wrapped his huge arms around her tiny waist. "We'll be back here in our own little nest by sunset, Saturday."

The log cabin had two large rooms on the first level, the kitchen and pantry held a well-constructed dining table that would comfortably handle six people. There was a good-sized cook stove, and Moose had built a counter that allowed for plenty of workspace. The living room's best feature was a massive rock fireplace that also featured swinging iron rods that would hold pots, and a large hearth out front where coals could be moved out onto the flagstones for open fire cooking.

The living room was open beam construction and their bedroom was a second level loft that overlooked the living room. When Clemmie first saw the cabin, she knew she had made the right decision marrying this monster half-breed Shoshone warrior. "This is always what I've wanted, Moose. It's beautiful. Our home," she said, many times.

Clementine was Iroquois by birth but had been raised as a white American and was fast learning the ways of the western mountains and the Shoshone. "Before long you'll have me wearing buckskins and moccasins, quilling war shirts for you, and learning to dance like your mother."

"That would be nice," Moose said, letting his hands roam about some, getting gentle, friendly sighs back.

"We may have to add on a room or two, you know. I do plan on presenting you with children and they would be happier living inside."

Moose was on his back with Clemmie cuddled up to him. "I remember you telling me you planned on presenting me with children. Should I start building those extra rooms?"

"Might not be a bad idea, big guy," she said. "What time should we leave in the morning? It's a long ride out there."

"It is, and we probably won't be able to ride to the farm, say hello, and ride back home. Let's leave at sunrise and then leave Sunday morning, early, before everyone is up."

"Your mother and your sisters all have Shoshone names as well as English names, but you only have Moose. Why is that?"

"It's Papa's fault," he said. "When I was born, Mama handed me to Papa and he said, 'What a Moose,' and that's what I've been ever since. It certainly wasn't a traditional naming and when I reached the age when I could make my own name, I stuck with Moose."

"Our babies will be big, too," she said.

SATURDAY MORNING DAWNED clear and warm with the slightest of breezes. "Just like I ordered," Travis joked slipping out of the canvas-covered lodge Elaine and Sarah had erected for them. "I love these Oregon mornings but I miss my mountains sometimes."

"When do you suppose the first guests will be getting here?" Elaine asked. "I wonder if Moose and Clemmie will really show up. If it was me, I wouldn't," she said.

"Now, now," he said. "Let's not have any of that. When the drums start, you'll be the first one dancing and you know it. Look, here come Hiram. He's already been out in the fields with his crew. He has grown into a man that fast, Elaine."

"Like our Moose, I think. Sarah and I tried to figure out just how old he is. He thought he was twelve when we left Bridger. If that's right, he's eighteen years old, Travis. He is a man."

"He and Moose will always be boys, dear lady. Always."

"Like his grandpa," she laughed. "Let's go get something to eat. I see smoke from the kitchen stovepipe and I'm hungry. Shoshone women are always hungry, Travis. Feed me." She was laughing and giving him little pokes with her doubled up fists, dancing away as he tried to wrap his big arms around her.

Hiram joined them on the walk to the kitchen door. "How are the fields this morning, Hi?"

"Still there, grandpa," he laughed. "As usual, we could use a little rain, but the planting went well. Sprouts are showing and look healthy. Mama's kitchen garden is doing well, too. Barbara and Angus should be here pretty soon. When do you expect Moose and Clemmie?"

"So far, young man, you are the fourth person to ask me that and I'll tell you the same as the others. We'll know that when he gets here."

Their laughter mingled with that coming from those in the kitchen as they walked in. Suzanne and Joanne were doing a little dance with baby Travis sitting in the middle of floor between them. Sarah was using the kitchen table as a drum and Elaine immediately joined the twins and the dancing continued for another several minutes.

"Seems like a Shoshone woman forgets her hunger when the drums start," Travis said, giving Zeke a solid whack on the shoulders. Within moments, Hiram had joined the women in their dance. Travis and Zeke sat at the table sipping coffee fully enjoying the entertainment.

The first to arrive that morning was a small surrey carrying Barbara and Angus, and Ted Chapman was less than fifteen minutes behind them. Mike O'Brien's family soon arrived, followed by Joshua Peterson and his wife, Edith. Almost unnoticed, Sullivan came riding up the lane. "Looks like some kind of party," he joshed. "Am I invited?"

An hour later, arriving on horseback instead of a wagon or carriage were Moose and Clemmie, both dressed in buckskins and finely beaded and quilled mocs.

Moose was wearing a Shoshone warrior's battle or war shirt and carrying a lance. "Now, that's what I call an entrance," Travis said.

"Couldn't find any buffalo," Moose quipped. "Scared hell out of a wagon full of immigrants, though."

"Lucky you didn't get shot," Travis yelped.

People continued to arrive throughout the morning. Lodges and tents were erected all around the farmhouse, and Travis, Moose, Zeke, and Hiram laid out the planks for the dance floor, a fire pit was ringed in stone, and flagons of beer, whiskey, and rum were passed about. Food was consumed by the hundred-weight, and as the evening began showing itself, Hiram brought out his traditional drum.

Sarah walked out onto the dance platform with smoldering sage and the drumming started. She blessed the crowd, and as she moved toward Moose and Clemmie to bless their marriage- the drumming changed pace. Elaine and Barbara moved onto the wooden floor and joined Sarah and the three began the Shoshone wedding chant. It was a moving, exciting, ten minutes, and only the chanting and drumming could be heard.

As the rhythm picked up, the crowd could feel an ending developing, and Moose stood, took Clemmie by the hand, and they moved onto the floor and were ringed by the women. He slowly started his part of the wedding dance and chant, moving around his beautiful bride, counter to the movements of the women. The drumming was getting faster, the feet were starting to hit the boards harder, Moose was jumping higher, and the climax found pounding drums, Moose leaping high in the air and falling in front of Clemmie, on his knees, kissing her hands softly.

For just a moment, it was absolutely still, no movement, no sound, and then the crowd erupted in howls of delight, storming the dance floor to hug and touch the performers. Zeke sat on one side of Hiram and Travis on the other, and they both whopped Hiram hard across his back. All he could do was sit with a huge smile splashed across his face.

Silas Williams pulled his fiddle out of his blankets and was joined by Judge Virgil Brown and his banjo. They played for hours, only taking breaks for beakers of beer and plates full of meat and fish. The dancing and singing might have been heard as much as five miles distant.

A lot of the singing was led by the new Willamette Valley Marshal, Slim Hastings. He seemed to know at least a hundred west Texas cowboy songs, south Texas cotton plantation songs, and Mississippi Riverboat songs. Silas Williams's fiddle kept right with him through them all.

Great platters of smoked venison, smoked salmon, roasted fowl, and vegetables were brought out and the feast continued. Barbara caught Elaine's and Sarah's eyes and motioned they should talk. They slipped into the kitchen, now void of people, and sat at the large table.

"I'm pretty sure I'm going to have a baby," Barbara said after Sarah poured coffee for them. "Angus doesn't know yet, but I'm pretty sure."

## 9

HIRAM WAS UP WELL BEFORE SUNRISE, DESPITE THE late night's activities. He was stoking the fire in his kitchen stove when he was sure he heard horses trotting away. He dashed out the door, grabbing the bow and quiver of arrows always standing close, and ran into the front yard. Did some horses get out or were horses being stolen?

*Am I being paranoid? These outlaws robbing and stealing from the immigrants, raiding the ranches and farms up and down the valley have all of us worried, I guess.* He had a good view across the broad side hill and down onto the main farmstead and spotted the horses. He smiled and wagged his head back and forth recognizing Moose's bulk and Clemmie's tiny frame as they rode down the long lane from his parent's home.

"You're a smart man, Uncle Moose," he chuckled. "Getting out early and not having to explain why." The morning air was brisk despite the fact it was supposed to be almost summer, and he slipped back into his kitchen to make coffee. Weekend or not, party atmosphere aside, he had a crew to put to work, and it would be a busy day. The heavy winter rains got the weeds all anxious, he liked to say, and he and the crew would be fighting them the rest of the summer.

The move from his parent's house into his own was more difficult on Sarah than on Hiram or his father. The two men spent most of the winter building the house in between storms, farm work, and territorial business. It wasn't a big house but it was impressive.

Zeke had spent the last few years teaching Hiram the art and craft of the cabinetmaker, and every part of that art was put to use in the home. Few nails were evident; instead the wood was made to work with mortises, pegs, and fitted joints. Wood panels were carved, the ironwork was extraordinary. Every set of hinges on every door and cabinet was hand forged wrought iron, some delicate as a butterfly's wing, some meant to hold off the barbaric Huns.

Hiram's new home had two bedrooms upstairs, a large kitchen and pantry, living room, and office downstairs. The flooring was inlaid parquet hard-wood, wainscoting was carved and inlaid as well. "We would never build a home like this, Hiram, except for someone very wealthy. What we've done here, is what every cabinet maker has always wanted to do. Pull out all the stops and let 'er rip."

Hiram still had his evening meals with the family, and on the few days that he didn't spend the entire day in the fields or in one of the shops, he brought the twins up and let them romp and have fun. He taught the girls how to ride, had Suzanne learning how to make the strings for his bows, and found that Joanne, despite her young age, was teaching herself to read. These times with the girls and his baby brother made him wonder if he would ever have a family of his own.

And then the thoughts of Barbara got all mixed up with thoughts of that beautiful young lady on the wagon train. *Gloria was her name and I sure wish I knew more about her. Why is she married to that old man? This is not right, either. I would run away with my Aunt Barbara in a minute, and I would break Gloria away from her marriage, too! I think I'll just be a fine farmer.*

DOWN AT THE big house and in the open areas surrounding it, life slowly emerged from bedrooms, tents, bedrolls, and the bunkhouse. Fires were lit, gentle cursing followed stubbed toes, and laughter came like steam from a coffee pot. Rebecca had the kitchen stove lit and had the first trays of biscuits out on the table. Sweet rolls would follow, and then platters of smoked side meat, bowls of scrambled eggs, and pans full of fried potatoes would be made available.

"I haven't danced that much since our own wedding," Zeke said. "I don't know what hurts more, my feet or my head." Sarah was dressed and smiling with no pity showing as Zeke struggled into his clothes. "I know, but how do you say no to your father? He can drink a barrel of rum and dance and sing for twelve hours, Sarah, and still be ready for another party.

"I'm not up to his standards, dear lady."

She giggled and patted him gently on the back, leading him out of their bedroom. "It'll take a week for us to even find the farm," he said. The aroma coming up the staircase helped get the big man started and he could almost smile by the time he stepped into the kitchen.

The twins raced to wrap their arms around his legs and little Travis scooted the best he could to be held by his Papa. "Good morning, all," he said and slumped into one of the chairs by the immense kitchen table. Remnants of the party, like elk bones, turkey carcasses, and empty pie plates were still strewn about.

"Somebody have a party down here?" he quipped. "No leftovers for the inn-keeper, eh?"

People moved in and out of the kitchen all morning long, getting breakfast, saying thank you for having them, and some leaving gifts for Moose and Clemmie. By two o'clock that afternoon, only Travis and Elaine, and Barbara and Angus remained. "I love this wonderful family, I really do, but at some point, I have to remind myself I'm not the man I think I am." Travis had limped about all day, moving from one chair to the next, from one stump to a log and back to a chair.

"If I ever say party again, somebody shoot me." He sat at the kitchen table, little Travis on his knee, nursing a cup of well-laced coffee. "I don't believe I insulted anyone, I don't remember smashing any heads or breaking any furniture. Elaine, oh love of my life, am I injured?"

"No, you brute," she laughed. "You were a perfect Rocky Mountain gentleman, dancing with all the ladies, drinking with all the men, and playing with all the children. You sang too loud and you cussed too often, and you had a grand time, as you always do."

"Well, we must leave, then," he said. "What are your plans, Zeke? You've been talking about a trip around the territory. Will you be leaving soon?"

"I'll leave in a couple of days, Travis. Spend some time in Portland, Oregon City, and into the great basin deserts of the eastern territory. I have to put an end to this slavery question, have to generate support for our constitutional convention and statehood. I'll never understand how someone can believe that it is right for one human to actually own another human.

"It's been a way of life for centuries, Travis, I know, but I believe as you do, that it is wrong." Zeke took a long drink of coffee and settled back in his chair. "We both know slavery has been going on since the dawn of history. We humans are pretty arrogant thinking we are the dominant species on this old earth of ours, that humans are the ultimate in the animal kingdom, and maybe that's why we can convince ourselves that it's quite reasonable for one man to own another."

"I'm glad sometimes that I'm getting to be an old man," Travis said. "You'll win this fight, Zeke. I'm sure of it. Just be careful. Some of these men you're facing are mean killers and you are challenging their very way of life. You're an enemy, you're backing them into a corner, and you'll have to be as wary as if you were back in the wilds of the mountains." He shrugged and sighed. "There's no such thing as a tame badger, Zeke. You're facing a mess of 'em, and you've got 'em pretty much riled up. Keep that knife of yours sharp and ready to hand."

"I understand how dangerous it is and I have my family in my mind at all times, Travis. At all times. Sometimes I feel that I was wrong in seeking this seat in the legislature and putting my family at risk. And then I think of just how wrong it would be if no one took up this fight and Oregon became a slave state.

"They really want families like ours to be illegal, Travis. The exclusion law exists in this territory and they have the votes to demand that it be included in a state constitution. I don't know if I can stop that from happening, but I'm going to fight to my last breath to keep Oregon from becoming a slave state."

"I KNOW you have to get back home, but we haven't had much chance to talk, like we used to. I'm glad you're married to Angus and happy. I just wish I had been older and it was us that was married." Hiram was sitting with Barbara in the chairs under the cottonwood trees, sipping some cold tea. He realized that he was blushing some, but had to speak his mind.

"I know I teased you something horrible, Hi, but please know how much I love you. You've grown to be a fine man, big and strong, and honest as the day. I have a secret that I'll share with you if you promise to keep it." She gave him one of those smiles that two years ago would have sent him into a panic of love-sickness.

"I will," he said. He still felt chills up and down his spine when he gazed into her eyes and often wondered if he would really find a woman as good as Barbara for his own.

"I'm pretty sure that Angus and I are going to have a baby. Promise me you won't say anything. I haven't even told Angus yet."

He promised and took her small and very dainty hand in his huge one. "I'm very happy for you, Barbara," he said. It was hard to watch them ride out from the farm, harder still to understand that he would never have her for his own. *I've loved her from the minute I saw her. The only other girl that has ever looked at me the way Barbara does is that girl on the wagon. The one married to the old man that whimpered from a little bruise.*

He wondered if maybe he would be able to ride south one day and see if those people were able to start their little community. Maybe see if that girl was still there. *Maybe when Papa gets back from his trip I'll make a little trip as well.*

"I HAVE three ten-gallon barrels of coal oil, Hank. We should be able to create a little fear, eh?" One-Eyed Frizell was grinning as he jumped down from the wagon. "There's considerable traffic on the River Road. Looks like half the east coast is moving to Oregon."

"When we're through they will ride with the bile of fear in their scrawny throats, One-Eye." Hank Jenkins had done his best to reinforce his gang of outlaws, bringing Lefty Thompson in. Lefty's brother, Sam, wanted to join but it was determined that with his bad attitude and no ability to keep his mouth shut, that he just stay at his run-down little farm and feel miserable. His son Michael, after working two seasons for Zeke Hawthorne had moved to Portland and become a dockworker.

Two young desperados from California had joined up, Leander Voss, missing part of his left ear from a knife fight, and John Sam, originally from western Utah and half Bannock Indian, who was known to kill with his bare hands in favor of weapons. A third man, Dick Crabtree, joined after a foray against a freight wagon. He had been riding as a guard and turned on his mates. That pleased Jenkins.

"Crabtree, I want you and Teddy Jewel to ride south to the Hawthorne ranch and see what it is we'll be up against. That half-breed sumbitch and his big shot father are gonna die and that farm will be ashes when we're through," he smirked.

"I want you to find a good way in and out without being on the main roads, and where we should hit to do the most damage. The house must burn, for sure, but find out what else is important for them to lose."

Jewel and Crabtree left as soon as they packed their bedrolls and filled their saddlebags with some food and coffee. The ride south along the River Road was an easy one and when they were within two or three miles from the farm, they moved east toward the hills and out of sight.

"We'll make a camp up in the trees, Crabtree. If we can get into a hollow of some kind, at least we can have a little fire for tonight. We'll move down in the morning to give that big shot and his kid a good look-see," Jewel said.

"I heard the stories about him taking out three members of the gang and putting old Hank and One-Eye to flight, but I don't really believe them. Must have been more than one kid."

"You don't want to talk that way about Hank," Jewel said, scowling at the man. "I was there. You weren't."

"Just sayin' that little half-breed boy had to have help."

"I seen that boy in Salem City one day," Jewel said. "He's bigger than One-Eyed Frizell and carries a knife that would bring a fortune on the streets of New Orleans. Word is, he made the knife hisself. He might be young but he ain't no little boy. I've seen Hank Jenkins in a fight or two and he ain't no coward, neither."

They ate fried side meat and drank water that night and the next morning, not wanting to build a fire that might be seen, just ate what was at hand. "There's a cattle ranch around here somewhere, too," Jewel said as they rode out in the morning. "I think the Hawthorne place should be over that rise yonder." He was pointing down the hillside and to the south to a ridge some mile and a half away.

"Looks like we'll have to do our lookin' from the trees, Jewel. Farmland is mighty open and we don't want to be seen. Let's stay up in the trees until we can see the place, then figure how to get close."

It was almost an hour before they found a spot where they could be hidden from view and still see the large farm. "They ain't nothin' to burn 'cept the main house, barn, and outbuildings." Teddy Jewell had crawled to a good spot to see the whole place. "Ain't gonna burn green corn stalks or beans. Hank can bring the boys to where we are. It would be easy to swoop right down and burn 'em out."

"I don't see a whole lot of people, Jewell," Crabtree said. "They must have farm hands, but how many? We ride down there and find five men with rifles, it would about end our play. Hank'll want to know how many men are there."

"I see a couple of men in the corn over there," Jewell pointed. "Probably the boy and his big shot father," he chuckled. "Let's get back to our camp. It's too late to start back, but we can in the morning. I got a jug of whiskey from that place in Salem. It's pretty good."

That was when they spotted the small house, on the hillside away from the main house. "Now, who lives in that house?" Jewell said. "We got to burn that one down too, don't you think?" He was almost cackling in anticipation of the gang riding down on the two large homes.

"Maybe steal us a woman or two while we're at it," Crabtree laughed.

It was still daylight when the two rode to their camp and broke out the jug. By sunset, common sense was out the window and they lit a fire for a warm supper. Down in the valley, Mike O'Brien was riding through his herd and spotted the fire. He rode toward it and dismounted some distance away. *That ain't no wildfire. Looks more like somebody makin' camp up there. Hope it's them rustlers.* Rifle in hand, he made his way quietly toward the blaze and heard two men talking.

It was a fast ride back to his ranch, and an even faster one in the morning to Hawthorne's place. "They were drunk and talking and laughing about burning you out, Hiram. Your Papa picked the wrong time to leave on his trip, I think." O'Brien was in the kitchen with Hi, Sarah, and Rebecca.

"Can you send one of your boys to find Slim Hastings?" Hiram figured he didn't have enough men to fight the whole gang, but if he could get help, he might be able to. "I'll keep the crew right here at the main house and we'll fight 'em off. Five men and two mean women, and they'll wish they never heard our name," he laughed.

Sarah whacked him across the back, chuckling as she did. "I'm not mean, son, but I am the wife of Sharp Knife." Rebecca blushed and didn't say anything.

"Did they talk numbers, Mr. O'Brien? Did they mention how many men might be in that outlaw gang?"

"I'll send for Hastings and then round up Joshua and K.C. and be back here tonight. I didn't hear any mention of how many were in the gang. Josh is a fighter and has a bone to pick with Jenkins, and K.C. has a couple of men working for him. We'll give 'em hell, my boy, we will. Pardon the talk, Mrs. Hawthorne."

"I'm Travis's daughter, Mr. O'Brien," she laughed. "I've heard worse."

O'Brien rode off to send his son looking for Hastings and for him to round up the ranchers. Hiram rode out to the fields and brought the crew in. "Meet me in the kitchen as soon as you get your equipment and animals taken care. If you have any weapons, bring them with you, we're gearing up for a fight."

## 10

SIX MEN RODE FROM THE HILLSIDE TOWARD THE Hawthorne farm just as the sun cleared the mountaintops to the east. It was a warm, early summer morning that already had the feel of a hot day in the making. Dust rose from the horse's hooves as they trotted in single file through scrub brush and high wild grasses, kicking up a stray jackrabbit or two. The only sound was of the horses and the gear they carried.

Before leaving the little campsite, Hank Jenkins had given a long talk on what to do and where to do it. "There are two things that are most important," he concluded. "That big house Teddy talked about must be ashes before we leave, and that half-breed boy must be dead.

"Whoever lives in the second house must be attached to that farm, so that house needs to be burned down, too. The barns and all the other buildings gotta burn long and hot. I don't nothin' left when we ride out."

"What about the women?" One-Eyed Frizell asked.

"What you find is yours," Jenkins answered. "Course, you want to share with your pards," he laughed.

Lee Voss struggled to his feet and walked up to the fire. "We rob and steel, Hank. I don't see the profit angle here. I ain't never had to kill nobody before that hadn't tried to kill me. Scare the gold right out of their pockets is my game." There were some snarls, and a couple of sounds that may have been in favor of what Voss said.

"That so-called little boy killed three of our gang, Voss," Jenkins snarled, letting his hand hover close to his big knife handle. "You knew when we rode up here what we were gonna do. You a damn coward? You the kind of man don't believe in protecting your pards' backs? You are about to die." The anger was written deep in Jenkins face, but he didn't seem to remember that he was one of those that fled in terror when the arrows started flying?

"I ain't no coward, Jenkins, and no man has lived after calling me one. You draw that knife on me, you're crow-bait."

The two men stood less that ten feet apart, to the side of the morning fire. The rest of the outlaws slowly withdrew from what was sure to be a bloody mess.

The situation ended in an instant when One-Eyed Frizell picked up his Hawken and shot Voss dead. "Worthless bastard. Those were my friends died at the hands of that filthy half-breed. Anyone else want out?" He quickly reloaded the weapon, glaring about the camp area.

"All right, let's get back to business. Crabtree, drag this vermin into the brush and out of my sight." Hank Jenkins gave Frizell a quick little smile. "Now, when we get down there, kill everyone in sight and head to the house and torch it. Each of you has enough coal oil?" He asked, getting nods from everyone. They had filled empty whiskey bottles from the barrel that was brought up from Portland.

"Two of you, torch the barns and outbuildings, and we ride back up here fast. Any questions, ask 'em now or keep your mouths shut." He looked around and everyone shook their heads. "Let's mount up. This is for Peabody, Ornery, and Irish Jack. Let's go."

If anyone mourned Leander Voss, they did it quietly.

IT WAS after three in the morning before everyone from the outlying farms and ranches had made it to the Hawthorne farm. Hiram had the group, K.C. Whitman, Joshua Peterson, Silas Williams, Mike O'Brien and his sons, and Marshal Slim Hastings at the kitchen table with plenty of hot coffee. Hiram had already sent the Saunders boys and the Stockbridge brothers out to do a little quick surveillance of the area.

"Thank you all for being here for us," he started. "Sam Saunders rode up to where Mr. O'Brien saw the gang members day before yesterday and just told me there are seven of them there now. My men have muzzle-loading rifles, so they will only get one shot off before they have to go to their knives. I will shoot once and then go to my bow."

He looked around at the men and knew he had superior manpower, but worried about firepower. "Mr. Hastings, you wanted to say something. Now would be a good time."

"Thank you, Hi. I think Silas, you'll back me on this. In Texas, when ranchers were facing an outlaw gang, the gang almost always attacked the main house first, tried to burn it down, then went after the outbuildings. I've heard of this Jenkins fool, and I'd bet that's going to be his plan.

"Mr. O'Brien moved Sarah, Rebecca, and the children to his place last night, so what we're doing now is simply keeping those outlaws from reaching this place. Hi and O'Brien know this property like the back of their hands, so here is what I'm proposing, and I'm doing it as Valley Marshal." It was necessary to assume that leadership position as early in this game as possible.

"Hi, you and your men, you have four?"

Hiram nodded.

"Good. Get out on the trail you think they'll be coming in on, and make your stand. O'Brien, take Peterson and Whitman and back up Hi.

"Silas, you will be here at the farmhouse with that nasty shotgun of yours and I'll be at the barn with mine. Anybody gets past Hi and O'Brien's people, we'll take care of them. Any questions?"

Coffee was taken down and the men filed out of the farmhouse to get to their posts. "I'm putting out all the lights here," Silas Williams said. "It will look like the family is asleep and not looking for trouble if some get through."

"I don't think anyone's gonna get past Hiram Hawthorne," Slim Hastings chuckled. "That boy is riled up like a sidewinder eyeing a kangaroo rat- up Pecos way. I don't think I'd want to face off with that one." Silas Williams was laughing hard at Hastings as the tall Texan walked out of the kitchen.

Most of the men carried shotguns and Colt Army cap and ball revolvers, and all of them had big knives, the real weapons of choice. Hi, Sam, and Skinny Saunders, and Toby and Brian Stockbridge walked out through the cornfields to the only possible trail the outlaws could use to get to the farm. O'Brien and his crew were right behind them. The sky was just lightening a bit as they set themselves for the attack.

The brush was thick and there were stands of timber on the slope that led to the farm, giving the men plenty of cover. These were the foothills that Hiram hunted in regularly, and he could probably follow the trails blindfolded. "I'll be right up here," Hi said. "I'll shoot my bow first, then the rifle, then back to the bow. Sam, you and Toby get across the trail from me. Let's not shoot at each other.

"It's important that we know where each of us is. Another thing, we will not yell stop or put our hands up, or give an inch. They are here to kill my family. I will not let that happen." He could feel tears begin and quickly turned away to march toward where he would hide.

"Brian, you and Skinny get about twenty yards or so down the trail from us and pick off anyone who gets through. If they get through you, they'll then be facing Mike O'Brien and his crew. Let's all get in position and stay quiet. No talking, no smoking."

Skinny stayed as close to Sam as he could and the two nestled down behind a bushy sage brush, clearing some rocks and debris out of the way of their old cap and ball rifles. "You'll be fine, Skinny," Sam whispered.

HANK JENKINS ALLOWED Dick Crabtree to move in front of him as they slowed their horses to a walk, coming down out of the trees and moving across one of the lower hills. The Hawthorne property was spread out in front of them and they could see young corn waving in the morning breeze. Jenkins slowed down again, and nodded to One-Eyed Frizell as he too passed the outlaw leader.

Jenkins wanted everyone to know this was the Hank Jenkins gang, but once a coward, always a coward. He was not going to be point man, not going to actually lead his men into his fight. Not going to be the target of choice.

They crested the hill and started down a trail that led through a stand of timber that included aspen, pine, cedar, and fir. The trail was easy to follow and the riders were each giving thought to what would be taking place when they reached the farm. Frizell had thoughts of a woman, and Crabtree just wanted to watch the house burn to the ground. How many guns might be waiting for them? Did anyone know they were coming?

It was one of those glorious Oregon summer mornings with high thin clouds streaming their colors across an endless sky. A sunrise breeze spread the aroma of mountain and meadow, but if one was seriously attuned to nature, one would not be hearing the birdcalls of morning. It was a dead give-away that the outland was being invaded. It was so quiet that when the bowstring gave its vicious twang, all heads jerked up.

Crabtree screamed and fell backwards from his horse, an arrow sticking out of the middle of his chest, blood arcing into the dust.

Before Crabtree's body hit the ground, a rifle shot took One-Eyed Frizell out of his saddle, half his head on one side of the trail, the other with his body. Jenkins' horse went down with an arrow piercing its neck and flung Hank Jenkins face-first into the dirt. Jenkins had his pistol in his hand and as he fell, he pulled the trigger. Sam Saunders screamed as he saw Hiram Hawthorne grab at his chest and fall to the dirt.

John Sam and Teddy Jewell whipped their horses around and put them in a full gallop back up the trail. Lefty Thompson had been riding directly behind Jenkins and gave the outlaw a hand up onto the back of his horse, turned it to flee and took a lead ball in his shoulder almost knocking him out of the saddle

Sam Saunders had leapt to his feet, pulled that old front stuffer to his shoulder and fired, before running to Hiram's side.

With help from Jenkins, Lefty stayed aboard and spurred his horse hard. The four men on three horses didn't stop at the little camp to pick up what was left, and made straight for the main hideout, almost killing their horses.

"Hiram's hit!" Sam Saunders screamed down the trail, bringing Mike O'Brien and his boys on the run. Saunders knelt next to Hi. "Where'd he get you?" he asked.

Hiram pulled his bloody hand away from his left shoulder. "I think it's just a nick, Sam, but damn me if it doesn't hurt some." Sam could see the tear in Hiram's jacket and pulled the coat back to get a good look at the wound.

"Yeah, boss, just a nick. Ripped a good ridge right across your shoulder. We'll get a bandage on there and you'll be fine. Sure, gonna be sore, though."

O'Brien got Hiram up on his feet after they stopped the bleeding with a pressure bandage, and the bunch made sure the outlaws on the ground were dead before trudging back to the big house.

"Did you hear that, Slim?" Silas Williams asked. "He took two of them outlaws to the ground, got himself all shot up, and he's wondering what's for dinner. That boy may think he's half-injun, but what he is, is Texan."

The two men got a good laugh out of the situation, some of that coming from the let-down that follows a quick battle.

Lefty was weak from loss of blood and shock and was held in the saddle by Jenkins. He helped get Thompson off the horse and laid him out as John Sam got the fire kindled. "Hang on, Lefty, we'll get you fixed up," Teddy Jewell said. He brought a pan of water and a couple of rags over, ripped the shirt away from the wound and was amazed how much blood was still pouring from the man.

He dipped the rags in the water and pressed them to the wound, once, twice, squeezing blood out each time. The flow simply wouldn't stop as the bullet apparently severed an artery and Jewell couldn't put pressure where it was needed.

Before he could get the blood stopped with pressure from the wet rags, it stopped on its own when Lefty's heart stopped. "He's gone, Hank. Bled out. We was seven this morning, now we're three, all because of a damn half-breed kid. I'm callin' it, Hank. It's over for me."

John Sam understood far more than Hank Jenkins ever would how it was that a half-breed kid could take out the gang. Sam was half Bannock, raised by his Bannock mother and outlaw, white father. He, too, was an expert with a bow and quiver full of arrows and wished he might have an opportunity to meet this kid, but knew one of them would have to die if they did meet.

"We got shot up because one man with a bow and quiver full of arrows can shoot many times while we reload, and that half-breed can shoot from hiding and quietly. There was many more people waiting for us than one Indian kid. They knew we were coming, Hank. We didn't surprise them, they surprised us.

"This so-called gang ain't no gang no more," Sam said. "I'm heading into the Snake River country. Take care of yourself, Hank. See you around, Teddy." Sam stepped onto his horse, turned it and quietly rode off, wondering if Hank Jenkins would shoot him in the back. *Of all the people I could have picked to ride with, I managed to tangle up with a bunch of fools. I've always been a loner, and I'm gonna stay a loner from now on.*

"I WISH NOW we had ridden our horses up here instead of walking," Hiram said as everyone gathered around Crabtree's dead body. After getting his wound well-tended, Hiram brought the Saunders boys back to the scene of the battle to take care of the bodies and look to see if anyone might be lurking around.

"Can't chase those fools on foot. I sure didn't mean to kill that horse. He reared just as I let the arrow go. That other one dead?"

"He's dead, Hi," Skinny Saunders said. "Think we should go get our horses and try to follow?"

"Let's get these fools buried and get back down to the house, make sure they didn't circle back around and then we'll decide on our next move. It will probably be Slim Hastings call, now," Hiram said. "I was sure you said there were seven men, Saunders, but I only counted six. Keep your eyes open, we might have a stalker out there."

It wasn't much of a chore to take care of the dead, and a short walk back to the main house. "They weren't carrying any identification, Slim," Hi said. "What's your plan?"

"Thanks," Slim Hastings said. "Got them in the ground? Good. I'll take up the trail and see where it leads. You said there were seven men at the camp you rode up on, Mr. Saunders?" Sam nodded.

"And, Hi, you said there were six riding down on you? I wonder where number seven might be?"

"Each of the dead men had whiskey bottles filled with coal oil, Slim," Hiram said. "We found a couple of bottles on the ground that must have been dropped during the getaway. Those men were going to burn us out. They would have thought everyone was in bed asleep. They planned to kill Mama and the children."

Hiram tried to hold back a river of tears cascading through the dust on his face. "What kind of man would kill women and children while they slept? My mama and those kids would be dead if you hadn't accidentally ridden up on that camp, Mr. O'Brien."

He slumped down on a piece of equipment near the barn, shaking with anger and fear, feeling the let-down that follows extreme action such as he'd just experienced.

"I'll ride with you, Slim," Silas Williams said. "You haven't even had time to pick a deputy yet and you're on a big case. Wish I was twenty years younger."

"You'd still be an old man." Hastings joshed him and

then ducked quickly as a big right fist narrowly missed his jaw. That was followed by laughter, so all was well with the Texans. "I ain't that old," Williams muttered through his laughing.

Hiram sent Skinny Saunders and his crew into the fields to commence another day on the farm, hitched up the spring wagon, tied his horse off behind, and rode to the O'Brien ranch to fetch his mama and the children.

*What an ugly bunch of men to simply come riding down out of the mountains with the idea of burning us out. Because of them, now I've killed another man, and even killed an innocent horse. I wonder if Papa was right, bringing us here? Yes, of course he was, and it's what he's fighting for right now, to make Oregon a good place to live.*

"I'VE BEEN FRANTIC, Hiram. I'm so glad you're safe. Is the house still there? Are our men safe? I wish your father were here. Tell me what happened." Sarah was talking faster than Hiram had ever heard and waited for her to calm down before trying to answer any of the hundreds of questions thrown at him. "I want to go home," she cried.

"Please tell me you're going to be fine. My son, shot! My God, Hiram I'm never going to let Zeke leave that farm again. Ever. Did they get the bullet out? We have to get the bullet out, Hiram. If it gets infected, you'll die." She was shaking and crying, fear written in broad strokes across her pretty face.

"It was just a nick, Mama," he said quietly, holding her close. "Like a big old scrape. I'll be fine, Mama. Let's get you and the kids back home. We're all going to be safe.

"They never got close, Mama. The house is fine." He sat down next to her and put his arm around her. "I'm not sure I like this growing up stuff, Mama. I wish Papa was here to tell me what to do."

"He doesn't need to, Hi. You already know what to do. You are a man, a grown man." She was bawling like a baby, letting him hold her tight. "Your Papa will be as proud of you as I am, and love you as much as I do."

It took many minutes of sitting quietly with Hi, and then Sarah gathered her wits, the twins and little Travis. Hiram drove them back to the farm.

THE WORD OF THE ATTEMPTED ATTACK ON THE Hawthorne farm spread up and down the Willamette Valley and through the streets of Salem City. It didn't take long for rumors to spread that George Belknap was behind the attack. Clarence Parson, sitting at his desk in the newspaper office was talking about the attempted attack with Ted Chapman.

"I've only met Belknap once," Chapman said. "Is he that kind of man? Would he send a band of outlaws to burn out Zeke, kill his family? He seemed rather well-educated, arrogant as most Virginians seem to be, but is he a killer?"

"I'm sure he has it in him to hire it done." Editor Parson was scowling at the thought. "He would never get another man's blood on his lily-white hands. He denies it, but I'm sure he was behind the murder of Nate Bishop two years ago. The old group calling themselves Oregon Firsters, pretty much broken up now, did the actual killing, but I'm positive Belknap was behind it.

"Can't print conjecture as much as I want to. What does Mr. Travis think about all of this?"

"My son-in-law, Moose Travis, rode to the farm this morning. He's ready to go to war. I haven't been near the Salem Trading Post, but I'm sure that old man Travis is sharpening one or more of his knives."

"Has anyone even heard from Zeke? Does anyone know where he is?"

"The farm and the wound he suffered in the attack are keeping young Hiram from leaving. This is a busy time on that farm and he has to run things. Right now, it's just he and four men that work for him, running that large farm. He's looking to hire more help but there isn't any way he can leave to search for Zeke. According to what I hear from family members, Hiram's wound became infected and is apparently very painful.

"All anyone knows is that Zeke left the Columbia River area and headed south to visit what's left of the Oregon Territory along the western banks of the Snake River. I hope that riders have been sent to find him and get him home."

"Maybe the word will spread and Zeke will hear about the attack." Parson leaned back in his old swivel chair, chewing on an ancient, previously chewed cigar. "I'm going to do everything I can to implicate Belknap in this attack. Oregon should be leading the west as a modern, sophisticated, territory ready to join the union, not filled with outlaws who could be hired to burn out families."

"Sounds like you're on a mission, Mr. Parson. You better make sure your little single shot pistol is loaded and primed." Ted Chapman was amazed that the man was still filled with fire after the attack he survived.

"I retired that old boy," Parson laughed. "I got me a double-barreled fowling piece loaded with buckshot right here," and he pulled a beautiful shotgun from under his desk. "Let 'em come, Mr. Chapman, let 'em come."

"My God, George, have you heard what's being said around Salem City about you?" Peter Flowers, the Willamette Valley rancher was pacing up and down the broad portico-type porch at Belknap's place south of Salem. "They're saying you are responsible for that attempted attack on the Hawthorne family."

"I've heard," Belknap snarled. He was sitting in the shade, a glass of Virginia rum in hand, chewing on a long cigar. "Wish they'd been able to make the attack. That bastard Parson is churning out those lies."

"What are we going to do about this, George? It's this kind of violence that will destroy our program, our efforts to bring slavery to Oregon. You didn't do this, did you?"

"No, of course not, Pete." Belknap's anger flared at the comment, and then he settled back in the chair with a hint of a smile. "I might have wanted to, but I didn't have anything to do with the attempted attack."

"People are bringing up the killing of old Bishop two years ago, too, George. You remember how our plans backfired on us then. People believed then that you were responsible, and now, they say you hired that gang. How do we stop that kind of talk?"

Belknap just sat in his big chair on the porch sipping rum, a dejected but maybe not completely beaten man. "I don't know, Pete. I didn't do it, you must believe me. You know I didn't arrange the Bishop killing, you must believe me that I'm not responsible for the Hawthorne attack."

"Unfortunately, it's not important what I believe, George. Our plans are going to be associated with the attack. How do we fight that?" Pete Flowers was at a loss as to what to believe and could see the great plans on bringing slavery to Oregon going up in the flames that should have destroyed Zeke Hawthorne's farmhouse. Flowers lacked the ability to think a problem through, simply reacted to situations as they developed, often in anger and violence.

"I'm going to ride through the territory, George, and spread the word that you were not behind the attack, that it was a gang of outlaws from California or something. We have to fight this. I have a man in New Orleans right now who is ready to sell us the slaves we will need once our program is in place. We have to fight this."

"That's a good idea, Pete. I also think it would be a good idea to make up some posters to hang everywhere you go, promoting Oregon as a slave state. Get the people to understand how important the issue is to Oregon's coming into the union as a slave state. Hit 'em in the pocketbook, Pete. Tell them how slavery will help their businesses, farms, and ranches. Do you need anything for your trip?"


"I WAS clear down near Fort Boise on the Snake River, re-supplying for the trip home when I heard about the attack, Sarah. I got here just as fast as I could. Thank God you and the children are safe. Tell me about Hiram. All I heard was that he was a hero and was wounded." Zeke carried a ten-day beard and just as much dirt on his clothing when he rode into the farmyard that morning. Hiram and the crew were already in the fields, armed now with shotguns and rifles.

"I haven't ever been that afraid, Zeke," she said. She threw her arms around the big man and held on tight. "You're home and we're safe. Don't ever leave me again. Promise."

"I'm glad I made the trip but I'm so sorry you had to go through all that," he whispered. "Is Hi okay? Was anyone injured?"

"Hi saved us all, and if Mr. O'Brien hadn't accidentally rode up on that camp we would be dead, Zeke. All the men up and down the valley came to our defense. The children and I stayed at the O'Brien's until it was over. Slim Hastings is out searching for the gang now. He thinks they rode south. He's been on their trail, but it's been hard to follow, he says.

"As you heard, Hi was wounded, and it would have been considered just a slight nick. The bullet tore some skin and meat off his shoulder, but the wound is now infected and I'm having a hard time controlling it. He's out with the men, Zeke. He needs to take it easy for a couple of days and let that wound heal, but he won't."

"I'll get cleaned up and get a good meal in me then go find Hi and the boys. Where is Hastings situated? Is he on that little piece of property near O'Brien's?"

"No, he's on the outlaws' trail," she said. "He's still looking for deputies, too, I think."

Zeke took a long bath, shaved, and had a platter of pork chops and mashed potatoes before heading out to the corn and wheat fields. He found Hiram in one of the cornfields talking with Sam Saunders.

"I'm glad you're home, Papa," Hiram said, hugging Zeke. "Mama and I aren't gonna let you ride off, ever again. Are you okay?"

"I'm fine, Hi, and I'm sure glad you and the family are." He held his son at arm's length, giving him a good looking over. He could see the bloody bandage under Hi's shirt. "You did a fine thing, son. How are things out here? And, tell me about this wound you won't let heal." He waved his arms, taking in all the fields, filled with growing corn, wheat, beans, hops, and even potatoes, and then tapped his son's shoulder, lightly.

"We'll have a fine harvest, Papa," Hi said, easing back from that tap. "We need to hire more people and soon. The Saunders boys and the Stockbridge boys are all we have. Come harvest, I could use another six to eight people out here. We've doubled our wheat and corn and added potatoes, Papa. Threshing the wheat will take a big crew, and the corn always does." He hadn't answered the big question and saw the look in Zeke's eye that told him he'd best say something soon.

"I'm gonna be fine, Papa. Mama wants me to sit around the house but you know I can't do that. We're working out here from sun up to sun down. The infection hurts, and it looks nasty, but mama's putting stuff on in the morning and when I come in at night."

"It's gonna take more than that, son," Zeke said. "Give this some thought. Bring your men out in the morning, give them their direction and return to the house and rest. Let Sam Saunders bring you a report at the end of the day.

Do that for just a few days and that arm will be good as new."

"Sam could keep things moving, I guess. I'll try, Papa. Can you find some help for us? I'm starting to worry about the harvest."

"I'll head into Salem tomorrow, Hi, and put the word out. Things are a lot different now than two or three years ago. There are people who want to work, so I'll get people for you."

"Tell me about your trip. Were you successful? Did you have any trouble?"

"Get your horse and we'll ride back to the barn. I'll tell you all about it," Zeke said. "I think we'll be farming in the free state of Oregon this time next year, son."

"AIN'T NOBODY knows who we are, Hank. Just a couple of hands moving south." Teddy Jewell was positive that he should have ridden off with John Sam and still had no idea why he was riding with Hank Jenkins. They'd left their camp following the attack and moved south about eight to ten miles a day, staying off the main road. They followed the foot hills on the east side of the valley, cold camped most nights, and were in the forest just north of Mill Creek two weeks or so after the near fatal attack at the Hawthorne farm. They weren't following a trail, but breaking their own as they went, which slowed them considerably.

"I've had the feeling we're being followed this whole time, Hank. We've done everything we can to not be seen by anyone, but I'm sure we're leaving a track that could be followed."

"I'd know it if we were bein' followed," Jenkins said. "Ain't none of them dumb farmers know enough to be able to follow us. I've been runnin' from posses all my life, Teddy. Just relax, we'll be free of this territory soon enough."

At the rate they were moving, it would be many weeks before they would cross the California border.

Among the problems was that of food. Jewell wanted to shoot a deer or other smaller animals but knew that a gunshot would alert anyone about. Despite all his big talk, Jenkins seemed to know nothing about living in the wild. What food they had came from Jewell's abilities.

They were riding toward Mill Creek Road, through stands of pine, cedar, and fir, when Teddy Jewell spotted what looked like a house, about two miles in front of them. "We better skirt around that house up there, Hank. No need to call attention to ourselves."

"Might be better if we check it out, Teddy. Might have some money, and I'm so hungry I could eat all their damn hogs."

"I don't think that's a good idea at all, Hank. They's just the two of us, and you ain't in the best shape."

"Well, I do think it's a good idea," Jenkins stormed. "That's exactly what we're gonna do."

Jewell knew it wasn't the right thing to do. He knew Hank Jenkins was weak from hunger, and knew they didn't have the necessary people to raid a farm, but he let himself be drawn along, as he always had. He had never had the guts to stand up to someone that demanded things. "What's your plan, Hank?"

There was no plan, and they rode up to the sturdily built farm house that was surrounded by a kitchen garden on one side, fruit trees on another, and barns and corrals off a bit and downwind. Barbara Whitell spotted the riders from her kitchen window.

*I don't know who you boys are, but you're not on a regular trail, you look scrubby as hell, and I'm not gonna welcome you.* She walked to the living room and took up the shotgun by the front door, made sure it was loaded and primed, and walked out onto the large covered porch as the two filthy riders came up.

"Hold it right there, you two. Just turn on around and ride on out of here. Ain't nothing here for you." All the memories of the attacks on her in Salem City and the recent attempted attack on Zeke's farm flushed through her mind. Anger boiled to the surface again. She pulled the two hammers back and kept the long barrels ready to bring up and fire.

"Don't want no trouble, ma'am," Hank Jenkins said, trying to smile, staring at that big gun that could cut him in two. "We've been on the trail and without food nor water. Could you spare a little? Even a biscuit would be a banquet," he said, all syrupy and smiley-faced.

Teddy Jewell started to move his horse a bit to the side and Barbara whipped that shotgun up and aimed it right at the little man. "No, no, buster. You two have to the count of three to turn those horses and move out now."

Hank started to say something but Jewell thought he was going for his gun, and he went for his. Barbara blew him right out of the saddle with one barrel of that monster gun and while she was catching her balance from the blast, Jenkins pulled his pistol and got one shot off before Barbara blew him into several pieces.

The lead ball from Jenkins' Navy slammed Barbara

back against the door with tremendous force and she collapsed onto the porch deck. She knew she was hurt and hurt bad, and tried to get to her feet. It was hard but she managed, ripped some material from her dress to stem the bleeding in her shoulder, and made her way to Jenkins' horse.

It took three tries before she could hike herself into the saddle, the stirrups far below her little feet, and she nudged the pony into a solid lope, heading for the mill and her husband, at least an hour's ride away. She fought off the weakness that came from a combination of shock and blood loss, kept her balance on an unfamiliar horse, and made the five miles in slightly less than an hour.

It was all she could do to not fall out of the saddle. In a daze, she spotted the belching black smoke coming from the steam engine, turned into the mill area, hanging onto the saddle horn with both hands. The tired horse stopped in the middle of the mill's large yard.

"It's Barbara, Angus," a mill hand yowled, running to the horse as she rode onto the mill property. Angus Whitell ran from the sawyer's platform as hard as he could and caught his wife as she brought the horse to a halt. She was barely conscious as she fell from the saddle.

He ran with her to the kitchen yelling for Moose and Beulah, flinging the door open and getting across the room in two strides. He laid her gently onto one of the benches and slipped the bloody material from her wound. Thankfully, he thought, the bleeding had slowed considerably. "My God, Barb, what happened? You've been shot. Who did this?"

"Two men," she whispered through the pain. "Never seen them," and finally she let the darkness overtake her and she passed out. Beulah was there with clean cloths and a pan of clean water, and started work on the wound just as Moose came rushing in the door.

"Barbara! No, no. What happened?" Between Moose on one side and Angus on the other, Beulah was getting pushed around a bit.

"You two, out," she stormed. "This girl needs my attention, right now. Send someone to Salem and bring Doc Spears up here. She's in no condition to be moved. Hurry now."

Moose ran out and found one of the mill workers and sent him off at a full gallop for Salem and Doc Spears. The mill was at least fifteen miles from Salem, a long ride. Moose turned to Angus. "What did she say? What the hell happened?"

"All she said was two men rode up to the house, and she passed out. I've got to get down there now."

"No, Angus. You stay here with Barbara. I'll go," and he ran to the stables to saddle his horse for the five-mile ride to the Whitell farm. An hour later, he found the two men, blown into many pieces and the bloody shotgun on the porch.

"You did good, little sister," he said. He looked through the pockets and Teddy Jewell's saddlebags and couldn't find any identification. He noticed that both men had drawn their weapons and both had taken the full load of buckshot from the scattergun. "She's good," he beamed.

*More scum moving through the territory. Get these fools buried and get back to the mill. Come on, Barbara, you're tough enough to take out those two, you be tough enough to live, now.* Sweat was pouring from the heavy work digging the pair of graves and he was taking a short break for some cool water when he spotted a rider coming up on the farm.

He raced to his horse and drew his rifle from its scabbard, slipped behind a pine tree and watched the man approach. "That's about far enough, pard. Who are you and what do you want?"

"Name's Hastings," he said. "I'm Willamette Valley Marshal Slim Hastings. I been tracking a couple of outlaws the last many days. You live here?"

"Glad to meet you, Marshal. I'm Moose Travis and this is my sister's farm. Zeke Hawthorne is married to my other sister, Sarah. Step down, I may have your outlaws spread out and ready to bury."

## 1 2

"THAT ONE THERE IS HANK JENKINS, FOR SURE," SLIM Hastings said. "I've seen posters on him. Don't know the other one. What happened that you killed these two?"

Moose chuckled some before he could answer. "Didn't kill 'em, Marshal, my sister did, and she got shot doing it. She's at the Donaldson Lumber Mill right now being attended to. How is it you were following these two?"

"They are part of the gang of outlaws that attacked the Hawthorne farm two weeks ago. They been zig-zagging all over these mountains trying to hide their trail, but until today, I wasn't sure how close I was to catching them.

"How bad is your sister hurt?"

"Real bad. Help me get these two in the ground and we'll ride back to the mill. We sent a rider to find Doc Spears, so he should be arriving in the next couple of hours."

It was another two hours before they were able to ride onto the mill property and up to the bunkhouse and kitchen. During the ride, Slim Hastings filled Moose in on the attack and Hiram's defense of the farm. "That boy's something else," Hastings said.

"I'm just glad all you men were there to help out. You say Hiram's gonna be okay? Nicked his shoulder? He's got rocks in his craw, Marshal. He'll be fine. Looks like the outlaw gang threat is over with," Moose said.

They piled off their horses and Slim took the lead ropes to tie them off while Moose scrambled for the kitchen door. "She's going to be fine," Angus said when he ran in. "She lost a lot of blood, but Beulah has done a wonderful job on her. Doc Spears hasn't got here yet. What did you find out?"

Angus was talking faster than a jaybird finding fresh corn, and pacing all around the kitchen and the dining tables.

"Slow down, Angus. She blew two men apart with that shotgun you gave her, and it looked to me that she shot them as they were drawing their weapons on her. She's one tough little lady." He looked up as Slim Hastings made his way into the kitchen.

"This is Slim Hastings, Angus. He's the new Willamette Valley Marshal that Zeke and the ranchers hired. He was tracking the two men that Barbara shot, and believes they were part of the gang that tried to burn out Zeke."

"Glad to meet you, Marshal," Angus said, shaking his hand. "Wish you'd caught up with those men before they shot my wife."

"They were desperate, Mr. Whitell. Hadn't eaten in a couple of days or more, and weren't willing to ask for help. Their kind just tries to take what they want and to hell with anyone who gets in their way. Unfortunately, your wife got in their way."

"And she got in theirs," Moose said, giving a high sign with his upraised fist. "She nailed 'em both, dead center with that shotgun."

It was almost another hour before Doc Spears arrived in his buggy and brought all his gear in. Moose was going to send his mill worker back to Salem to bring Sheriff Fred Sharp back.

"I'll go find the sheriff," Hastings said. "I'll make the formal report. He'll probably want to get a statement from Mrs. Whitell, but that can wait until she recovers. Nice to have met you all and I'm sure we'll be running into each other from time-to-time."

"Looks like Zeke and the ranchers hired the right man for that job," Angus said as they walked back into the kitchen. Spears was just starting to work on Barbara.

Doc Spears had the dressing off and cleaned the wound. He added some powders to the wound and redressed it. "You did a good job, Beulah." He looked up to Angus. "Is your wife pregnant, Angus?"

"My God, doc. Yes, she is. Probably about three months, she thinks."

"That's not good," Spears said. "We need to get her in a bed where she can be kept warm and comfortable. This isn't good," he said, again. "That girl lost a great deal of blood and she needs to be comfortable and build up her strength."

"Bring her to my old house here," Moose said. "I have a fine bed. Angus, you can stay here for a few days. I'll send someone to your place to keep care of your animals. I can get Clemmie to come down and take care of her."

"That would be best," Doc Spears said. "There really isn't much more I can do. I'll leave these sulfur powders for you. She needs as much rest as she can get, plenty of liquids, and lots of food. Change those dressings at least twice a day and sprinkle the wound with the powder."

He motioned Beulah aside. "That girl may well lose that child, Beulah. Don't let those men move her or make her get up once they get her in bed. She needs to stay in bed and you need to keep her there."

"I will, doc," the large woman said. "I wonder what brought all this on? She's so beautiful, so fragile."

"That girl is far from fragile, Beulah. She's a tiger in a kitten's coat. Keep her warm, fed, and in bed," and he patted her on the shoulder. He rode off in his buggy knowing full well he could not do anything more. "It's up to the universal powers now," he murmured.

Moose sent another employee to his new home to fetch Clemmie and she arrived an hour or so after Doc Spears left. "That poor girl," she said. Moose, Angus, and Beulah had relayed the story to her, and Beulah took her aside to tell her about the pregnancy and Doc Spears's worries.

"I've done hospital work, Beulah," Clemmie said. "We'll work together to save that baby."

"So, I guess that wraps up the story on the Hawthorne farm attack," Sheriff Fred Stone said after Hastings gave him his report. "Were you able to talk to either of those men?"

"No, they were dead long before I got there. Mrs. Whitell took care of that for us."

"She may be tiny, marshal, but she's a wildcat. A couple of fools threatened her in town here a while back. I know what happens when that girl gets her anger up. There's rumors all over Salem that George Belknap may have hired that attack on Hawthorne's. I wish those two boys weren't dead."

"Word was, seven men were riding toward the farm, but only six showed up. Three of them died, and now two more are dead. We have two men unaccounted for, Sheriff," Hastings said. "It is possible that Belknap may be one of those two. Might not hurt to talk to the man."

"He lives several miles south of Salem, actually almost half way to Eugene. Puts him way out of my jurisdiction, and yours, marshal. I hope the legislature can clear all this up in their next session. We're building too fast," he grouched. "They call it progress, that Oregon will be a strong economic entity when statehood comes, but they've left too many things out of the picture."

"Like law enforcement in the rural districts," Hastings chuckled. The irony of the two lawmen willing to discuss a planned attack on a farm family with a possible perpetrator and couldn't because of jurisdictional questions did not evade their quick minds.

"Is there anyone associated with Belknap that might live within our jurisdictions?" Hastings was still chuckling softly as he asked the question. "Maybe spread a little fear among the troops, ask some seriously leading questions, and see who might fold if Belknap is involved?" There was a twinkle in his eye and a long Texas drawl when he asked.

Stone gave him another long look. *This is one tough hombre despite that deep chuckle and the humor in his eye.*

*Man would be nuts to go up against Marshal Hastings without having a decided advantage.*

"Belknap is the one promoting the issue of slavery for Oregon if we should become a state. He's also been known to support the old Oregon Firsters bunch, and they were extremely dangerous. Known to be involved in killings, attacks on women, owned slaves, and probably killed a member of the territorial legislature.

"I'm telling you this just so you know Belknap's background," Sheriff Sharp said. He got up from his desk and walked to the stove for some coffee. "To the best of my knowledge, Belknap has never been personally involved in any of what I just said. But he has always been nearby, closely associated.

"Would he attack the Hawthorne farm? My thought is, no. Would he hire such an attack? I'd say, yes. Did he? You got me, marshal." He sat back down at his desk and pulled a sheet of paper out. "There is one man, Peter Flowers, has a ranch north of Hawthorne's place, and who is one of the loud voices in favor of slavery. In fact, I believe he actually owns some slaves. He and Belknap have worked closely during past legislative sessions.

"I do believe the man might just be in your jurisdiction, Marshal Hastings," he said. "The man can be tricky. Likes to give the impression that is calm and open to new ideas, but he has the temper of a cougar. Be wary, Hastings." He wrote the name on the paper along with directions to the Flowers' ranch, folded it up and handed it to Hastings. "Let me know if you find out anything. That session two years ago was frightening and I don't want to have to go through that again. The slavery issue will be a very hot potato this time around, and I've got all I can handle right here in Salem City."

Hastings shook hands with the sheriff and walked out to his horse. *That man's a lot sharper than I was led to believe. He'll be good to work with. I need to know more about Belknap and Flowers before I go off half-cocked.*

## 13

PETE FLOWERS WAS AT THE OREGON CITY HOTEL restaurant and saloon enjoying their free lunch, holding down a meeting of property owners from along the Columbia River. "Our ranches could be so much more profitable if we didn't have to pay wages to these trail bums to watch our herds. I tell you, I've seen herds in the east twice the size of ours, and the cost to maintain less than half what we have to pay.

"Yes, sir, gentlemen, owning slaves is the only real pathway to financial success in the agricultural world. There are men in New Orleans right now willing to ship hundreds of slaves to us. All it would take is enough votes in Salem this August, during the Constitutional Convention to make that happen."

Flowers planned on having these little chats with major ranchers and farmers along the new eastern territorial border as well, but was running up against some serious opposition. Ezekiel Hawthorne had been through this territory just weeks before, talking with the same people, promoting Oregon as a free state.

"Tell me, Mr. Flowers," Nick Wallace asked, "why you believe that it's right, morally or otherwise, for a man to own another man? I've heard the argument that it's been a way of life for thousands of years, but that still doesn't make it right. Why do you believe it's right to own another human being?"

Wallace ran cattle and sheep a hundred miles of so south of the Columbia River in what some call an almost desert area of the great basin. He was probably mid-forties, tall and heavy in the chest and shoulders. He had large hands and long fingers and held a water tumbler about half full of Kentucky's finest.

"It takes fifty acres to feed a steer in my country, Flowers. Tell me why I should have the right to own another man."

"I've read about scientific tests being done that prove these black people really aren't completely human. They are treated just like one of your fine ranch animals. Well fed, doctored properly, not overworked."

Wallace cut him off, slamming his glass down on the bar. "Damn fool lies, sir!" He stood tall, glaring at the Willamette Valley rancher. "Those stories have been proved false for years. Next, you're gonna try to tell me their heads aren't big enough to hold a human brain.

"I've seen how slaves are treated. That's one of the things that drove me west, Mr. Flowers. Owning slaves is wrong on so many levels I find it incredible an educated and intelligent man would even give the idea a second's notice. I stand with Hawthorne on that question, sir. Oregon must enter the union as a free state."

Flowers ran into this kind of opposition to the slavery question at every stop and was on his way back to the Willamette Valley a few days later, planning to spend several days at his ranch before meeting with George Belknap. It was still a long hard ride from Oregon City across the mountains and into the broad valley.

It was late in the summer when he arrived at his ranch. He put his horse and pack mule up and made his way to the big house, a hot meal, hot bath, and warm bed was first and foremost on his mind. "Food, Bertha," he said to the large black woman who greeted him.

"Glad you're back, Mr. Flowers, sir. Meat and potatoes coming up." Bertha had been with Flowers for many years and was one of only two of his slaves who had house privileges. The other, Johnny, was the man who kept the others in line and who reported every misdeed to the boss.

"Where's Johnny? I want a full report on what's been going on while I've been away. Were there problems?"

"No sir," Bertha said. "No problems. Johnny does a fine job keeping them boys in line out there. He's moving some cattle right now, sir. He will be here pretty soon."

It was the next morning as Pete Flowers was getting ready to make a ride through his large ranch that he spotted a rider coming up the pathway. Flowers pulled his rifle from the saddle scabbard and stepped off his horse. "Hold my horse, Johnny," he said, handing the reins to him. "Recognize that man?"

"Don't believe I do, Mr. Flowers, sir."

"Help you with something, mister? You're on private property."

"Good morning, I'm looking for Peter Flowers. My

name is Hastings, Willamette Valley Marshal Slim Hastings."

"I'm Flowers, what do you want? What do you mean, Willamette Valley Marshal? What kind of nonsense is that?"

"May we talk, sir?" Hastings asked, still sitting tall in the saddle.

Flowers knew the ranchers and farmers along the valley had formed an association and hired a marshal. He would not join the association and wasn't willing to accept this concept of a marshal in the first place. "You have no authority on this property, Hastings. I have nothing to say to you." Flowers turned to take the reins back from his black overseer.

"I'd like to talk to you about an attack on one of the farms in this district, Mr. Flowers. Men were killed, and I believe the attack came from men who were hired to kill and burn out one of our farms."

"I have nothing to say to you, Hastings. Get off my place. You're trespassing." He still held the rifle but did not attempt to point it or use it as a threat, but Hastings knew just how fast it could be brought into play.

"I'm sorry you feel that way, Flowers. I was hired to keep the peace in the valley and work under the authority of District Judge Brown. There were seven men known to be in the gang that attacked the Hawthorne property. Two are missing, sir. I was hoping you might be able to shed light on those two."

"Get off my place Hastings. Get off now," and he brought the rifle up fast. Hastings saw that he had it cocked. He smiled, tipped his hat, turned his horse, and rode off wondering if he would take a big chunk of lead in the back.

"That didn't go well," he chuckled, putting the horse into a gentle lope. "Man's carrying a load of hate. Somebody who won't talk, is willing to point a weapon at someone who isn't being a threat, is dangerous indeed." He decided his best bet would be to have a talk with his fellow Texan, Silas Williams.

The ride down the valley toward Williams' place was easy on a warm summer day. Hastings took in all the beauty of the Willamette Valley, the river, shining in the hot summer morning, every tree at full leaf and fruit trees beginning to bear their sweetness. "In west Texas, when you look out yonder you can almost see the curvature of the earth. Here, mountains east and west, and even a magnificent volcano to break things up. I like Oregon," he murmured turning into the path leading to Silas Williams' ranch.

Cattle were grazing on lush grasses, and Hastings could see about an acre that had been set aside for corn, now towering in the breeze. *Them steers'll be fat and tasty when they finish off that corn. I guess I just don't have the right approach to farmin'. Everything I planted died a horrible death.* Even so, Hastings had a smile on his face as he rode up to the ranch house.

"Mornin' Slim," Silas called from a rocking chair on his broad veranda. "By golly, it's a grand day, ain't it?"

"Good mornin' to you, Captain," Slim said. He stepped off his horse and walked up onto the porch. "Wouldn't happen to have something cold for this here pilgrim, would you?"

"I'd have to get up to get you something cool. But, my

fine friend, I have my flask right here, and I can just hand that to you." He cackled at his little joke and Slim Hastings took a seat on the porch and a long pull on the flask.

"Thankee," he said, wiping his lips with his shirtsleeve. "What do you know about this Pete Flowers? Man just throwed me off his place."

"He's a nasty one, Slim. Ain't got many friends. Thinks he's some kind special like those southerners that tried to run Texas for a while. He thinks he's running a southern plantation while the rest of us call our places ranches or farms. Those black people that work for him are slaves, from what I've been told. Never did cotton to slave owning, myself."

Slim Hastings took another sip from the flask and handed it back to Williams. "Rumor running through Salem City is that George Belknap may have been behind the attack on Zeke Hawthorne's farm. Flowers and Belknap are close as bourbon and branch, and right now there are two men from the group that attacked Zeke's place missing."

"Interesting, Slim," Silas said. He got up and paced about on the veranda, spit some tobacco juice out into the dust, and sat back down. "Most interesting. Belknap's a dirty, back-stabbin' sumbitch, for sure, but not the kind that would actually get his hands bloody. Flowers, though," and he let the comment just hang in the hot breeze.

"Flowers pulled that fully- cocked rifle down on me and I could see in his eyes that he would have gladly pulled the trigger," Hastings said. "All the people we know that were in that gang are dead, Silas. If Pete Flowers or

George Belknap were involved, there ain't no way to prove it unless one of them would confess."

"That ain't gonna happen." Silas took a pull from the flask and handed it to Slim. "You gone over where those boys were camped the night before the attack?"

"I think I'll ride up there and look around some more. Don't you be workin' too hard, Silas, and I'll see you again soon."

Hastings could still hear the chuckles from that veranda many yards down the pathway that led back to River Road. "He's an old codger," Slim muttered, more to his horse than himself. "Wish I would have been along with him during his Ranger days. I bet there were storms flailing the desert when he got his blood up."

III

BOOK TWELVE: POLITICS:
PISTOLS AND PALAVER

## 14

ONCE AGAIN, SARAH'S KITCHEN WAS FILLED WITH men eating everything she took out of the oven of her large wood cook stove. "Better make some more coffee, Rebecca," she said. "There's more sweet rolls in the oven."

Zeke had five of his legislative brothers in for a meeting to discuss how to get that constitutional convention called. These men were from mixed political philosophies but all were solidly behind the move toward statehood. "I've been to each of the districts in our territory this spring and early summer," Zeke said, to open their meeting. "There is opposition to statehood, but it is weak and there aren't that many men involved. Our fight isn't whether we move toward a constitutional convention, gentlemen. Our fight is whether Oregon is a free state or a slave state."

Sitting around the large table, the men all nodded in agreement. John Bradley had spent many happy hours in this warm kitchen, argued many legislative proposals over cups of coffee laced with rum at this very table. "If we simply concentrate on the moral implications of slavery, we should silence most of the opposition," he said.

"That may be a bit naïve, John," Sam Chastain from Portland said. "I agree with you that slavery is as immoral as one can imagine, but those I've discussed the concept with don't see the immorality. They believe a slave is less than human. I'm not sure taking the high moral road is our strongest argument."

"I agree with you, Sam." Logan Mac Dougal was in his third session as a member of the territorial legislature and represented the area along the Columbia River near Oregon City. "On the other hand, which argument would be stronger? It is simply wrong, in my opinion, for one man to own another man. Should we concentrate on the freedom aspect? That's a strong argument. How can we claim to be a freedom loving people when we deny men their inherent freedom?"

"I like that argument," Fred Fowler said. "We aren't free because the government says we are. It's the government's responsibility to guarantee that we remain free. Yes, slavery is morally wrong, and we must always remember that in our discussions, but it is the individual's freedom, his liberty to be free, that must be defended by law."

"I think we are all in agreement with that," Zeke said. "I'd like to suggest that we write up a paper outlining our platform on this issue and then go back to our districts and hold public meetings to fully discuss this issue. Our arguments are morally strong, and legally strong.

"The convention dates have been set for August, and we will have to be ready. During the convention, we'll be fighting for this position, and if we do form a constitution we need to be ready to make it fully acceptable to the population. This is a two-pronged fight."

"With your knowledge of the language, Zeke, I think you would be the right person to write this up." Harold Meir, usually the quietest member of the legislature, made his comment into a formal suggestion and those at the table agreed.

The constitutional convention delegates included the legislature and prominent members of the general population. "We're going to have to sell the convention delegates first, and the general public, second," Zeke said.

"To make this work," he continued, "I think our proclamation should be short and to the point. Something that could be quoted easily, remembered easily. As Jefferson said, Life, Liberty, and the Pursuit of Happiness. Would you agree to something like that?"

Rousing approval by the five brought another voice into the kitchen. Young Travis Hawthorne was awakened from his late morning nap and wanted to be heard. "I think we're about to be evicted," Zeke laughed. "Will you join me at the tables under the trees, gentlemen?"

"I'll bring coffee and some dinner out shortly," Sarah said. Her eyes told Zeke thank you for clearing out. "I have two young chickens roasting in the oven for you, and you'll be most comfortable under those cottonwood trees."

The roasted chickens were moist and tender, and Sarah served them with some early sweet corn followed by peach pie and ice cream. Coffee laced with the ever-present rum finished off the mid-day meal.

"Most enjoyable, Zeke. I'm going to spread the word

throughout my district as soon as I get home," Sam Chastain said. The others all joined in saying about the same thing.

"When we meet at the convention in August, at our first opportunity we must bring these ideas to the floor for debate. At that point, with all of us in agreement, we can each take a turn and show solidarity to the point of overwhelming any opposition that might still be there." Meir hadn't made a speech that long in the many years Zeke had known him.

"I'll write our proclamation and see to it that hundreds of copies are printed and sent to each of you to distribute in your districts," Zeke said. "This is now a fight for freedom, for a free Oregon, for Oregon statehood." Sarah thought that Hiram, way out in the wheat fields could probably hear the hurrahs that followed.

"THIS IS REALLY WELL WRITTEN, ZEKE," Roland Sullivan said. "I like the way you have brought the words of Thomas Jefferson, John Adams, and good old Ben Franklyn into the essay on freedom. Without coming right out and moralizing, you have made the point of slavery being immoral. Well done, my friend."

Sullivan held the broad sheet up to read from the parchment. "This part, about the government's responsibility to guarantee that freedom really says it all." He read, "In this country a man should be born free, it's an inalienable right, and it's the government's job to guarantee that right to be free. It is not the government's right to deny that freedom, it's the government's obligation to preserve it." Sullivan was beaming as he finished.

"I want to stand at a podium and read this proclamation to a crowd of people, Zeke. I want to do that." The rotund man seemed to be quivering in excitement and Zeke had to chuckle, watching him.

"Mr. Sullivan, you are a piece of work, indeed. Your glass has never been half empty, I'm sure. Probably closer to three-quarters full. I've sent copies of this to all our members and to the various newspapers in the territory. If we do have public meetings, I would most enjoy hearing you read from it.

"What has been going on with our opposition, Sully? Between the farm and my continuous meetings, I haven't been off the farm in weeks. Slim Hastings comes by once in a while and other than family and fellow legislators, I haven't talked to a soul."

"My brewery will collapse if you keep it up, Mr. Hawthorne," Sullivan laughed. "We need your business. What's Hastings got to say?"

"He found a body a few weeks ago near where that gang camped before their attack on my place. He thought it had been there for some time and figures it belonged to one of the gang, which means he's still short one man from the seven that Sam Saunders saw that morning."

"George Belknap has been quiet around here. I think he and his following fools are concentrating all their efforts on the eastern section of the territory and south of here, around Eugene. Who's the representative from Eugene?"

"Belknap's district includes Eugene," Zeke said. He had a frown spreading across his broad face thinking about that. "I think I need to take a couple of days and travel through that country. I'll bring a couple hundred copies of my broad sheet and make a nuisance of myself." The smile retuned immediately. "When was the last time you were in Eugene, Sully?"

"If that's an invitation to ride with you, my friend, I accept."

## 15

"HE'S FAR TOO BIG FOR HIS BRITCHES, GEORGE. JUST who does this Ezekiel Hawthorne think he is riding into your jurisdiction preaching his personal moral code? A good whuppin' is what that man needs." Pete Flowers had ridden south after Zeke and his followers had distributed his 'Freedom Proclamation' up and down the Willamette Valley north of Salem.

Zeke and Sullivan were now in Eugene for a series of public meetings to promote Oregon statehood and most of all, Oregon as a free state. Flowers was sitting in one of Eugene's many saloons, this one near the ferry crossing, having whiskey and enjoying the free lunch. "We're just a few weeks from the convention, Pete. Hawthorne knows this is my district, that's why he's here, to challenge me in my own district. I would give anything to walk up to that man, shove a pistol up his nose and pull the trigger, but I won't and I don't want anyone else to, either.

"Every time violence has been used against that man it has backfired. Even when I've had nothing to do with it,

I'm blamed. No, Pete, we can't whup on him. Instead, I'm going to challenge him to a debate, to argue in front of all our friends, this issue of Oregon being a slave state. With my powers of persuasion, I'll whup that man properly and the newspapers will have to say that I'm right."

There were groups of men that moved through the streets of Eugene, bullies- every one of them, keeping order as dictated by Belknap. "George, that town marshal of yours, and his so-called peace squads, could make quite a show of it," Flowers said. "I ran that valley marshal off my place. Just aimed my loaded, primed, and cocked rifle at him and he fled like the cur he is.

"You could put Hawthorne out of the district with a simple visit by some of your men. The man needs to be shut down before he destroys our efforts to bring slavery to the west." Flowers' anger had been rising regularly as the summer wore on, with visits from Slim Hastings adding to his fervor. Now, he found Belknap pulling back from the aggressive stand he had always taken.

Belknap had learned the art of arrogance from those southern landowners, the planters of Virginia, at an early age. They dominated public life in Virginia, had the finest properties, the finest horses, their plantations were beautiful and bountiful, and they used their power and influence with heavy hands. Belknap had the arrogance, he just didn't have the power and influence he thought he did.

"That marshal the ranchers hired for the north valley is sure you were behind the attack on Hawthorne's place. I've throwed him off my place twice now. He's spreading the idea that seven men were seen in the area before the raid and only six can be accounted for. He's suggesting that you might be the seventh."

"You and I know that's a lie," Belknap said. "If he comes on your place, that's trespassing. Shoot the bastard. When and where is Hawthorne scheduled to speak next? I want to be there and challenge him to a public and open debate."

"He's speaking tonight at the school house, George, but you shouldn't go there alone. Bring some men with you. I'll be with you, but bring others. Hawthorne gets these people all riled up and it might be dangerous for you." Flowers hoped that it might, because that would give him the opportunity he needed to beat or kill Zeke Hawthorne.

"That's probably a good idea, Pete. Bring a few of our people with you but don't start any trouble. If trouble starts, make sure it's their people who start it."


"I LIKE THIS LITTLE TOWN, Zeke. Used to be called a mud hole, but old man Skinner knew what he was up to when he built that little trading post down here. It's right on the road to California, and there's ferry service across the river. I think Eugene Skinner started that, too, and the steamer runs all the way to the Columbia."

"Is there any single place in this territory or ours that you don't like, Sully? You know more of the virtues of Oregon than any man alive, I do believe."

"And I'll talk about those virtues at a moment's notice, my friend." They were laughing as they rode down a muddy street toward the schoolhouse. "I put notices up all over town that you would be here this evening to discuss statehood and Oregon freedom. Should be a good crowd, I hope."

"I'm glad you decided to come with me, Sully. No one I know could hold a negative thought if you were around. Will you do the honors of introducing me tonight?"

"What a pleasure that will be, Zeke. Anyone else we know going to be here?"

"The only people I know in the Eugene area are that bunch that were in the wagon train that Hiram ran into. Of course, George Belknap has his holdings several miles north of here."

"Wouldn't it be nice if he showed up? I can almost see it, Zeke, him getting rowdy and you challenging him to a debate. Would you do that? Would you debate George Belknap?"

"Without the least hesitation, my friend. Let's find a café and have something to eat and talk about tonight."

Eugene was just a village but growing rapidly as more and more wagon trains were moving along the Oregon Trail. The tiny town was also a major stop-over for travelers and merchants on their way to or from California. Just a small trading post, a few years ago, now there was an actual business district, even a small central park with a gazebo in the middle.

IT WAS quarter to seven when Zeke and Sullivan left the Eugene Men's House, a popular boarding house that acted as a hotel. It was a short walk to the Methodist School of Eugene and the talk about freedom. The crowd was already filing into the large building with its auditorium that doubled as a church on Sundays. Zeke was dressed in clean canvas pants, a wool shirt, and wore a frock coat and floppy slouch hat.

"I really thought you would wear more formal attire, Zeke," Sullivan said. Sully was fitted out for the governor's ball, in Zeke's mind. From his black boots, polished to a gleam, to his fine beaver flat-crowned hat, starched white shirt with collar, and brocaded vest, he was the epitome of Oregon's civility.

"I'm a farmer, Sully, not a city feller. This is who I am, and these people need to understand that. You might get at least one of your wishes, Sullivan. Look over to your left, sir."

"My goodness, will you look at that? George Belknap in person. You think he'll start trouble? Maybe we should have invited Travis." He still talked about the time Travis drove off a rowdy at a meeting to promote Zeke's first run for a seat in the territorial legislature. "Travis knows how to handle ruffians," he chuckled.

"He might want to interrupt the proceedings some, but I doubt he's here to start trouble. I can handle him or even his ruffians if I have to. Slim Hastings is still sure that he was behind that planned attack on my place. He says that Pete Flowers has run him off, even threatened him once. If you see Flowers, make sure I'm aware. He would be the one to start trouble."

Zeke recalled that because of Flowers, he'd had his only argument with Slim Hastings. Zeke felt that Hastings should have charged Flowers for an attempt on his life when he aimed the rifle at him. The argument didn't affect the feelings Hawthorne had for the man, or the respect, but it had been a quarrel.

They made their way through the crowd, saying hello to many along the way, getting words of encouragement, even strong pats on the back. Eugene was a small village and most of the people that lived in the general area were hard-working farmers, ranchers, fishermen, skilled craftsmen, and unskilled laborers. Zeke Hawthorne was among men of his own ilk and was fully enjoying the moment.

Zeke took his seat on the podium and Roland Sullivan moved to the lectern to welcome the crowd. Zeke watched Belknap and when the legislator looked toward him, he nodded in welcome. The nod was not returned, Zeke noted and then saw Pete Flowers enter the auditorium accompanied by several other men. Sullivan was in his own world talking about Oregon and all the splendors of the state. He quoted parts of the flyer Zeke had written, and was filled with zeal.

He wrapped up his little speech by saying, "Here now, is the man that will help lead us into statehood for Oregon. The Constitutional Convention is just a couple of weeks away, so please welcome Assemblyman, Ezekiel Hawthorne."

The crowd was loud and boisterous, friendly and warm in their welcome, and Hawthorne let them carry on for a few minutes before raising his arms to bring some quiet to the hall. "Thank you," he said several times as the crowd slowly came to order and most took their seats. One man didn't.

"Mr. Hawthorne, sir," George Belknap said, loudly, stepping forward and half turning to the crowd.

"Good evening, Mr. Belknap. I'm pleased you're here tonight. I know you've represented this district for some time and these are your constituents. Did you wish to make an announcement before my little talk?" Zeke was overly nice, pleasant even, and held a smile through his anger at being interrupted before he could even begin.

"I only wish to make one quick statement, sir, and I'll be gone. I challenge you to an open and public debate on the question of slavery." There was a smattering of favorable comments, a boo or two, and most in the crowd were waiting for the fireworks they felt were sure to come.

"That's a splendid idea," Zeke said after getting the crowd quiet again. "It would be interesting to see how you will justify the concept of slavery. Did you have a time and place in mind, sir?"

"I do," Belknap snapped at Zeke's comment. "Sunday afternoon in the town's plaza. Will you show up?"

"Indeed, I will. Now, sir, if you don't mind, these folks are here for my little speech and you'll have your turn on Sunday." The crowd loved the repartee, and Belknap stormed from the hall to many jeers and some clapping and hurrahs. Zeke noticed that Flowers and several of the men that came with him, stayed for the speech.

"THAT WENT WELL, Zeke, and you were splendid in how you handled Belknap. He didn't take kindly to your comments."

Zeke had to chuckle at Sullivan. "No, he didn't, but I do like the idea of a full debate on the subject. I'll never turn him, I know that, but it might be possible to educate a few of these people."

"Are you the least worried that Belknap might be leading you into a trap of some kind? Have rowdies on hand to break heads and all that? There are reports of roving gangs of rowdies in this little village, you know."

"I've read the reports, Sully," Zeke said. "George Belknap might be a snake, but this is his district. I doubt he would set up such a thing. If this was Flowers' area, I would be worried."

They stayed at the school for several minutes following the speech, talking with many of those in attendance, getting a good idea of how the people were thinking about statehood and the question of Oregon being a free state. They were walking down the muddy street back to their rooms on a cool summer evening, joshing each other and having a good time of it.

It was the dark of the moon, but there were enough lights from buildings they could see the Willamette River down the hill from them. Shimmering in its broadness, Zeke was always taken by the sight. *I've seen that river from so many different angles and it's always beautiful, winter or summer. I love being along the river with Hiram fishing for salmon, watching the flocks of water birds, and the sight of a steamboat is always a thrill.*

"You're gonna be sorry for comin' to this town, you injun-lovin' bastard," a voice cried out from behind a hedge. Three men stepped out from the shadows, two of them carrying stout lengths of hardwood. "You about to be ejicated, you nigger-lovin' bastard," the largest of the three challenged.

Zeke recognized the men as having been at the speech with Pete Flowers. He saw rage in the men's faces, and strength in their bodies. The loud one was glaring at Zeke and his slurred speech told him that considerable alcohol was fueling the talk. The big man took a step toward Zeke, and raised the club to swing it when Sullivan whipped a little pepperbox pistol out. "I don't think so,"

Sullivan said quietly, aiming the gun at the man's head. His two companions spread out and one of them snarled back.

"You only got one shot, porky. They be three of us."

"How much did Pete Flowers pay you for this?" Zeke asked. "I saw all three of you with Flowers earlier." Zeke opened his frock coat and pulled his beautifully honed knife from its leather sheath. "It looks like one of you will die from a gunshot, and one of you will die when this knife opens you up, top to bottom. Maybe, one of you might live. Who's first to die?" he said, letting the knife catch a glint of lamplight as he slowly swung it back and forth. Sarah would have reminded those boys that Zeke's Shoshone name was Sharp Knife.

The largest man swung the club and the little pistol flashed. Sullivan took the club's whack across his shoulder, everyone heard the crunch of bone breaking, and fell to the ground. The man with the club jerked up straight, blood gushing from a great gash in his neck, and he too, fell to the ground.

"That didn't have to happen," Zeke said. He glared at the two men left standing, staring at their companion, who was now staring back with dead eyes. "You men take your dead friend and leave. Tell Flowers he failed."

"We ain't goin' nowhere," the man in the bearskin coat said, waving his oak branch. "Gonna teach you a lesson, boy," and he lunged at Zeke, swinging the club wildly. Zeke was quick, big and strong. He danced out of the way of the club, swung that knife quick, and found his mark. The man dropped the club, grabbing his side, feeling the blood pouring through the rent in the coat. He stumbled a couple of steps and would have fallen face first into the street's dirt and rocks, but caught himself. He staggered toward Zeke.

"Need to get that looked at before you bleed out," Zeke snarled, moving in a half circle around the man, keeping his eye on the third man, too. That third man had grabbed the oak branch when it dropped. "One more swipe, like this," and he lunged, whipped the knife around, almost taking the man's head off. The third man also lunged with his club, smashing it into Zeke's head, knocking him back and almost down.

Zeke gripped the knife, slipped down on one knee, felt the blood dripping down his neck and across his shoulder. He was dazed but not out and watched that third man slowly circle in for the kill. He knew that he couldn't take another hit to the head, that he would be knocked out and then be killed.

He gathered as much strength as he could, pushed back onto his feet, spread his legs to give him balance and power, and watched the man move. It wasn't his first time attacking someone, Zeke knew, could feel the man's hatred, and had the knife ready for whatever move the man made.

*Take your time*, he told himself. *Let your strength come back, circle, move, give yourself some time*, he told himself over again. His head ached from the blow it took, his eyes weren't focused, and his knees were wobbly, but he was ready to take this man out. "Your friends are dead, mister, and you're going to join them in hell's fire when you make your next move."

He saw the man's eyes narrow for a charge and also saw Sullivan slowly get to his feet, nursing a broken arm. Sullivan was behind the man with the club, and he bent down next to the man he'd shot and picked up his length of oak. One step, a vicious one-armed swing, and the third man's head exploded in skin, blood, bone, and brain matter. Sullivan dropped the cudgel and grabbed Zeke before he passed out again.

The noise from the fight brought a few people out onto the street, and one of them ran as fast as he could to find the town marshal. "My God, it's Mr. Hawthorne," another man shouted as he ran to the scene. "What happened? You're bleeding. My God, is that Mr. Sullivan? Somebody get the doctor."

Zeke let himself slowly slip to the dirty street and sat next to Sullivan's unconscious body. Two men eased Zeke back to his feet and two others helped Sullivan up as he regained his senses. They ushered the two into John Blairsden's house and got them settled into overstuffed chairs. Everyone was trying to talk at once.

"Let's calm it down, men," a new and stronger voice said. "Make way, now. Let me in, damn it. Mr. Hawthorne, is it? And Mr. Sullivan? Looks like you two got the tar whupped out of you. Can you talk? I'm Eugene City Marshal, Zeb North."

"Got jumped by those three out there, marshal," Zeke said, rubbing his head gently. "Me and Sully were walking back to our rooms when they attacked." He wanted to tell North that the three were at his speech with Pete Flowers, but maybe not yet. "Don't know any of them. I think we need a doc."

"Doc Shadows will be here shortly. What brought this on, robbery?"

"No, I don't think so," Sullivan said, trying to sit up

straight. "They were at Hawthorne's speech tonight and said some foul things before the attack."

"I saw them there," a voice piped up. "They work for one of the ranches north of Salem City."

"What makes you sure of that?" Marshal North turned to the man. "You're John Blaisden aren't you? A cattle buyer for Klepton's?"

"You're almost right. I'm a hide buyer. I've been to the ranch north of Salem and seen those three there. The man that owns the ranch, Flowers is his name, also owns slaves and these men work the niggers."

"Did you come to Eugene to stir this kind of stuff up, Hawthorne?" The marshal wasn't sure exactly what to do. "We've got a nice little community here and we don't much care for people looking for trouble."

"Marshal North, this territory will become a state soon, and every person here has a stake in how that state will be. Will it be a state where men are free to build good lives, have happy families, and prosper? Or will some of its citizens be slaves, denied their freedom, forced to live by someone's brutality, have no dignity?

"If you consider that asking those questions makes me a trouble maker, then yes, that's why I'm here, and that's why those men attacked Mr. Sullivan and myself. Why weren't you at our meeting tonight?"

Several men in the room said, yeah, Marshal, why weren't you there? Another voice popped up. "He wasn't there because he works for George Belknap instead of Eugene City."

"Is that true, marshal?" Sullivan's arm hurt bad and he wasn't as fully conscious as Zeke, but was just as amazed at the comment. "Belknap pays you to do his dirty work? Does the county commission know that?"

"That's enough of that kind of talk. I want written statements from you two tomorrow before you leave town."

"Oh, we're not leaving, Marshal. I have an engagement Sunday afternoon in the town square. But you will get my statement, you can be sure of that."

Marshal Zeb North stormed out of Blairsden's home almost knocking Doc Shadows right off the porch. "Easy there, North," the doc said. "Before you go off half-cocked, better have some of these men get those bodies up to the mortuary."

"Humph," is all North said, motioning some of the men to help him get the bodies moved. Shadows was shaking his head as he came into the room to attend to Zeke and Sullivan.

"Must have been a nasty little fight," he said, getting his tools ready. "Who wants to go first?"


"WE MUST BE a sight in all our bandages and wraps," Sullivan joked as they found seats at a café for breakfast. "I hurt everywhere, and that doc wasn't really trying to not hurt me, either." When Shadows was setting the bone in Sullivan's arm, there were squalls of pain voiced loud and long. "I'm sure that man has a great dislike of me, Zeke." Zeke had to laugh at the comment.

"I hope this place or someplace close is one of your customers, Sully. I could use a big mug of cold beer right now. I know it's early morning but my head is killing me. I've never been hit that hard, ever."

"Don't ever quote me, Zeke, but right now the last thing you need is beer or rum. You've sustained one hell of a whack to the head, probably have a concussion, and you don't need to make it worse. Your brain is probably scrambled and swelled tight against that thick skull of yours. Eat your food and let yourself heal some."

"I guess I know you're right, old man, but I could drain a keg right now."

## 1 6

"AFTER THE OTHER NIGHT'S ACTIVITIES, BELKNAP, I really didn't think you'd have nerve enough to show up." Zeke's anger was barely held in check, his knife just under his frock coat was cleaned of recent blood and easily to hand. "I said I would be glad to debate you in an open forum and I'm here to do that.

"I am curious, though, George. What happens following our little presentation? How many men will attack me this time?" Hawthorne's eyes were slits and Belknap could see Zeke's jaw muscles working as teeth were gnashed. The hit to Zeke's head was so fierce that both his eyes were blackened. The face was fearsome to look at and Zeke was working to make it just as angry looking as he could.

"I had nothing to do with that, Hawthorne. Don't accuse me without proof." Belknap stepped back, ready to run at the first move by Zeke.

"I saw those men with your rancher friend, Flowers, at the meeting. Belknap, your friend, Marshal North, suggested I leave town, and you, sir, are a bald-faced liar. I'm ready to mount that platform yonder and begin this debate. Are you man enough to face me?" All the while, Zeke's hand was close to where he could flip his coat open and grab that knife.

Before Belknap could answer, Marshal Zeb North mounted the steps to the speaker's platform in the middle of the park. "I declare this gathering a public nuisance," he said. "You will disperse immediately. Leave this park now. My deputies have orders to arrest anyone in this area five minutes from now." He looked down and nodded to George Belknap and stepped off the platform.

"That was well done, George," Zeke said. "You get out of having your ideas blown to hell, get out of having to make an ass of yourself in front of your own constituents, and you can blame the marshal for not allowing you to speak. You're a serious stain on what a legislator should represent."

The marshal stepped up to Zeke to give him a little prod, using a cudgel he carried. "You touch me with that and I'll have you before a judge in moments."

He looked Belknap in the eye. "We'll have this debate, Belknap, at the constitutional convention. It's in Salem, Belknap, and you'll wish then that you had allowed it here. There won't be any hired marshal to protect you." Anger flowed through his veins and bile grew in his throat as he spoke, glaring those blackened eyes at the former Virginian.

Hawthorne spun on his heels and stalked out of the park and found Sullivan standing near the street. "Concussion or no, I am going to that little pub near the ferry and have a cold beer, Sullivan."

GEORGE BELKNAP WAS in a rage when Pete Flowers rode up to his ranch house later that week. "We've lost the fight, Pete. Your stupidity has cost us the opportunity to have Oregon admitted to the union as a slave state. You can get back on that horse and ride off. You're not my friend, you're not a supporter of the cause. Flowers-you're nothing but a thug masquerading as a rancher."

Flowers' anger erupted at the comments. "How dare you, Belknap?" He dismounted, had his quirt in hand, smacking it solidly against his leather chaps and high boots. It was a seriously menacing threat. "You who saw to it that a member of your own legislature was murdered, shot in the back, how dare you call me a thug." He glared at Belknap, almost pulled the long-barreled pistol, and stepped back into the saddle. Belknap had taken three steps up to his veranda style porch, as Flowers continued his tirade. "You'll regret those words," he snarled, jerking the horse around and riding off fast.

Belknap just stood there, a half-filled water tumbler of whiskey in his hand. "It's over," he said for about the tenth time, and sat back down. How long had he sat in that chair? He wondered when he realized the sun was going down. He reached for the bottle and found it empty, and remembered it was almost full when he sat down. He knew he was hungry, wanted another drink, and all he could say was, "It's over."

As the days and weeks went on, George Belknap realized just how much damage had been done as friends evaded him, constituents asked embarrassing questions, and supporters withdrew their support. The time for the convention was fast approaching and he knew he'd find little support in Salem City.

*I must salvage something. I must see to it that our race cannot be polluted, and salvage the laws we have dealing with mixed bloods. It's the only thing left.* His followers weren't as willing to concede the argument, he would find out, but he'd lost so many with the attack on Hawthorne and Sullivan even they were wavering.

BARBARA WHITELL'S wound was healing rapidly but the rest of her body was fighting a losing battle. She had lost so much blood that the baby inside her was denied all its proper nourishment, and was wasting away instead of growing. "Barbara," Doc Spears said, "I'm afraid we aren't going to be able save that dear child."

Barbara felt she already knew that answer but wasn't willing to accept it. "Isn't there something I can do?" She was sobbing, pleading. "Something you can do? I want this baby, doctor." He took her hand and rubbed the knuckles gently, trying to sooth the tiny woman with the huge heart.

Doc Spears couldn't remember how many babies he'd delivered over the years, and was painfully aware of how hard the frontier was on women. How many babies never quite made it? How many never made their first year even if they were born alive? He would be the first to say, frontier women were strong, and the first to say, often the frontier was stronger.

"You fought off two killers, saved yourself through shear will, and I'm not willing to give up, either," he said. He shook his head again, looked deep into her sad eyes, and squeezed her hand. "I can't think of anything that we haven't already tried. You lost so much blood, your baby starved. Those men couldn't kill you, but they did serious harm to your baby.

"All we can do is keep feeding you as much as you can possibly eat, hope that your blood is as rich as we can make it, and pray," he said. She saw tears form and drop onto his wan cheeks. "We'll have our answer within the next few days, and I'm not very hopeful, dear lady. Eat and sleep and pray," he said.

She cried herself to sleep each night for a week, ate everything that Beulah and Clementine fixed for her, and knew it wasn't working. Beulah heard the scream clear across the lumber mill facility and ran to Moose's old house. Clemmie was already at Barbara's bedside.

All they could do was try to calm Barbara, take care of the fetus, and cry. They cried right up to the time of burial, and into the days after that. Moose cried for one of the few times in his life, holding his sister, rocking into a Shoshone death chant. The two quietly sang and chanted for several hours.

Angus Whitell was helpless. He had no idea what to do. He hugged Barbara and caressed her lovely face, told her how much he loved her, and cried as only a broken hearted Irisher can cry. He sat by her bedside for hours every day and slept next to the baby's grave every night.

It was a full two weeks before Barbara could move around some, close to ten days before Angus could get a full day's work in at the mill, and at least a week before Beulah had her schedule back in order. Donaldson's Mill was finally back in business. Clemmie moved back to her and Moose's new home, Barbara and Angus made the long trip back to their home, and logs were rafted down Mill Creek to be turned into lumber.

"We'll try again, Angus. My strength will come back, I can feel it already. It was just bad luck that those men showed up here."

"It was the best of luck that you survived," Angus said. "We'll get you good and strong and then we'll have seven or ten children," he laughed. "Maybe not all at once, though."

"My God, no," she squealed. "Is the farm okay? I need to get out and do some work around this place. Are the animals okay?"

"Everything's fine, little darlin'. Sydney did a wonderful job of keeping the place up while we were gone. The doctor said you can do light work, and I want you to promise you won't be over working while I'm at the mill."

"I'll be more careful than you can imagine, Angus. My kitchen garden is ready to harvest and I know at least one hog is ready to be taken care of. I'm glad Moose said we could keep Sydney. He's a good worker and I'll let him do the heavy work."

"I'll miss him at the mill, but Moose said we can keep him for as long as we need him. Might that be a couple of years?" They laughed and hugged, and knew they were lucky beyond words that they hadn't lost more when those outlaws showed up.

IV

---

# BOOK THIRTEEN: THE CONSTITUTIONAL CONVENTION

AUGUST 17, 1857 ARRIVED WITH A HOT SUMMER SUN in Salem City. Some felt the humidity was higher than the temperature. Legislators and visitors from the far corners of Oregon Territory were in town and the Constitutional Convention was going to be called to order at the stroke of twelve o'clock noon. Activity in the capitol city varied from raucous to sublime, with many simply looking on the festivities as an excuse for a party.

Buildings were decorated with bunting, flags flew from every pole or porch, and bands of every organization were playing rousing marches and patriotic ditties. Every church had been filled that Sunday, every saloon was filled that day, as well. What would be the outcome? Who would be considered the winner... the loser?

Some of the more sporting saloons had chalk boards posted behind the oaken plank, and based on the betting, odds were calculated, just as they often were when the finest horses were raced. The cigar smoke was so heavy in one saloon, the fire boys were called out with their hose carts and hand pumpers.

Many representatives had to leave their farms and ranches at the height of harvest season, with crops ready for market, animals at their peak, and their government demanding their services. The intensity of the situation was discussed openly, at the barbershop, at the saloon, at the dress shop, and in the smoky back rooms.

Everyone who called themselves, Oregonians, were concerned about whether their particular philosophy would be represented in the new state constitution. It was a busy time for members of the legislature. They met with supporters, heard every argument possible for and against every article that had been proposed, and the convention hadn't even convened.

During those several days, Zeke Hawthorne spent hours with his committee, George Belknap with his, and other factions were meeting in various locations as well.

"Can we pull this off without anyone getting killed or maimed?" John Bradley was sitting at a large table in the conference room of the Salem Hotel, surrounded by assemblymen, senators, businessmen, and hangers-on. He tried to make light of what was on everyone's mind. The session of 1855-56 was a disaster following the brutal murder of Nate Bishop.

"I'm wondering if there isn't some kind of plan behind all the violence. Is this a deliberate distraction? If we spend our time discussing what has happened instead of what we're actually here for, we might not get much accomplished." Zeke wanted to put all the talk of past violence and that of the attack on he and Sullivan to rest, wanted to discuss how to get their programs pushed through all the committees at the upcoming convention.

He tried to put aside discussions on the attack on his farm, the injury to his son, and the attack in Eugene. "That's old history. What we're doing right now is current history, something that will be remembered for generations, eons, taught in schools a hundred years from now.

"We need to be the leaders of this march to statehood, not be worried sick about what those who oppose us might be planning. Forget George Belknap, forget the Oregon Firsters, push aside any threats that may have been rumored about by those doing their best to upset our cart. Bribes may have been offered, maybe even accepted, but set that aside, and think only how we should work toward our goal."

"Hear, hear!" Bank of Oregon president, Obediah Sinclair, barked. "The future of this wonderful territory should be built on the solid foundation of what you gentlemen put together during this session. A constitution that all Oregonians can cherish, one that will create an economic climate that allows business to flourish, and one that guarantees freedom to everyone."

"I wonder why you're not in the legislature, OB?" Sam Chastain laughed, "But you are absolutely right." He opened a large buckskin pouch he had slung over his shoulder and brought some papers out. "I've taken it on myself to put together a rough draft on the most important points I think we should concentrate on during this session.

"If you'll give me a few minutes, I'll read them off to you and maybe we can have someone copy this off so we each have copies."

"You've got a quick mind, Sam. I want to hear what you're thinking," Zeke said. The others around the room nodded and Sam Chastain read off ten points he felt needed to be attended to in any potential constitution that might be proposed.

"THESE POINTS, as most of you are aware, are not mine, but come straight from those brave men who stood up to the king and thumbed their collective noses. These are our Bill of Rights straight out of the constitution. And the point those men made then are as valid today as they were seventy-five years ago. The thing that stands out in that document is the concept of individual freedom, and that, gentlemen, is what we're all about."

"There are many in the territory that don't believe Indians, Negros, and half-breeds should have any freedoms, Sam." Zeke was going to force these men to realize that they were up against strong opposition that needed the strongest argument. "There are several states in the union that don't allow anyone of color or mixed color to have those freedoms you call precious. I, too, call them precious, and for all men regardless of race, but we have to have arguments to counter what the opposition thinks."

Sinclair said simply, "Our territorial constitution has a restricting clause in it right now that denies citizenship to Negros and those of mixed races. Denies the right of land ownership, too. We're all too familiar with the Exclusion Law that found its way into our current document.

"There's a serious threat to include that in our new state constitution." Sinclair said. "Zeke's right, platitudes, regardless of origin, are not the answer. We need strong arguments against their policies and platform."

The arguments and discussion went on through the rest of that day and the next, finally concluding with a platform that Zeke felt sure would be ripped to shreds by Belknap and his followers. "I'll help lead this fight with this platform, gentlemen. It's a good one, solid in every way, and those who favor slavery and a separation of the races will attack it vehemently, I'll guarantee."

"If Belknap's against it, that means I strongly favor it," John Bradley quipped, getting hurrahs around the table. "Should we have this published? Should we ask the newspapers around the state to publish what it is we are planning?"

"It would give the opposition prior knowledge of our plans," Chastain said.

"Yes," Zeke said. "It would, but I'm sure they will have that prior knowledge anyway since we'll be talking to our supporters. The convention starts in two days. Here's what I propose. Make this document available to the press, because every newspaper in the territory will have reporters right here. What say you?"

It was agreed and OB Sinclair said he would take responsibility for getting copies available for all the newspapers in the territory and have copies available for distribution as well. "The more people are talking about this, the better," Sinclair said. "We're not only denying the concept of slavery we're promoting the idea of individual liberty and freedom."

"It's the liberty word that sticks in Belknap's craw. We're not defending our position gentlemen; we're promoting our position. Let them try to defend their position of denying liberty and freedom." Sam Chastain got in the last words and a solid round of applause for his effort.

THE CONVENTION WAS LED by the president of the Council or Senate, the Honorable Hugh D. O'Bryant, and the Speaker of the House, the Honorable, Ira F.M. Butler. They called the convention to order, and made opening statements. Rules were given the okay by voice vote since they were basically the rules of the legislature. Members were assigned to committees, which were named and approved, and the first day's business was finished.

"Well, Mr. Sullivan, we made day one," Zeke laughed. "We must now get down to the hard work." He was joined in the dining room of the Salem Hotel by his wife Sarah and son, Hiram. The small children stayed on the farm to be looked after by Rebecca. "I'm glad you two were here for all the pomp. You'll be able to say for the rest of your life that you were there when this fine territory became a state."

"I'm going to say that my father helped that happen," Hi said. "I'm very proud of what you're doing, Papa."

Sarah blinked away tears, and had a vice grip on Zeke's hand. "You will always be the man that defended me in front of the Fort Bridger people, my Sharp Knife," she sobbed. "I can't keep the tears from flowing, Zeke. I've never been more proud of you."

"My fear, and my family's a part of this, is the exclusion law. I'm almost sure we're going to win the battle over slavery, but the exclusion law worries me. The way it's being promoted, it goes way past those of Negro or mixed Negro blood and includes any race mixed with the whites. That includes my entire family. Everyone except me, Travis, and Angus.

"The background that some use to justify it is messy at best and is difficult to argue because it's so nebulous. In the early days of territorial settlement, an Indian tribe along the Columbia River was decimated by disease brought by white missionaries. The tribe believed they were poisoned and counter-attacked, wiping out the mission. The exclusion law came from hatred and that hatred is perpetuated into this generation.

"Everyone else in this family is of mixed white and Shoshone blood. Even Clemmie is Indian. I'm going to fight this proposal with every drop of blood I have. This will not become a part of Oregon's state constitution."

It was Sullivan who did his best to lighten the atmosphere by talking about the many people continuing to arrive from the east, about how many new businesses were being opened, up and down the Willamette River Valley and the Columbia River basin.

"There's great development along the coast and inland to the coastal range of mountains. The Columbia River areas are filling with people and townships, the area along the western banks of the Snake River, and the great inland deserts are filling with people, cattle, and sheep."

He talked about great cattle and horse ranches being organized all over the state, and how available transportation was now- compared to just five years ago. "Between great transport wagons and teams, magnificent steamships, and the international trade through the Portland docks, this state is one super-powered economic engine," he almost shouted, his jowls quivering with delight.

"At some point, Sully, you will run out of good things to say about Oregon," Zeke joshed. "You are, of course, absolutely right. There's no finer place to live and raise a family."

"I was up at the Trading Post today to see Grandpa," Hiram said. "He said something about Moose planning another trip to the Green River country. Have you heard anything, Papa?"

"No," Zeke said. He had heard all the stories from the immigrant trains coming through, about the Bannock, Paiute, and Western Shoshone Indians raiding the wagon trains, particularly those heading for California. The Oregon Trail along the Snake River and the Lassen Trail across the Black Rock Desert were prime targets.

"Moose will always feel it's his duty to protect the people," Zeke said. "Let's get together with the family, maybe at Travis's, when this convention is over. There will be more and more confrontations, and we've known for some time the government's position on the matter. This concept of eminent domain is now government policy."

FOR THREE DAYS, committee meetings hammered out what would be brought before the convention for a yea or nay vote. Zeke was called to speak before several of the committees, particularly one's debating slavery, the Exclusion Law, and education.

"I'm here this morning to discuss the issue of whether Oregon should be admitted as a slave state or not. I believe my position is well known amongst you of the committee, but I also feel it's important for me to make an opening statement before you begin to ask questions. I have offered each of you gentlemen a copy of my statement."

Zeke's opening remarks only lasted for about ten minutes, brief by legislative standards, and were not interrupted even once. "In conclusion," he said, "Slavery exists in the world because it is *allowed* to exist. Some societies are not as moral as others, some societies believe that money is more important than liberty. I don't believe that the United States of America is morally deficient and I don't believe that liberty is simply a word, not an edict.

"When I talk about liberty and freedom, I'm not talking about the white race or the red race or the black race. I'm talking about the human race. We are humans and we come in a myriad of colors, but in every race, we bleed red. Dogs don't cohabit with cats for a simple reason. One is of the canine race and the other of the feline race.

"There are some that believe that whites shouldn't cohabit with other colors, but we are all of the, human race. Each individual should make that decision, not government. It is not the government's responsibility to say who a man might fall in love with. Nor is it the responsibility of the government to say that one man might own another man. Slavery is wrong on every level of discussion, as is the concept of excluding certain races or mixed races from being citizens or owning land."

The discussion following his short speech was led by George Belknap who many felt gave the appearance of a beaten man. The committee was split on the question of slavery, voting nine to three to ban slavery, the sale of slaves, and the prior ownership of slaves in the constitution. It was the question of exclusion of certain races and the mixed races that drew the most attention.

By the time the dust settled, what was proposed and accepted by a bare majority, was a law to deny Negros and Mixed Blood Negros from owning land and even from living in the state. The debate was vicious in some respects, with men like Belknap calling non-white people less than human, and making other ugly comments. Most of the arguments were aimed at those of Negro blood, but Indians and mixed-blood Indians were also included in the arguments.

"I've never felt more ashamed of my fellow legislators than I do at this moment," Zeke said when the final committee vote was announced. They called for exclusion only of Negro and mixed-Negro people, only after it was pointed out more than once that at least three members of the legislature were of mixed Indian blood. Oregon was settled first by the fur trade trappers, many of whom were married to women of various tribes in the west.

Some of their children were now community and territorial leaders and were about to vote themselves right out of the potential new state. The humiliation factor was not lost on some sitting next to the mixed-blood legislators. Friendships were challenged during those debates and the vote would be discussed over many bottles of fine liquor over the next months and years.

"What these men did today," Zeke said, sitting at a table in the Salem City Hotel Saloon with Sullivan and Chastain, "will be brought before the convention tomorrow and if it's accepted by the convention it will be a stain on this state for a hundred years or more.

"We'll have one last chance to debate this question, but our arguments will be limited to five minutes by our own rules. I'm almost sure the slavery question is now a dead issue, but the exclusion law is very much up for grabs at this point."

"Are you going to be the speaker against?" Sullivan probably felt he already knew the answer but asked anyway.

"I'm speaking against the issue and Harry Proctor from Oregon City will speak in favor. I'm not sure at all how the convention will vote on the exclusion question."

Sarah and Hiram returned to the farm the next morning, after having a quiet breakfast with Zeke. "I feel I've let the family down," Zeke said as they walked out to the buggy. "All I can do is talk my fool head off today, Sarah. Give me a big hug, pretty lady, and wish me luck."

They hugged for several seconds, Zeke kissed her and shook hands with Hiram. "Remember now, you two be back here day after tomorrow so we can get together with Travis and Moose. This question of attacks on the wagon trains is going to have a big effect on the Shoshone Nation and I know Moose must have some information that we don't have."

Zeke watched as they drove out of town and then made his way to the Capitol Building, remembering the horror of two years ago when Nate Bishop was gunned down at this very doorway. He stood next to the door and looked around, remembering the sound of that heavy lead ball hitting his friend in the back.

*That man died right here. Right where I'm standing at this very moment, and died for the cause that I'm going to fight on the floor in less than an hour.* He wiped away a couple of tears that could have become a torrent if he let them, remembering his friendship with Nate Bishop, the times they'd rode through the territory together, the committees they sat on together, and the many tankards of cold beer they had consumed at Sullivan's brewery.

"All of this because one man wants to dominate another, because greed and the love of money is stronger than the sense of right and wrong. How many men have died fighting this piece of hell called slavery? How many more will die if we let it continue?"

No answers, he knew, as he slowly opened the door and walked into the capitol building to slay his dragons. He had to chuckle as he thought about that. "Who will be Dulcinea?" he whispered.

## 18

"WE WILL NOW VOTE ON EACH SECTION OF WHAT IS about to be the constitution of the great state of Oregon," Council President O'Bryan said to rousing applause and howls of delight from the room filled with delegates, reporters, and the general public. "As each part of this document is brought to the floor, the committee vote will be recorded, and one person from each side of the question will be given no more than five minutes to make a statement.

"I will not hear any arguments on this, and if necessary, I will have the sergeant of arms escort any member that refuses to stop talking at the sound of my gavel from the floor. I will remind you again that we will be gentlemen at all times during this period, at least." He got generous laughter at that.

The debating went well through the morning readings. There were a few comments from the visitor's gallery that drew the attention of the sergeant of arms, but no one was asked to leave, and what disruption there was, was considered mild. The question on whether slavery would be a part of everyday life in Oregon finally came to the floor. George Belknap rose to speak in favor of the question.

"Libraries around the world are filled with accounts going back to the time of Babylon of organized slavery. It is a way of life, an economic stabilizer, and an opportunity for the races that are not fully human to have productive lives." There was a general outcry from the visitor's section and it took President O'Bryan several minutes to restore order.

"Another outbreak like this and I'll clear this hall," O'Bryan thundered. "Mr. Belknap, your clock is running."

Belknap used up the rest of his five minutes with equally atrocious comments, the crowd was somewhat calm, and O'Bryan called on Zeke Hawthorne to make his statement. He made a rather simple speech, one he had used before, in Eugene, in Oregon City, and from the back of one of his mules while plowing a field. Sarah could have repeated it word for word if she had been in the gallery.

"Human beings come in many colors and shapes. Our eyes are not the same, nor are our noses. Some human beings have big ears, some have big feet, while others can't seem to grow a full head of hair," he said. The gallery laughed along with many of the legislatures. "The point is, though, we are still human beings, despite our differences. It may be that some societies throughout history have allowed, even promoted slavery. That doesn't make it right.

"There is a dignity that comes with being a human and

that dignity is sundered by slavery. One race is not superior to another, any more than one country's citizens are not superior to any other country's citizens. We say that we cherish liberty, freedom. We even wrote that into our federal constitution, and it has been discussed about putting the concept into the Oregon state constitution.

"Maybe we should write that we cherish liberty for white people? Nonsense. If you believe that every human should be free to live a life of liberty, then you must vote *No* on the question of slavery. If one person in Oregon is freer than another because of that person's color or race, Oregon will never become the great state it should be destined to become."

By way of thunderous applause, President O'Bryan almost didn't have to call for the vote, but of course he did. Zeke was ecstatic when the floor vote was overwhelmingly against Oregon being a slave state, but found it was impossible to quell the anger that still existed because of the Indian massacre of the missionaries so many years ago.

TYRUS AMES, representing the Columbia River district presented the argument in favor of the exclusion law. He particularly wanted Indians, half breeds, and those married to whites to be excluded from land ownership and voting rights. "It was in November of 1847," he said, flourishing a document of some kind, "that the Cayuse horde descended on Whitman's Mission and murdered that fine missionary, his wife Narcissa, and eleven other wonderful people.

"It was a massacre," he thundered. "They killed every

single person at the Whitman Mission. Every one of them, dead, murdered... slaughtered by savages after all the hard work Whitman had done to civilize the heathens. Indian blood is savage blood and they must be separated from the white folk."

Zeke did his best to fight those comments. He reminded everyone that it was the Whitman's who brought the white man's diseases to the Cayuse tribe. Those diseases almost wiped out the tribe, and the Indians believed they had been purposefully poisoned by Whitman. His arguments fell on deaf ears. The Whitman Massacre was burned into the collective minds of the representatives and nothing would change that.

"I call your attention to the fact that several members of this august body carry the blood of several tribes of Indians. It was fur traders and trappers that first came to this territory and many of them had Indian wives. Their children are now sitting in this hall being called savages, and told they aren't welcome here.

"The exclusion law is wrong. We just voted Oregon to be a free state, to not allow slavery. Now you want to vote that we won't allow a black person or one of mixed blood, or an Indian or one of mixed blood to own land or even be allowed in the state. All this while some members of this body are of Indian mixed blood."

Zeke's arguments did not fall completely flat, though. The exclusion law would be a part of the Oregon State Constitution. His only consolation in the matter was that Indians and those of mixed Indian and white blood could own land and be considered full citizens of the state. Some considered that a victory for the Hawthorne group, but Zeke knew that in the long run, it was far from a victory.

"I'll never understand that vote, Sully," Zeke said, sitting at a table at Sullivan's brewery. "It will be a stain on this state for generations to come."

"You made history, Zeke. Look at it this way, you have seen to it that your family and all the families with mixed Indian blood are not going to be excluded."

"Yes, I did," Zeke said. "But what about the free negroes? What about mixed blood negroes and their families? They will be forced to leave Oregon or stay and be whipped in public by law. That's wrong."

"You fought a good fight, Zeke. Let's concentrate on getting the general public to vote yes on this constitution. Are you spending the night, for if you are, I know a place that is serving roast elk for supper."

"I'm spending the night," Zeke smiled.


"WHAT HAPPENS NOW, PAPA?" Hiram and Sarah were in Salem City following the convention. "Are we a state?"

"Not yet, son," Zeke chuckled, "but we're working on it. We'll all go to the polls on November ninth to vote yes or no. If we vote yes on our constitution, then the document will be sent to Washington and congress will mull it over for God knows how long. Hopefully, it will find its way to the president's desk and we will become a state on his signature."

"Are you going to be home now? Our farm is in need of many hands, Papa. I haven't hired extra until you give me an okay, but harvest time is here and it's going to be a big one."

"Between now and November ninth, I'll be in and out, Hiram. Never more than a day gone, though. I'll be campaigning for the constitution up and down the valley within my district. We'll get all this started as soon as we get back home, Hi."

## 19

I'M GLAD WE'RE ALL TOGETHER LIKE THIS," SARAH said, helping her mother prepare supper for the huge family. "Even without the youngsters being here, this will be a full table tonight. Do you know what Moose is so excited about?" Sarah and Zeke had discussed the Indian problems that immigrants had been facing along the Oregon Trail and how Moose felt he was letting his people down by not being in the Rocky Mountains with them.

"I tried to pry it out of Clementine but she wouldn't say a word," Elaine chuckled. "Moose is worried on the one hand and seems pleasantly excited at the same time. He and Clemmie should be arriving shortly."

It was during the time of the constitutional convention that Moose said he wanted to have a meeting with the family when the convention was over, but wouldn't go into any detail about what was so important. Conjecture of course ran the gamut from Clemmie being pregnant to

Moose quitting the lumber business. And Moose wasn't talking until the family gathering.

"I think you've done a splendid job on this statehood thing, Zeke." Travis, Angus, Zeke, and Hiram were sitting on the veranda enjoying some of Sullivan's fine bourbon, waiting for Moose and Clementine. "That exclusion law sticks mighty deep in my craw, though. The only time my wife's a savage is when I do something wrong." That broke the tension and the laughter rang through the surrounding forest.

"My little girl proved her savagery," Angus laughed, "but we lost in the long run. We had a man show up at the mill, looking for work, and told us about two Indian attacks on their wagon train. One between Salt Lake and Fort Boise, the other between Boise and the Columbia.

"Is the Oregon Trail going to get any kind of army protection, Zeke?"

"It's being talked about. I know California has sent some California volunteers onto the Lassen Trail, in Utah Territory. The Pitt River area is ripe for attacks, and of course the Snake River has already been the scene of attacks. Maybe we'll know more when Moose gets here."

"I think I just heard a couple of horses come up to the corrals," Hiram said. He jumped off the porch and ran around the building. "About time you got here, Moose," he said, taking the reins from the two horses. "Hi, Clemmie."


THE TABLE GROANED from the weight of food spread across it, and the family settled in for a long discussion, led by Moose. "I guess I'm bringing some good news and some not very good news," he said after everyone's plates were full.

"I have a letter here I want to read. It's from Buck O'Keefe."

"Buck," Zeke said. "I hope he's okay. He's one fine lad. Go on, Moose."

"Buck went to Missouri and hitched up with the army as a scout and has been working at the new Fort Bridger. They rebuilt the place, Papa. Can't be as nice as when we were there," he chuckled. "Anyway, Buck has been working with Broken Hand and is working with our people, having the Shoshone help with keeping the Oregon Trail as safe as possible in that area, anyway."

"Broken Hand is one of the most honest men I've ever known," Travis said. "He and old Gabe were quite a pair when I was younger. Keep going, Moose."

"It seems that the Sioux and the Crow are really fighting the encroachment of the immigrants, and the army is taking a strong stance against them. They've come to the Shoshone asking for help. Buck wants me to come to Bridger and spend a few weeks helping negotiate the treaties."

"What a wonderful opportunity, Moose. When do you leave?" Zeke seemed as excited by the idea as Moose. "You've had it in your mind to help your people, and now you can."

"Yes, and Clementine is coming with me. Angus will be the mill manager while we're gone, and we'll be on the trail by the end of the week. We're going on horseback with one pack mule each, so travelling light and fast."

"Do you have any idea how long you'll be gone?"

Barbara asked. "You won't be spending the winter, will you?"

"No, we'll be back before the first snows, I'm sure. According to Buck O'Keefe, all the preliminary talks have taken place and it will simply be developing that evasive trust thing. The people don't trust the army but do trust Broken Hand. Broken Hand trusts the people but doesn't trust the army. Right now, no one knows Buck O'Keefe well enough to trust him or not."

"And the people trust you and Broken Hand," Travis pointed out. "Take the army out of the equation and your job is done, old man," he laughed. "You've got some work to do, Moose. Just remember, simply because whatever army general signs whatever treaty, it's worthless until congress approves that treaty."

"I think I understand the process, Papa, but I still worry about how this will affect our way of life. That is, the people's way of life. Working as scouts and guides for the army is going to change how they live. Shoshone have been mountain people, hunters," Moose said, an almost longing in his voice. "I just hope that I will make some positive notch in the life calendar of the people, with a treaty that all can live with."

"Don't bet it'll hold up even if congress approves it. What a politician says today isn't what he'll promise tomorrow, and if you don't believe that, talk to some of the tribes in the Great Lakes areas." Zeke appreciated Travis's attempts at humor, but wanted to make sure that Moose was aware of the duplicity involved in politics.

"Some of those people in congress talk out of many sides of their mouths, Moose, and generals will often promise things they can't produce. Don't get caught up in army politics or find yourself promising something only Congress can offer."

"There was a couple of paragraphs in Buck's letter that said almost that same thing. He was telling me what Broken Hand had told him."

"All of this talk about treaties and wagon train attacks, and danger are one thing, Moose, but don't forget the most important," Elaine said.

"What's the most important?"

"You bring buffalo meat home when you come back," she laughed, getting a thumb's up from Sarah and Barbara. "Buck's a good cowboy, so gather a fine herd of buffalo and bring them here."

Supper went on for several hours, not breaking up until after Elaine served fresh peach cobbler topped with fresh whipped cream. "I could eat three of those all by myself," Travis said. "Maybe even four."


"MOOSE WILL BE ALL RIGHT, won't he?" Sarah, Zeke, and Hiram were spending the night at the Salem Hotel following the long supper. Hiram had his own room, and Sarah and Zeke were already in bed. "Life for our people is changing so fast. These times are so filled with danger. Can the Shoshone trust the army?"

"Government policy fluctuates wildly based on which faction is in power, Sarah. It appears that right now, the government is in favor of eliminating the buffalo herds and forcing the various tribes to relocate to specific areas and become farmers. They could not be more wrong in their thinking," Zeke said. "Like Moose said, your people are hunters.

"There is a tidal wave of people moving from the east to the west and those already in the west must make way for that tidal wave. They can ride with the wave, be awash in a complete change of life or swim against the tide and drown. I think what Broken Hand is offering is a way for the Shoshone to ride the wave and survive."

"Moose said the Sioux are already at war."

"That war will be hard fought, Sarah, but just numbers alone tell me that the Sioux will win many battles but will lose the war. Which path is the right one? Work with the concept of eminent domain or fight it to the death? I think what Broken Hand is trying to do is right for the Shoshone. What needs to be answered, and won't be for some time, is whether the treaties will be honored. I think you understand as I have discovered, there is no honor in politics."

"WILL WE BE IN DANGER, MOOSE?" Elaine asked as they finished packing their mules for the first stage of their ride east. "Those attacks we've heard about scare me."

"We won't be riding the main trails, Clemmie. We'll go north through the Yellowstone country and drop south into the Green River area. We have friends with the Nez Percé, but we'll have to be particular when we move through Crow and Black Feet territory. You've never seen country like what we'll be travelling though. The mountains reach deep into the clouds, the trees are immense, and game is everywhere.

"We'll be eating mostly what we find along the way. If we spend time with friends, we'll be eating buffalo, but if we're not, we'll be eating rabbit," he laughed.

"Maybe some venison if we're lucky. We can't take the time to smoke out a venison and I don't believe in wasting food."

They rode through the mill property, saying goodbye to all there, stopped briefly at the Salem Trading Post, and arrived at the Hawthorne farm well after sunset. "I'm glad you're here, Moose." Zeke walked out of the kitchen along with Hiram and the twins. "Let's get your animals taken care of and get you some food."

Clemmie grabbed the twins and headed into the kitchen while Hiram took the horses and mules to a corral. "You just here for tonight?" Hi asked.

"We'll be gone by sunrise. I wish you were riding with us, Hiram."

"I wish so, too, Uncle Moose, but this old farm needs me here. The election is coming up and Papa needs to be out campaigning. There's still the possibility of more trouble from outlaws, and we're not through with the harvest, by any means."

"They want me to help move my people from being warriors and hunters to being farmers, Hi. For you and Sarah and Barbara, that's working out fine, and I'm doing well being a lumber man. I'm not a warrior any more, haven't been since we moved to Oregon, so maybe it will work out. I just don't know."

Hiram was at a loss for words. This was the first time he had ever seen his uncle in this kind of mood. "I don't fully understand, Moose."

"According to what Buck O'Keefe said in his letter and what Zeke has said about the government's policies toward the Indian nations, the tribes will be moved from their traditional hunting areas to land the whites don't want to be turned into farmers because the whites want the traditional hunting land.

"When they are moved, the government will supply food until the tribes can grow and raise their own. I fully understand why the Sioux are at war, Hiram. What's happening is wrong and I also understand what Zeke says. Regardless of wrong or right, the simple over-whelming numbers will crush the Indian nations and nothing will stop those numbers of people."

Zeke helped the two get the mules unloaded and feed was distributed before they headed for the house. "You have a huge heart, Moose, and a level head. You will need both during your negotiations. Think of what's best for your people and know what will happen no matter what. The immigrants will continue to come in ever increasing numbers and your people will need to make changes to survive. It isn't right but it is going to happen that way."

Hiram was in the corral well before sunup helping Moose and Clemmie load the mules and saddle the horses. "You hurry back, Uncle Moose." He held the tears back until the little caravan was well down the trail leading to the River Road.

## 20

AUGUST SLIPPED INTO September and the campaign for Oregon statehood was livelier than the campaigns for assembly that Zeke had faced three times. He organized helpers in the Willamette Valley district and they spent countless hours promoting the constitution to anyone and everyone they encountered. Zeke found that his idea of only being gone from time to time was very wrong.

Zeke became the organizer, putting people into the different districts to promote the yes vote on the constitution. He had people in Eugene, Portland, Oregon City, along the Oregon side of the Snake River, and along the Pacific coast. If it hadn't been for Sullivan taking over after several weeks, Zeke would have missed harvest entirely.

"I can't thank you enough, Sully. My God, old man, if we weren't doing this there would be no one out there promoting the yes vote. It didn't enter my mind until after the convention that we would need to heavily campaign this. You should have kicked me hard, Mr. Sullivan for not having this program put together a month before the convention."

"You have it organized, Zeke. I'll take over now and run the campaign. You bring in a good crop, and we'll all be living in the grand state of free Oregon soon."

Zeke was back at the farm that night, ready to join his son and their hired hands the next morning.

"I SENT word to Mr. Johnson in Portland to get me five people, Papa. I have started the harvest. I had to do that or we would start losing some of it, I contracted for extra wagons, mules, and for Johnson to distribute our produce. He will begin bringing in those wagons in three days or before, if this weather holds as it has been."

"That's fine, son, just fine. I'm going to make one more swing up the valley and back, and then I'm all yours. Everyone else is also scheduling their harvest, so campaigning would be a wasted effort. Five people? On top of the four, full-time help?"

"I'd like more, if I could find them. We'll have wheat, corn, hops, beans, and barley to bring in and I don't think the eleven of us are going to be enough. We've added a full plot for potatoes, remember, and they will be as labor intensive as the corn and beans. All that extra land we planted and a wet winter and spring, and we've got a big harvest looking at us." He laughed and said, "You should stick around once in a while."

"I will, Hi. Politics, government, public service is over for this old man. If this constitution is ratified and if congress finds time to vote for it, I'm through with it all. You'll have to put up with me on a daily basis."

"My heavens, Hiram. How much corn did you plant? Seems we've been harvesting corn for months now." Zeke was chuckling, driving a wagon pulled by four mules and loaded above the side boards with sweet corn."

"This is just the sweet corn, Papa. For the public markets. The rest will come when the corn still in the field dries good. There's another fifty acres to go, so don't wear out on me. Sam and Skinny Saunders are working with Toby and Brian Stockbridge in the bean fields, and the five of us are bringing in the corn.

"I'm sure glad we were able to get these men from Portland and Salem. I still want another three men, but there simply aren't any available. Everybody has an exceptional harvest this year. Probably because of such a wet winter. I wish I could put five men in the wheat fields right now, too."

"I'll never be able to say thank you enough, Hi. You're an amazing son. Your mother and I are so glad you found us," he laughed. "Amos Johnstone and Silas Williams have already brought their herds in and moved them north to the sale yards. They're sending some men down next week to help us out.

"You'll have your five, but I don't know how much they know about threshing wheat or cutting corn. Silas told me they were all good workers, so that's a help."

"Thank you, Papa. I'll take over the threshing with those men and leave you with the ones here in corn. Are you still having headaches from that beating you took? I'm really worried that you're okay."

"They've mostly gone away, son. Sully said with a concussion like I suffered, there might be problems for some time to come. The only thing good to come out of that trip was Sully and I being able to leave with dignity. The people in Eugene were some of the nicest I've come across on my trips, but Belknap and his hooligans are another story."

"Did you really threaten that marshal? I read what they said in the papers. Did you really tell him that you would tear his throat out if he touched you?" Hiram's eyes were wide and he was trying his best to hold in a chuckle. "It made you sound like grandpa."

Zeke had to laugh right out loud. "No, son, I didn't. I did tell the man I would see him in front of a judge if he used that little stick of his on me, but I think it was Sully having fun with the reporter that caused the comment about tearing the man's throat out.

"I'll tell Travis what you said, though. He'll love it."

"Will you make any more trips before the November election? I sure don't want you to. When will we know about statehood?"

They had the wagons almost back to the corncribs, Zeke driving one with Hiram on horseback alongside. There were two more wagons, each with a driver and outrider behind them. "I'll have to go to Salem once or twice, but those will be day trips. Out and back in one day. Statehood is some time off, I'm afraid.

"We've hammered out a constitution, you remember, and submitted our constitution to the voters. They'll make their decision in November. If all of that is accepted, then we will ratify it during our regular session, and it goes to the president and congress. Our regular session might be a little longer than those in the past. I'll be gone often at those times. Most of it during winter months."

"That's good," Hiram laughed. "You will be home for Christmas, won't you?"

"I assume your grandpa will be in charge, as usual, so you can bet that I'll be right here. You look at Travis and say party, and then hang on tight." Zeke and Hiram were laughing about that as they started to unhitch the wagons.

"I'm sure glad Barbara is well again. I was really scared when we heard about those men showing up at her place. Will she be able to have another baby? I still wish she was my wife, you know."

Zeke had to step back a little and give his son a long look. *He's a man and I tend to forget that. He stands taller than I, weighs more, and just told me he wished he had been able to marry Barbara.* He stood very quiet for another moment, taking it all in. *Where on earth has the time gone? That skinny little kid of ours is all grown up.*

"I know how much you love her, Hi. Only time will tell whether she'll be able to have a baby. She's tough, that girl is, but she's so tiny, we won't know for some time. On my next trip to Salem why don't you ride with me and we'll take a run up to their place and say hello."

"You bet, Papa. Yes sir," he yelped.

It took several hours to get the three wagons unloaded and the teams taken care of. The other crew brought in wagons loaded with fresh green beans to add to the stock. "Mr. Johnson is supposed to have wagons lined up tomorrow and for the next three days, Papa. The fresh sweet corn is going to Oregon City, Portland, and Salem

City, and these first wagonloads of green beans are heading to Salem and Eugene. Next week's beans are going north."

"I'm sure glad you took command of this old farm, Hiram. This is my last term as an assemblyman, and my last year in politics. From now on, you and I will be running this place. You'll finally get some help."

"And I need it," Hi laughed. "Are you sure you'll be able to walk away from politics? You enjoy what you do and everyone says that you're good for Oregon. You've been the lead man on bringing this territory to statehood, Papa, can you really just step aside?"

Zeke had to take a couple of moments to think about what Hiram said. "You're right about being involved up to my neck in the statehood program. There's no doubt about that, but it's the rest of it, Hi. The nasty people I've had to deal with, the criminal element in politics is more than ugly.

"No, son, there's no doubt that I'll miss some of the life of an assemblyman, but I won't miss the backbiting, the fools and their little games of one-upmanship, or the seriously ugly things like Sully and my fight with those men in Eugene. I'll quit and walk away, you can put your chips on that."

The boys remembered to shuck their boots before slipping into the kitchen. "Something smells good."

## 2 1

THE MEETING WITH BANKER, OBEDIAH SINCLAIR, AND the old convention committee, now a Vote Yes on Oregon committee, broke up late in the afternoon and Zeke wanted to meet with Roland Sullivan before making the long ride home. It would mean not getting home much before midnight but talking with Sullivan always made him feel better.

*I doubt that man has ever even heard the word pessimist. He's a dreamer and that isn't always bad. His dreams tend to find the light of day more often than not. Maybe I'll just spend the night and leave early in the morning.* He wouldn't admit it to Hiram or anyone else, but these past several weeks of hard work on the farm had left him very tired.

Sullivan had seen it, even commented on how tired Zeke looked. Zeke sloughed if off, but Sullivan said it was probably partly caused by the concussion and the fact that Zeke didn't take proper care of himself. *He's probably right about that, too.*

*A good long sleep on a soft mattress just might put these old bones back in shape. All those hours of sitting at meetings and listening to the droning on of platitudes and paradigms has taken its toll,* he chuckled, feeling the soreness in his shoulders.

Sarah said it often, Sullivan had said it often, and Zeke was determined to ignore their pleading for as long as possible. "You've had a serious injury to your head, Zeke," Sully would say. "If you don't ease up, learn to take a rest, you're going to compound that injury, and it's your family that will pay the consequence."

Sarah said it a little differently. "You need to rest, Sharp Knife." He knew they were right, knew he wasn't helping himself, but as he said often, "I have obligations, people have put their trust in me."

Sullivan had a broadsheet printed and delivered to the Hawthorne farm that simply read, "It's the most successful man that recognizes that it isn't he that does the job, but rather he that sees to it the job is done." The broadsheet had a signature block, all in flourished penmanship that couldn't actually be read. Only Sully and Hiram knew it read R. Sullivan.

Hiram designed and built the frame for the poster using some of the finest white oak on the property, antiquing it, working in fancy scrollwork, and the two of them presented it to Zeke at the kitchen table to squeals of delight from Sarah. Sarah and Hiram demanded that the framed broadsheet be hung prominently in Zeke's office, just off the living room.

During the meeting Zeke had discussed his concerns that the exclusion law that was inserted in the constitution would continue to lead the new state toward accepting slavery. "It will continue to bother me," he told

John Bradley. "We're saying that it is all right to deny some people their inalienable rights. What is the difference between and Indian and a free black and me? Only the outer color of our skin.

"It's not right but there is no other choice for people who think as I do. We'll not be able to draw up a constitution that would be passed," he all but sighed.

He was hailed by a gentleman on the boardwalk as he walked down the marble steps from the hotel. "I say, Mr. Hawthorne, may I have a moment?"

"Well, Mr. Blairsden. It's nice to see you again. In fine health, sir? How's the beef hide market these days?"

"It's a strong market, sir. It's those Californios that are changing the cattle market, and for the better. They are feeding the animals so they gain weight fast then taking them to market earlier. The meat is far better than it's ever been. We have a commercial market for beef."

"That's good to hear, Mr. Blairsden. I grow that feed you're talking about," he said with a chuckle. "What else is on your mind?"

"There is a group of people in Eugene, another one of those religious sects that we seem to draw down there," he said, "that wish to have a talk with you about these liberties and freedoms that you defend regularly. They did not attend your public meetings in our fair town but got the word secondhand, so to speak."

"Is this an invitation to come back to Eugene and speak again? I'm not sure my head can take another thrashing," Zeke laughed.

Blairsden laughed, shaking his head at the jest. "No, Mr. Hawthorne, I'll guarantee it. The group calls themselves the Church of Eternal Peace," Blairsden said. "The leader, a Johnny Clapper, says he believes you're familiar with them."

"My son saved them from an outlaw gang some months ago. I've never met any of them. Are they having a problem of some kind in Eugene?" *Thoughts of religious sects being denied opportunity because of their beliefs is something George Belknap just might approve of.*

"I'm under the impression that Clapper and two others want a meeting with you, but they are afraid of having that meeting in Eugene. It seems that Marshal Zeb North has been pretty hard on some of the sects.

"They would like to meet with you here in Salem City and asked me to set it up with you, if possible. They would like to meet with you on Monday of next week."

"All right, I'll meet with them. If they're getting trouble from North they just might need some help. Tell them to be at the Salem Hotel- Monday, at one. I'll be here." They shook hands and Blairsden walked off one way and Zeke the other.

*There have been several sects that have moved into the Eugene area seeking religious freedom, and looking to be free of persecution for their beliefs. To have the town marshal doing the persecuting is strange indeed. Hiram knows these people since he saved them from that gang of outlaws. I think I'll bring him with me.*

SARAH AND REBECCA stood on the porch of the big house watching Zeke and Hiram ride off to Salem City. "Hi's shoulders are just as wide as Zeke's," Sarah said with a smile. "He was so skinny and frail when he came to be our son, and just look at him."

"He's a fine man, Sarah. Some young lady will be happy with him one day. He's taught me how to read and write, how to do my numbers, even how to draw pictures of buildings the way he does. He made beautiful drawings of his house before he built it, and it looks just like those drawings."

Sarah chuckled just a bit at the comment since she remembered being in as much awe of Hiram's abilities herself not too long ago. "He and Zeke are more alike than I can imagine sometimes. It's as if they were really father and son, as if Zeke fathered the boy." She'd told her mother many times that the two men were best friends more than father and son and remembered Elaine saying it was the same with Travis and Moose.

"Zeke will be involved in the legislature again starting next week, Rebecca, and once again won't be around while we plan for our Christmas family holiday. My goodness, this family has grown since we moved to Oregon. I don't think that kitchen is big enough to hold everyone." The women were laughing together when they walked back into the house.


"I'm glad you asked me to come with you, Papa. That Clapper fellow wasn't too smart, but he did seem willing to learn when I had a chance to break through his nasty personality. I've wondered, often, how they were faring."

"Don't you mean how a particular young lady was getting along?" Zeke was chuckling some as he asked and noticed a definite coloring in Hiram's face.

"Her name is Gloria, Papa, and she's married." He clammed up for a minute and Zeke wasn't about to take his joshing any further. Riding quietly along the Willamette River, seeing high early winter clouds sparkling in the sun, hearing the activity of water fowl in for the winter from their arctic summer homes, gave Hiram time to put some thoughts together.

"It would have been very wrong for me to make any kind of advance, regardless of my wondering how they were getting along, Papa. But I have had thoughts about the lady. She is about my age, maybe a year or two younger than me, and most attractive. But, as I said, she's married.

"What bothers me, I guess, is that she's married to a very old man and they don't seem to be friends. You and mama are married, but what stands out in my mind is that you are really good friends, too. Shouldn't husbands and wives be friends?"

"You're amazingly astute sometimes, old man," Zeke said. "I haven't given much thought to what you just said, and probably because you're right. Sarah and I are best friends as well as husband and wife. I can't imagine being married to someone who wasn't also a good friend.

"When we meet with this Johnny Clapper and his two friends you can discreetly ask about the welfare of the other members and that would include Gloria. That must have been quite a show you put on for those folks," he chuckled. "I've heard it retold so many times, and it's bigger and more ferocious with each telling."

"It's Silas Williams and Josh Peterson that make up those stories. It's embarrassing sometimes having to listen to them. I did what had to be done because that's what you would have done. I thought really hard that night. I had a small fire going and was wrapped in my blanket and kept asking, 'What would Papa do?' and then, I went and did it."

That was the first time Hiram had told that part of the story and Zeke just sat straight up in the saddle, looking hard at his son, feeling waves of love flow through his body. "That's the way I do most things, Papa. You're the smartest man I've ever met, the toughest, and the bravest. If I take the time to think about something, and ask that question, 'what would Papa do?' I know I can do it right."

The rest of the ride into Salem City that morning was quiet as both men had galloping thoughts raging through their minds. Zeke was more and more amazed by this son of his and Hiram had thoughts of Gloria that could not be shared with anyone.

THEY TETHERED their horses outside the Salem Hotel and walked in, swiping at considerable trail dust. "Looks like we're a bit early, son. Let's have something cold while we wait," Zeke said. They slipped into the ornate barroom and took one of the tables near the window so they could see Clapper when he arrived.

"My head still hurts when I think about that evening in Eugene," Zeke said. "Zeb North, the town marshal is nothing but Belknap's mouthpiece, and what Blairsden intimated is that North has been giving these people some trouble. What's important, Hiram, is that we listen carefully.

"Often when people talk about something that bothers or frightens them, you have to listen for what they don't say. Understand?"

"I'm not sure I do. Listen to what someone doesn't say?

Or do you mean that what they do say might have two meanings. That they hint at what really troubles them." Hiram was shaking his head but also had a slight grin on his face. "Kind of like when you used to reprimand me by way of a lecture rather than a stern talking to."

Zeke was laughing at that and drank down the rest of his beer. "You're amazing, Hiram." He looked up as three riders approached the front of the hotel.

"That's them," Hiram said. "My God, will you look at that? That's Gloria riding with Johnny Clapper and the other man is Tobin, Gerald Tobin. He's the one that finally got Clapper to get the wagons moved. Gloria is riding with them? Clapper didn't have a lot of good things to say about women making their ideas known." He and his father stood up and welcomed their visitors.

"Hello again, Mr. Clapper," Hiram said, shaking his hand. "Meet my father, Ezekiel Hawthorne. Mr. Tobin, it's nice to see you, and Mrs. Law, it's a pleasure." They all shook hands.

"There's a nice little parlor just off the hotel lobby. We might be more comfortable there," Zeke said. He led the procession into a small meeting room lined with Oregon wood panels. The ornate table was elegantly carved and finished, and the matching chairs shone in their natural state. "This is much nicer," he said.

"How have you been faring, Mr. Clapper? I've wanted to ride south and visit, but that farm keeps me pretty busy." Hiram was speaking to Johnny Clapper but spent most of the time looking at Gloria Law. She spent an equal amount of time looking right back at him, and included a generous smile with those looks.

"Our land was just as it was advertised, and we have a

nice community building now. Our first crops are smaller than we would have liked, but clearing the land and getting a late start too, created that problem." Clapper was more forward than Hiram remembered.

"Mr. Blairsden indicated that you might be facing some problems, Mr. Clapper," Zeke said. "Please tell me about that."

"I guess our problems started when some young rowdies, real hooligans, began giving us trouble when we came to town to shop or visit. We are looking for new members of our society and they tried to stop us from discussing what we are doing in our community. Mr. Tobin can explain one of the incidents better than I. He was there."

Hiram noticed that Gloria lowered her head some as Gerald Tobin began to speak, not looking at him at all. "Earl Sorenson, Hubert Law, and I rode into town on a Monday morning to meet with a couple of families that indicated a desire to join with us." Tobin glanced at Gloria as if to say something, didn't, and continued.

"Hubert Law was still nursing a bad leg he broke when we first arrived and that wouldn't heal right. He stepped off his horse, twisted an ankle or something, and almost fell down. Four rowdies on the street started calling him vile names, suggesting the poor man was drunk. Before long, another man showed up and introduced himself as the town marshal. Said his name was Zeb North, and challenged Law."

"Challenged him? How or why would he do that?" Zeke asked.

"North said public drunkenness was a crime in Eugene. He was going to put Mr. Law in irons and take him to jail. I said that Law was suffering from an injury to his leg and simply twisted it getting off his horse, causing him to stumble.

"North struck me across my face with a riding quirt he carried and told me to shut my filthy mouth. It was then that Earl Sorenson whipped North around and was about to smack him a good one, that the rowdies started flailing away on poor Mr. Law who simply could not defend himself.

"The whole scene was out of control when North pulled his revolver and fired it straight up. Everything quieted down, but Mr. Law had been seriously injured by the four men. He never recovered from the beating, Mr. Hawthorne. We had to bury the poor man two weeks later. The problem right now is, Marshal North won't arrest the four men for the beating. Intimidation by the rowdies have increased, as well.

"North is claiming that Law died from a drunken binge, from alcoholism, not the beating. North even claims there was no beating, and he's threatened anyone who says they were a witness to the beating."

Hiram's head twisted quickly at the news of Law's death, and he found Gloria crying quietly, looking right at him. *She's so pretty and now a widow. She's my age and a widow. I must say something. I must.*

"I'm so sorry, Mrs. Law," he stammered and without thinking reached out and took her hand. She grasped his with strong fingers and they simply stared into each other's eyes.

Zeke broke it up asking if Clapper or Tobin knew who or what was behind North's behavior. "Generally, there is something to kindle that kind of attitude. Has anything been said that you could say brought it on? Those rowdies are being goaded, probably even paid into attacking, but why? And who controls the purse strings?"

"I think it has something to do with the land we've staked claim to," Gloria said before Clapper could answer. Hiram saw anger flash across Clapper's face and then ebb quickly when she said that.

"My late husband said that another group of people had discussed filing on the land but we filed our claims first. Mr. Law said that a territorial official named George Belknap was one of those involved and had complained to the marshal about us." She lowered her eyes, her cheeks reddened a bit from the little speech. Clapper appeared to be furious with her.

Zeke could feel the tension in the little parlor and wondered just what Clapper was so upset about. "Is there something you would like to add, Mr. Clapper? I'm very familiar with Belknap and North," he said, continuing. "I've had my dust-ups with both men. Is this about land or what might be on the land?"

Clapper sat quietly steaming. Zeke saw it too, but it was Tobin who finally spoke. "We filed on two full sections of land, Mr. Hawthorne. Each of our families filed on their quarter sections just as the territorial land commissioner told us we could. Within those two square miles, there are two fair-sized streams that come together to make a nice river.

"I was told by more than one person in Eugene that Mr. Belknap and two of his business partners were planning to build a grist mill at the confluence of those streams, but we filed our claims before he was able to file his. I believe his plan now is to drive us from our sanctuary."

"Tell him the whole story, Mr. Clapper," Gloria said. "Hiram, there's more to this."

"Mr. Clapper," Hi said. "I tried to help you once before and you shoved me off. Now, you ask for my father's help and when we offer it, you're trying to shove us off again. If what Mr. Tobin just told us is the whole story; then we might be able to help, but if you're holding something back, we might just get up and ride for home."

"No!" Gloria said, grabbing Hiram's hand and holding it. "No. Please, Mr. Clapper. Tell them."

## 22

"BE QUIET, WOMAN. You don't know what you're talking about." Clapper was red in the face, and perspiration streamed off his forehead. "I should never have allowed you to come with us." Zeke could see more than just anger in his eyes. There was fear as well.

"I most certainly do know what I'm talking about," she stormed. She was squeezing Hiram's hand, and staring at him. Finally, she continued. "Mr. Law told me all about it before he died."

"Let's calm down just a bit," Zeke said. "It seems there's more to this than persecution or threats because of beliefs. Mrs. Law, just what did your late husband say?"

"She's just a woman, Mr. Hawthorne. She don't know, nothing." He started to get up from the table. "I think it's time for us to return."

"Sit down, Clapper," Hiram said. He looked into Gloria's eyes, which were the color of green-blue water cascading from a falls, and wanted to talk about things not related to this problem he was facing. "Mrs. Law, what did your husband tell you?"

"Before Mr. Clapper, Mr. Sorenson, and my husband went to file on our land, they were approached by another man who offered them what Mr. Law called an opportunity."

"Be quiet!" Clapper was furious and it was Tobin who forced him into his seat.

"I've not heard any of this," Tobin said. "Continue, Gloria, please."

"This man's name is Pender... Julius Pender, Mr. Law said. Mr. Pender came to Mr. Clapper to adjust his filing request to incorporate where those two streams come together. He also said that if he could, Mr. Pender would finance the building of a gristmill. Our initial filing was more to the east, Mr. Law said."

"Why weren't we told about any of this?" Gerald Tobin asked. "We've never been involved in any kind of business, Clapper. We believe in peace and you've always preached that it's business that brings conflict.

"Now, we're in the middle of serious conflict because you've gotten us involved in more than just business. I fear that you've now involved us in politics, and dirty politics at that. You would do well to answer now, Clapper."

Tobin was a large, robust man who had felled the trees to build the houses, and who forged the iron to build the plows, and who nursed the livestock when they needed it.

Hiram could see Tobin flexing the muscles in his shoulders, and wondered if the big man would smack Johnny Clapper right at the table. "I think this, so-called, persecution we've been led to believe, isn't quite what you've said it is, Mr. Clapper."

Hiram was well aware that many eyes had noticed he was still holding hands with Gloria Law.

He did not let go of that hand and continued. "If this is a business deal that's gone bad, you've come to the wrong people to help you. Am I to believe that someone representing George Belknap came to you to file on this section? If that's the case," Hiram said, "Why is Belknap's guard dog, North, fighting you?"

"Because, Hiram," Gloria said, "Mr. Law told me that Mr. Clapper and Mr. Sorenson were going to build the mill and cut Mr. Belknap out of the deal." She gave Hiram a solid squeeze and did not let go. "Our people are being lied to everyday. We're not being persecuted."

Tobin sat across the table from Clapper, glaring anger flashing from his dark eyes. "You've lied to us, Clapper. What more have you done? Have you spent our money on some wild venture? You would be wise to answer my questions before I reach across this table and break your neck."

"No need for that, Mr. Tobin," Zeke said. "There's no need for more violence. One man is dead and others may have been injured because of all this, but to continue the violence would be against what you say you believe in, Mr. Tobin."

Tobin shook his head, then got control of himself and nodded, giving Zeke the slightest smile.

"I wouldn't really do that," he said, nodding again. "Thank you, Gloria, for telling us this. Mr. Hawthorne, we appreciate you meeting with us. The situation is at least understood now, because we met. I'll escort Clapper back to Eugene and we'll hold a meeting and decide what to do."

Tobin looked across the table at Gloria Law. "Is this why you were so adamant about coming to this meeting? You planned the whole time to tell your story to someone you knew would listen?"

Gloria nodded, her head lowered a bit, still holding fiercely to Hiram's hand. "I couldn't tell anyone in our group what Mr. Law told me," she whispered. "Mr. Clapper would have me beaten or worse. Thank you for standing up for me and allowing me to come and tell the story."

Clapper was incensed, jumping to his feet. "You'll do no such thing, Tobin. This is my group, I make the decisions. If you don't like my decisions, leave. Take nothing with you, give up your property rights, and leave." He started to walk out the door and Zeke grabbed him by his coat collar and jerked him back. Clapper was slammed back into his chair.

"No, Clapper. Laws have been broken- by you, by Marshal North, and by Belknap. I think it's time that Judge Brown hears about these problems. Hiram, would you run and see if the good district judge would like to hear about this little problem of ours?"

"I'm on my way," Hi said, jumping to his feet. Gloria got up and walked out the door with him. All eyes were on the two, and Zeke's had a glowing smile attached to his gaze. Clapper was struggling to get up and away from Zeke, but Tobin walked around the table and put a big hand on his shoulder. His fingers drove deep into the man's muscles, and Clapper slowly sank back down in obvious pain.

"We'll just sit quietly and wait for Judge Brown," Zeke smiled, retaking his seat.

"How far is it to the courthouse, Hiram?" Gloria asked, keeping a vice-like hold on Hiram's hand as they walked from the hotel. "Thank you for being here. There are so many things I want to tell you. Will we have time?" The tears had stopped and were drying on her cheeks, but her lips were quivering. "I'm afraid, Hiram."

"We'll have as much time as it takes," he smiled. *She said she's afraid and she just stood up and braced Johnny Clapper. I doubt this lovely creature is afraid of anything in the world.* "I've wanted to come south and visit, but it would have been wrong, you being married and all."

"That's what I want to tell you, Hi. I'm not married, never have been. Mr. Law and I were never married, never lived together as man and wife. I'm Gloria Nesbitt and when my parents were killed in a fire, Mr. Law took me in. We were friends and that's all we were.

"Johnny Clapper never knew that. He and Mr. Law formed this group to come to Oregon to make money. Only Mr. Law and Mr. Clapper knew that. Mr. Sorenson became an active partner later. I didn't know that until Mr. Law told me just before he died." She took a long breath, gave a sidelong glance at Hiram and continued.

"Mr. Clapper and Mr. Law created this Church of Eternal Love to make money. It is not a religious sect, it's a corporation. Those that joined were never made aware of that. They gave Clapper all their money and swore allegiance to him. The entire program is a fraud."

Hiram's heart was racing millions of beats per minute

as they slowly strolled down the street toward the court-house. "I'm a free woman, Hiram, and Mr. Clapper knows that now. I won't be going back to Eugene."

"No, Gloria, you won't," Hiram said. The smile lit the street far more than gas lamps ever could. He felt her fingers tighten even more.


"WELL, this is a bit of a pickle, isn't it?" Judge Virgil Brown coughed, looked about the room, and slowly sat down. "This is the kind of conspiratorial nonsense that tends to keep people like me awake at night. I don't like to be kept awake at night," he growled.

His long hair, hanging in waves shook with his anger, his eyes glared at Johnny Clapper, and he reached into an inside pocket of his frock coat for a cigar. "More than one business had been created by way of a lie or two, but I believe I'm seeing out and out fraud. Not just between businessmen but including the feckless souls looking for a religious experience."

He got the cigar smoking much like Moose Travis's, Rumely steam engine, and shook his shaggy old head. With a wry grin aimed at Zeke, the judge continued.

"There's only one answer to this and that's to have everyone involved arrested." It wasn't clear whether the judge was making a small ironic joke or was being dead serious.

Brown loved the law. He had law books shipped around the horn from the east coast regularly, and had several rooms of his home filled with book shelves over-flowing with tomes. "Most irregular. Every single person or group involved appears to have committed a crime," he chuckled, nodding vigorously to Zeke. "What have you brought me, Zeke Hawthorne? A swarm of bees and you want me to sort them out?"

Brown looked around the table. "Where are those two, young people? Hiram! Get in here." Hiram and Gloria were sitting on a couch in the hotel lobby, still holding hands, and talking a million miles an hour.

"Coming, Judge," Hi said, getting to his feet. He slipped into the parlor, Gloria at his side.

"You two skedaddle down to the sheriff's office and send Fred Sharp up here. Hurry," he said, waving the two back out the door.

"We'll make our plans, Gloria, while we fetch the sheriff. I have a thousand things to tell you about me, about this huge family I'm a part of, and an equal thousand things to promise you for our future."

He blushed, stammered, and continued. "That is, if you'll even consider having me in your life, forever." Her only response sent his heart into a reckless pounding when she simply squeezed his hand even harder and sighed a soft yes.

"In the meantime, Mr. Clapper," Judge Brown continued, glaring at the man. "I'm asking you not to move before Sharp gets here. You'll see to that, Hawthorne?" Zeke nodded, still smiling as he watched Hi and Gloria, holding hands, walking out of the hotel.

"Until we get this figured out, we'll just sit quietly," Judge Brown said. He pulled a flask from an inside pocket of his elegant frock coat, took a healthy swig and offered it to Zeke.

Zeke nodded with a smile. "Thank you, Judge." Between finding out that Clapper was a complete fraud, knowing the election was just around the corner and that he should be campaigning, and now, his son is acting like a puppy in love, Zeke could only smile and take the offered flask.

*I wonder what on earth is going on between Hiram and Gloria?* They had been holding hands since this discussion began, and in the last half hour seem to have gotten even closer. *I think Gloria knows more than she's let on. Has she passed that on to Hiram or is she leading him into something? Please be careful, son. She's a very recent widow and still in mourning.*

"Are you going to hold Mr. Clapper, your honor?" Gerald Tobin had a worried look on his face. "No one back home knows anything about any of this. What if that Mr. Belknap or the marshal, decides to seek revenge? I'm worried about our people."

"I think you should be," Brown said. "That's why I've asked for the sheriff. I'll authorize him to extend his jurisdiction south to include the Eugene area, and he will in turn arrest Marshal North and George Belknap. You and your people, including the lovely young lady, will be called on to testify."

Brown looked over at Johnny Clapper and shook his head. "Your best move right now, Mr. Clapper, is to find the best attorney in the territory, because you're gonna need one."

"WHAT AM I going to do, Hiram? I can't go back there. I don't belong, never did. I was there only because of Mr. Law. You've helped everyway since I first saw you, and now, I'm begging for help." Her eyes, still the lightest color of blue he'd ever seen, were sad, and overflowing.

"I don't want you to go back, Gloria. My father will have Clapper's problems under control before the end of the day and we'll have a talk with him about this. Everyone believes you were married to Law and it would be unseemly in their eyes for us to do anything.

"I would like you to come home with us and for you and me to work toward being husband and wife. I have my own home, but you could live with my parents. Mama would cover you with more love than you've ever known."

"No, Hiram," she whispered. "You have already done that." She wiped away her tears, smiling and crying at the same time. "I know what you're saying, trying to protect my reputation, but the only people in the world that think I was married are those few in the group.

"If you ask, Mr. Hawthorne, sir, I will answer."

There was no hesitation and Hiram stopped them right in the middle of the boardwalk that led to the sheriff's office. "My dear Gloria Nesbitt, I find that I will not be able to live my life out without the presence of a loving beautiful wife. I offer my love, my life, and my soul, for you to keep forever. Will you marry me?"

The two stood in the middle of the boardwalk holding each other, rocking back and forth in broad daylight. Gloria was bawling like a baby and more than one resident of Salem wondered if they shouldn't intervene in some way. Finally, Hiram eased them apart and took the last two steps to the sheriff's office.

SHERIFF FRED SHARP couldn't make sense out of what

Hiram told him and it took some strong arguing to get him to come to the Salem Hotel and meet with the judge. "Judge Brown is a demanding man, Hiram, and I'm not his little puppy dog to run and fetch every time he says so." He grabbed his hat and winter coat and trudged out the door. "Why would I care if somebody wants to build a gristmill near Eugene? All right, let's go."

Judge Virgil Brown didn't mince words as he explained what Clapper and company had attempted in Eugene and the complicity of Belknap and Marshal North. I'm appointing you, temporary marshal, Fred. I know you can't be here and there at the same time, so name a chief deputy marshal, probably your own man here, and send him down there.

"Everything we do for the next several months is going to be temporary anyway," he continued. "After the election and we become a state, then all the new laws will have to take effect. All the offices and positions will need to be filled. You got a problem with any of that, Sharp? No? Good. How about you, Hawthorne? Good." Judge Brown didn't mince words.

Sheriff Sharp took Clapper into custody, put the irons on, and marched him toward the jail, muttering the entire time. "Just a damned puppy dog. Sure, Judge, I'll take over the marshal's job in Eugene, too. What the hell, why not?"

Luckily, the muttering was under his breath and Brown didn't hear any of it.

GLORIA NESBITT STOOD at the table after Sheriff Sharp had put Johnny Clapper under arrest, but before anyone left the hotel, and told her story. There were tears cascading down her cheeks when she finished. "I had no relatives, I was fifteen years old, and Mr. Law took me in. Not as his wife but as a girl in trouble, and saved me from a horrible life. When Clapper made him the offer on his western adventure, Law said it might be best if everyone thought I was his wife."

"That's an amazing story, Gloria," Judge Brown said. "This entire situation is amazing. You couldn't possibly have been involved in any of the antics perpetrated by Clapper and the rest, so you're free to do whatever you choose."

"Let's find a quiet little café and have some fried clams," Zeke said as everyone filed out of the hotel. "This has been an amazing day and I'm not sure I've caught up with everything that's taken place." The three were still chuckling when they found a table at Irene's, near the river and ordered baskets of fried clams. Zeke and Hiram had cold beer and Gloria had coffee.

"I'll send for your belongings," Zeke said, "and you'll become a part of this family very quickly." Zeke gave her a warm smile and patted her on the shoulder. "I've got to get back on the campaign trail, Hi. The election is just a couple of weeks away, and the session will get underway a few weeks after that."

"I'd like it very much if Gloria could live in your big house until we are able to get married. I think Grandpa would like it if we got married during the Christmas party, don't you?"

Zeke had some beer dripping out his nose, went into a coughing fit, and it was several long minutes before he could get any kind of an answer out. "Travis will think he's dead and gone to heaven if you ask him," Zeke finally sputtered. "I don't know if the farm will survive, though. I think if might be best if you give that a lot more thought before you make a decision." The rest of their afternoon meal was much quieter.

"There isn't enough time in a day or a year to get my work done. How well did we do with our crops?" Zeke asked, changing the subject to one he hoped he could control.

The conversation went on for about another hour and the three mounted up and made the long ride back to the farm. Zeke rode in front and Hiram and Gloria rode side-by-side, talking for the entire time.

*I guess that son of mine knew what he was doing building that home of his own. We'll have another one of Travis's grand wedding parties but I sure hope it isn't right along with one of his grand Christmas parties, I guess.*

## 23

THE DATE FOR THE GENERAL ELECTION, NOVEMBER 9, 1857, was approaching fast, and debate over the issue of Oregon statehood was at a fever pitch in every community. The issue of Oregon not being admitted as a slave state was one hot topic and the issue of exclusion of negroes and those of mixed negro blood was equally discussed. Many were still demanding that Indians and mixed-race Indians be included in the exclusion law.

"Here's something you need to accept, Zeke," Roland Sullivan said at the kitchen table one day. "Those along the eastern Columbia River have this continuing hatred and fear of Indians. They would vote for statehood in a minute if the exclusion act also included Indians."

"So, the missionaries brought disease that almost wiped out the tribe," Zeke responded. "Later, the tribe retaliates believing they were poisoned, and wipe out the missionaries, and we're supposed to be ignorant enough to justify condemning all Indians for this?"

"No, Zeke, not all of us. What I'm saying, though, the

people along the river are not fully satisfied with the new constitution. The vote, my friend, is going to be close, and that is one of the reasons. It's not being helped as the wagon trains pass through and talk about the Indian problems they've had most recently along the Snake River. The Shoshone, Bannock and Paiutes have been raising all kinds of hell."

"I suppose it would have been nicer if all humans were the same color," Zeke said, "but the irony of that is, we would then condemn each other because of eye color or hair color or some other damn difference. That's what it is, Sully. We fear those who are different, and fear breeds hate and contempt."

There were many arguments for and against statehood, some discussed openly, others whispered because of fear of retaliation. What were the benefits of statehood? Would the average citizen even recognize a difference between Oregon as a territory and Oregon as a state? Would the army pay more attention to the building Indian problems if Oregon were a state? How would this affect law enforcement and the judicial system? Zeke entertained those questions at every rally he attended up and down the Willamette River.

Emphasizing economics helped bring most of the business community to favor statehood. The issue of slavery simply wouldn't go away. So many of the immigrants arriving within the last fifteen years, from the end of the fur trade years, were from Missouri, Virginia, New Orleans, and Texas, that the issue was still viable despite the fact it was not included in the constitution they would be voting on.

"I'm very tired, Sarah," Zeke said one night, long after

supper. He had been gone three days, made five meetings, and had to be back on the road in the morning. "Only a few days to go, sweet lady, and I'm never leaving this porch ever again." He chuckled and took a sip of brandy. Sarah stood behind him kneading his shoulders, smiling, watching an autumn storm sprinkle welcome rain onto their farm.

She spent countless hours worrying about Zeke's health since that terrible beating he took in Eugene. Because he wouldn't let up, and continued at a pace that would tire a buffalo, in her words, he wasn't healing properly, was always tired, even cranky from time to time. She did everything in her power to slow him down, force him to rest, to get well and most important, spend more time with her.

Evenings like this, just the two of them, sitting on the porch, watching the sun slip into those western mountains, were pure joy. "I think I'll have Hiram build a set of chains that I can attach to your legs and then attach the other end to the porch railings, Sharp Knife. That will keep you right here on this porch with me." They laughed and he gave her a strong hug and murmured in her ear. She was giggling like a little girl, continuing their conversation.

"Hiram and Gloria are making some wonderful plans for Hiram's big new home. They want to get married before the spring planting. Do you know what he said?"

"No, tell me. I know it'll be good and I need some good thoughts right now."

"He said if they get married in the early spring it will be too muddy and wet for Travis to be able to throw a huge party. Isn't that something?"

"That eldest child of ours amazes me every day," Zeke said. "Too muddy for a party. Better not tell Travis, that'll just goad him on," he laughed. "I'm glad this is all working out for those two. Hiram's heart must be four times larger than the rest of ours. He seemed to see right through old man Law's situation with Gloria but didn't know the details. He knew from the minute he met her that something was wrong."

"She's an amazing woman, despite her young age, Zeke. She was almost killed in the fire that killed her parents. She tried to save her mother and her dress was in flames when they pulled her free. She was very lucky to survive." She sat back in her chair, looking deep in Zeke's eyes and chuckled.

"Next year at this same time, Ezekiel Hawthorne, Sharp Knife, we could very well be grandparents."

"My God!" Was all the man could get out before her chuckles turned to laughter and both of them laughed long and hard for several moments. "I better have another brandy, dear heart. I hope we can spend a hundred years or so, sitting on this porch talking about our family." His spirits were dramatically lifted after their conversation.

"There's more, Zeke. We're gonna have another one, too." He just sat there, grinning like a ten-year-old boy, not saying a word. It was much later that night when everything she'd said, actually hit him.

"RIGHT IN THE middle of the biggest election this state will face in a lifetime, we have good old George Belknap being arrested and claiming the charges stemming from his attempts at fraud were perpetrated by me and Judge

Brown. Hiram is planning to get married come spring and Travis thinks that's more important than the election, and now, right in the middle of all this, you tell me I will be a father again come the summer heat. My cup runneth over, Sarah Hawthorne."

"I'm not worried about Mr. Belknap, or the election, or the marriage, Mr. Hawthorne," she said. "I'm worried about you. You haven't been at full strength ever since you took that horrible beating in Eugene. You need a long rest, Sharp Knife."

"The election is next week, we'll have a longer than usual legislative session because of it, but when that's over, I'll get my rest. No more earth shattering issues for this old Missouri farmer, my Shoshone bride. You'll get so tired of finding me sitting and resting at that kitchen table of ours, you'll demand that I plant even more crops."

"Where are you going tomorrow that's so important? Why can't someone else do it? Why do you always have to be the one to do all these things?" The questions had been asked before, and answered, but never to Sarah's satisfaction. "Yes, oh mighty husband of mine, I know," she laughed. "Because you can."

She poured him another snifter of brandy and curled up on his lap. He wrapped his old buffalo robe coat around the two of them. "Yup," he said, holding her tight. "I never saw any of this coming that day I walked into your school house at Fort Bridger and asked about books. The twins are riding the mules and pestering the daylights out of Hiram, and he loves it, little Travis is walking and talking, and now we're gonna have another one around here," he paused, smiling gently.

"That's why I'm doing all this, sweet lady. I'll be going

up to Joshua Peterson's place, and he and I will ride through the valley talking with all the farms and ranches along the way. After this trip, I'll be home until the legislature convenes in December."

"I wish the Peterson's lived a little closer. I really like his wife. Edith's a fighter, Zeke. She'd make a good Shoshone." They laughed and talked for another half hour or so and finally came inside, banked the fires, and slipped into bed, cuddling like a couple of young people who had just found each other.

"WELL, Joshua, it's been a good trip. I think we've just about talked ourselves out of words," Zeke joshed. "Are you folks still going to run your trap lines this winter?"

"We've been doing it for so many years, it would feel wrong not to. Most people want a mild winter and we hope for a cold and bitter one," he laughed. "The foxes, wolves, coyotes, and lynx have the most wonderful fur when it's miserable for humans.

"How about you folks? What do you do to pass the time in the long winters?"

"Mend everything we broke during planting and harvest," Zeke laughed. "Hiram is getting very good with his wood working and we've been taking orders for furniture and I still do a lot of iron work during the winter." He noticed Joshua looking off in the distance. "What do you see, old man?"

"Is that Slim Hastings riding toward us? Looks to be in a hurry."

The marshal waved at the two while he was still some way off and rode up to them at a lope. "Glad to see the two of you," he said. "That fool Flowers is up to no good and I need some help."

"I hope this level of chaos comes to an end soon," Zeke snarled. "What's Flowers up to? Belknap's in jail, so he might not be behind this."

"He has nine men ready to ride with him and he's going to go to every polling place on the ninth and terrorize the voters. Anyways, that's what the word is. I went to talk to him this morning and he took a shot at me before I got a word out. I need to put together a posse and stop this nonsense."

"That man's been a fool and a problem from the day he came out of the mountains and settled on that land of his," Peterson said. "He shoots first and doesn't care. Anarchist, that's what he is. He was against Oregon becoming a territory, too. Said this was open country and it didn't need laws and rules. He's trouble, Zeke. Dangerous trouble."

"What he's done now is called- attempted murder of a law officer," Slim Hastings growled.

"Let's do this, then," Zeke said. "Joshua, you ride through the farms and ranches to the north, I'll ride through the south, and we'll meet with you, Slim, at O'Brien's place early tomorrow. We'll stop this before it gets started. You weren't hit?"

"No, but I heard the bullet sing as it went by. Not a friendly sound. I'll go find Silas Williams while you boys round up the others. We could use a beat up old Texas Ranger on our side. Tomorrow morning then," he said, waving as he rode off at a strong trot.

"Glad we hired that man," Peterson said. "See you in the morning, Zeke," and he turned his horse to trot north along the Willamette River Road. Zeke rode south toward Mike O'Brien's ranch to gather that big man and his two boys. He already knew that with his four hired hands and Hiram, just his little party would outnumber Flowers' gang of troublemakers.

*They aren't troublemakers, old man. They are plain and simple outlaws and I won't have this election jeopardized by outlaws.*

---

## 24

IT WAS A LARGE CROWD SITTING THEIR MOUNTS IN front of Marshal Slim Hastings' little office just off the O'Brien ranch. Zeke had the Saunders boys, the Stockbridge boys, and Hiram with him. Mike O'Brian had his two boys and three of his cowhands with him, Joshua Peterson brought Amos Johnstone and his two hands, and K.C. Whitman had one hand with him.

"You sure you're up to this, Papa?" Hiram asked. "You've been working awfully hard and your head is still giving you fits."

"I'm fine, son. How about you? You got shot last time something like this came up. You don't have to ride with us if you don't want to."

"I want to, Papa. I'm about to have a family, too, remember? This is my Oregon and there's no room in my Oregon for men like Pete Flowers." Zeke just sat on his horse, a huge smile splashed across his craggy face. He found he couldn't say a word, he was so choked up.

Slim Hastings stepped onto the porch with his new

deputy, Gregory Pilgrim, and Silas Williams standing behind him. "We'll be riding in twos, side-by-side to the Flowers' ranch. When we get there, I'll lead us in. There's twenty of us, so here's my plan. Four squads of five each; I'll lead one squad, Greg here will lead one squad, and Silas Williams will lead one squad. We all have lawman backgrounds. Who will lead the fourth squad? Someone with leadership qualities."

"Gotta be Zeke Hawthorne," Mike O'Brien said. "I'd follow that man to hell if he asked me to." General laughter was followed by nodding of heads, and all eyes were on Zeke. "'Course we wouldn't be havin' this trouble if old Zeke hadn't demanded we become a state." That lightened the mood, but only for a moment.

"When we ride onto the property, let's break into squad formation and spread out wide. There was no discussion of any kind yesterday. As soon as I hit that property, the rifle barked. If we spread wide, ride hard and fast, we should be able to get them bunched up.

"If Flowers is smart, he'll call it off. If not, be prepared for a long fight. There are lots of trees for those men to hide behind, outbuildings to shoot at us from, and a couple of irrigation ditches they could jump in. Check your weapons now, gentlemen, and know where your extra rounds are. Let's ride."

Within minutes, Slim Hastings led twenty men onto the River Road and the five-mile jaunt to Pete Flowers' ranch. Every man knew the danger, tasted the fear, and was ready to fight. Silas Williams rode alongside Hastings. "We're an organized militia, Slim, old son. Just like the old days. Let's remember this first ride of Able Company of the First Oregon Volunteers."

"Sit tall, Captain Williams, and ride proud," Slim Hastings said in the finest Texas drawl he could put together. The two of them were suddenly back to fighting Comanche warriors, chasing immigrants trying to put up fences, and eating Texas dust. "I think Oregon dust tastes just as rotten as Texas dust," Silas laughed.

The dust plume from the twenty riders was seen at the ranch and the word spread quickly that a large mounted group was fast approaching. Pete Flowers walked out onto his porch and watched the men turn off the River Road toward his home. He picked up his rifle in one hand and a telescope in the other.

"It's that damn marshal, bringing the whole valley here," he muttered. He ran to a steel triangle used to call the men to meals, and rang it long and loud. The men, mostly hanging around the bunkhouse, came running.

"You men spread out, but don't shoot unless I do. I counted twenty riders." He saw the seven men he had hired just for something like this. He wondered where the other two were. Each man found something to get behind and had weapons in hand. "These men are riding here to throw me off my own land. They aren't anymore the law than I am. They are hooligans trying to be somebody important. I'm paying you good wages to defend this ranch, and I want this ranch defended. These men are acting illegally, and I want them stopped. Dead."

"Looks like they're spreading out in small groups, boss," one man yelled.

"I see 'em," Flowers snarled. He pulled the big rifle to his shoulder and took a long aim at the lead rider. His finger slowly squeezed the trigger and fire flashed from the muzzle.

"Damn!" Hastings said, almost falling from his horse from the impact as the bullet slammed into his left leg. The thwacking sound of the impact was heard by many of the riders. "Sumbitch, Silas, take command," he said, pulled his horse aside, and slowly fell to the ground, holding his leg. Blood was flowing and he whipped his kerchief off and tried to stem the flow. "Ride boys," he yelled out. "I'll be fine."

The four squads were spread wide, and when Silas Williams gave the signal everyone leapt into a hard gallop, weapons screaming death with every bound. Flowers saw them coming and fired wildly. "Kill them all. Kill them!" he screamed, reloading. No one heard him in the din of gunfire.

Flowers dove to the boards of his porch, bullets whistling just inches from his head, and chewing up wood and glass. He felt splinters of the wood cutting through his shirt and pants, and continued jacking rounds through his rifle.

Zeke brought his group through some tall dry corn, taking considerable fire from one of the irrigation ditches. "Ride right through 'em, men. Ride hard, duck down low, and shoot straight," he yelled, sinking his heels into the sides of his horse. It was a hard charge, withering return fire that slowed quickly as he and his men hung off the sides of their horses, Indian style, firing their weapons.

Men were hit and their screaming was different from the screaming of the attacking horde. Hiram seemed to be floating, his horse was running so hard and fast. He saw the irrigation ditch coming up fast, laid himself low across the neck of his horse and fired one more time before leaping his horse high over the ditch.

The three men in the ditch didn't hold up, and Zeke jumped his horse over the ditch, pulled it up and turned it back quickly, his rifle at the ready. Only one man stood up, hands high, when Zeke dismounted. His two companions were not moving. "Skinny, disarm this fool and hold him while we settle this problem."

Skinny was off his horse in a flash, roughing the man to the ground and tying him up. Hiram rode alongside Zeke as they made their way toward the barn and the large cottonwood trees. Gunfire was slowing considerably.

Silas Williams rode his horse right up onto the veranda style porch on Flowers' home and knocked Pete Flowers onto his back. Williams jumped off his horse like he was a twenty-year-old again, and shoved his old Army revolver into Flowers' face. "It's over, Flowers. Make one little move and your brains will be spread on the ground for the ants and crows."

A bullet passed close to William's ear, he twisted, found his target and dropped the man with a single shot through the middle of his chest. "Damn fool," he snarled. He whipped back around, and in anger smashed the long barrel of his revolver across the head of Flowers. "Call 'em off or die," he screamed.

Before he could, a single gunshot rang out from the barn followed by a loud yelp, and Josh Peterson could be heard using extremely profane language. Zeke ran to the barn to see if the rancher needed help and started laughing hard when he got into the darkened building.

"What in the name of Hannah are you doing?"

"I chased this fool in here," he said, aiming his rifle at a man sprawled in a pile of horse manure. "He slipped and fell right there, firing his pistol on the way down. I was right behind him and stepped on this pitchfork, which whipped up and slapped me in the face. Damn it hurts." He was wiping blood from his forehead and knew he would be sporting black eyes for the next several days.

"Just quit your damn laughing," he tried to snarl and found himself chuckling right along with his friend.

Zeke jerked the filthy man to his feet, but was still laughing as he and Peterson escorted the outlaw out of the barn. "Gotta watch where you're going, old man," he chortled, prodding the outlaw.

Along with Slim Hastings, Flowers and two of his men were wounded, and one man died when a bullet drove wood chips into a man's neck and he bled to death. There were also two men dead in the irrigation ditch. The only other injury was a serious black eye and welt on Peterson's forehead. Williams and O'Brien brought Hastings up to the ranch house.

"Attempted murder of a lawman is a serious crime, Mr. Flowers. I'm pleased to put you under arrest and I'll be even more pleased to see your sorry ass hanging loose and dead." He eased himself into a large armchair on the porch, taking pressure off his wounded leg. "You are mighty lucky that I'm not one to carry a grudge, Mr. Flowers. You shot at me the other day, and you shot me today. Then again," he said, "you might not be so lucky," and he pulled his old hog-leg and it was quick thinking by Silas Williams stepping between the two that kept Flowers alive.

"Let's collect personal information on those dead ones

and get them buried," Silas Williams said. "We'll need to patch up the hurt ones, and probably bring them in in the back of a wagon. We'll put all the bastards in the back of a wagon."

"Somebody's gonna have to keep an eye on this place," Mike O'Brien said. "He's got corralled animals and some in pastures that will need caring for. Jackson, can you take care of these animals until things get straightened out?" Jackson was one of O'Brien's hired help and gave him a nod.

Hiram had a team harnessed and hitched to a wagon, and helped get the wounded on board and comfortable. Hastings sat with his wounded leg wrapped well, holding a shotgun on the rest of the prisoners. "Let's get this show on the road, it's gonna be a long ride."

It was a long and slow ride for the group as they escorted the prisoners all the way to Salem City since Hastings little jail had just one cell. The twenty-five-mile ride took the rest of the day, through the night, and into the next morning before they pulled up in front of the sheriff's office riding along the well-marked River Road. Sheriff Fred Sharp had to put three men in each of the two-man cells he had available.

"Mr. Hawthorne, I'd just as soon you didn't come to town any more. Every time you show up, I have to put more people in jail."

Zeke laughed. "I'll be here in a few weeks for the opening of the legislature, Fred. Better build a new jail." Sobering, he thought, *I hope I never have to bring you another man. I'll be so glad when this election is over. What the hell was going through Flowers' mind to pull such a stupid move? He proclaims his status as an anarchist, but shooting a lawman riding with a posse the size of ours isn't anarchism, it's just stupidity.*

"Before we break up and head back to our homes, I'd like to take just a minute more of your time," Zeke said to the men as they gathered outside the jail. "As farmers and ranchers of the Willamette Valley Farm Protective Association, we have proved the value of forming the association, but we have also proved just how right we were in hiring Slim Hastings to be our Willamette Valley Marshal.

"Slim's already at the hospital so I can't say this right straight in his face. I wish I could look in those Texas eyes of his and say, 'Thank you.' Let's never forget what we did yesterday. God only knows what kinds of problems Pete Flowers would have caused on election day if Hastings hadn't discovered the plot.

"That's all I've got to say, except this. Thank you, each one of you. Thank you," Zeke finished. Hiram was standing right beside him and the large son whacked his father across his shoulders.

"No, Papa. Thank you," he said, and most of the men nodded, smiled, and started to mount up.

"Let's go home, son. I am one tired old farmer."

## 25

---

IT WAS A WAVING, SHOUTING ROLAND SULLIVAN WHO rode up the farm path from the River Road to the Hawthorne's large farmhouse. It was the twelfth of November and there hadn't been any word one way or the other since the election on the ninth. "Looks like Sully's got some good news," Zeke said. Sarah and Gloria joined him on the front porch, hearing the ruckus clear in the kitchen.

"You did it, old man. I'm riding on Oregon state dirt," he shouted, jumping from his fine trotter. "It wasn't as close as we feared. All you fine legislators have to do now is ratify the vote."

"We'll do that," Zeke smiled. "Can you prod congress to finish the process so the president can sign the papers?" He was joking, but also worried about how long the rest of the process might take. "Come on in, the coffee's hot and I have a little bottle of Willamette's finest bourbon to give it some flavor."

"Are you feeling any better, Zeke? Between your heavy

work load, getting the stuffing whipped out of you, and then getting in a gunfight of all things, you have a lot of people worried."

"I've been keeping him as quiet as I can," Sarah said. "He thinks he's fine, but he's not. He's worn down to the bone, Mr. Sullivan."

"That beating he took in Eugene is behind most of the problems, Sarah. A whack on the head from a hard, oak club isn't something to sniffle at." Sullivan looked over at Zeke and continued. "You suffered a concussion, Zeke, and you've been ignoring the consequences.

"If you don't take some time off and let your old head come back to normal, you're gonna find yourself in a big old box heading for a deep hole in the ground. Sometimes, old friend, you just have to let other people lead the trek."

"Mr. Sullivan, you're the best friend a man could have," Zeke said. "We have almost finished what we started. I can't back off now. My God, man. The legislature will meet in one month for our early session. Statehood, Sully! We're not quite through."

"I see," Sullivan said, sitting down across the table from him. He poured each of them a hefty dose of Sullivan's Distillery bourbon in their almost empty coffee cups. "Let me fully understand the situation. There are some twenty thousand people in Oregon right about now, and there is a score involved in legislative matters. Probably five or more fully capable of ramrodding statehood through the coming sessions.

"And you, sir, are the only one that can see to it that it is done properly? I understand," he said, sitting back with a mock satisfied look on his face. Zeke broke out in laughter, slammed his fist on the table, and held his hand out to Sullivan.

"You do have a way with words, my friend. Your point is well made and taken. Sullivan, my dear friend, I have one request. Ride back to Salem City, find John Bradley, and suggest that he take front position on the statehood matter when the session opens. I will stay on my little farm, bother Sarah constantly for the next two weeks, attend the session, and let Travis handle the entire Christmas party by himself."

"I'll hold you to that, Sharp Knife," Sarah laughed.

FALL RAINS BROUGHT the Hawthorne farm to a standstill as far as getting any work done in the fields. By the first week of December most of the family was ready to ship Zeke off to Salem a week or so early for the legislative session. "I'm sure glad you got some rest, Papa," Hiram said one day, hammering some hot iron near the forge. "You're looking much better, good color, and your eyes sparkle more." Hiram smiled and saw Zeke smiling as well. "No more headaches?"

"No headaches, no dizzy spells, and my energy level is excellent, son. Working with you on these furniture orders, and spending time at the forge have made me right with the world."

"Me, too, Papa. What will the process be at the legislature? Will you simply accept the vote or what?"

"The results of the election were sent to Washington immediately, Hi. We'll conduct the last of the territorial business starting on December 6, break for the holidays, and pick up again during the first week of January. Everything is up to Congress and the president now."

"There's no huge problems that are going to get in the way of statehood?" Hiram was smiling, leading his Papa into a corner.

"None at all, son. Why?"

"Suzanne and Joanne and I have decided it's time for you to teach those young ladies how to fish. I have taken the lead on this and built them each proper fishing rods, found reels and line, and they want to know the secrets of fishing."

"You've passed on the parable?" Zeke asked, laughing and taking a friendly poke at Hiram.

"Yup," he said. "Give a man a fish and he eats for a day. Teach a man to fish and he never goes hungry. If you take a peek out the barn doors, you'll see two charming ladies waiting for us."

Hiram had taken the girls fishing several times after the harvest was over and it was his hope that they would get Zeke seriously involved again in fishing. He remembered how Zeke had taught him simply by going fishing as often as possible. "I remember fishing in the Snake River when we were on the road from Bridger to Oregon," he told the girls.

The rest of the day was one disaster following another, accompanied with more laughter than the great Oregon outdoors had heard in a long time. Tangled lines, hooked frocks, stubbed toes, and crying jags when everything failed all at the same time filled the rest of the hours.

Suzanna caught the first fish, a nice trout but stuck herself with the hook trying to take it out, then Joanna fell in the creek and got sopping wet. At first, Zeke was a little exasperated about the little problems, but his sense of humor and deep affection for the twins came to the surface quickly.

"You are feeling better, Papa," Hiram said more than once. The steelhead run had started and Zeke caught a beauty of about seven pounds or so.

Two laughing men with two giggling little girls in tow clambered onto the weather porch late in the afternoon. "Well, now, I proclaim this to be a fine day, indeed," Zeke said, hanging his rod and reel on hooks. "Looks to me like there are more than enough fish to feed this family."

Joanne was squealing in happiness, holding two very nice trout, almost more than she could lift. Suzanne held her one trout, equally big, and Hiram had three, each with holes in their sides made by his arrows. "Why can't you catch fish like we can, Papa?" Joanne was holding up her fish for Papa to see.

"I guess I just need to practice more." He was laughing, thinking she saw numbers of fish while his one steelhead outweighed all their fish combined. "Maybe we ought to do this more often, eh?"

It was a loud, fish-smelling bunch that stormed the kitchen, to Sarah's delight. "Fresh trout for supper tonight," she said.

"Can we go again, Papa?" Suzann was going to be the fisherman among the ladies and jumped up and down when Zeke said something about tomorrow morning when the fish were looking for breakfast.

"You've created a monster," Sarah laughed.

DECEMBER SIXTH WAS a cold and snowy day in Salem City,

but the atmosphere in the capitol was anything but cold. The gentlemen of the Territorial Legislature gathered for their last session. "I've said it before and I'll say it again," Zeke said. "These are my last days in politics. No more. I'm satisfied with the work we've done, and will let others lead the way through the early years of statehood."

The first day's session had been purely ceremonial and he was enjoying supper with Roland Sullivan and OB Sinclair from the bank. "I was talking with Ted Chapman yesterday and he plans to seek the office of state treasurer. He'd be good in that chair, I think."

"You'll miss it, Zeke," Sinclair said. "It's in your blood now."

"No, on many counts, OB. My farm has grown and needs me. My family is still growing and needs me. I'm glad I contributed to this, but Oregon doesn't need me. She will need many men and women and they will flock to her bosom."

There was work to do in the legislative halls and for ten days they wrapped up as much territorial work as possible. They couldn't make a new law since it would be nullified as soon as the president signed the statehood papers, and for some that was a frustration. There were some that disdained the title representative and were enthralled when they were called lawmakers.

"We got as much done as possible," Zeke said. He and Sarah were enjoying a late morning cup of coffee in their warm kitchen. "When we go back after the holidays, we'll put the final dots and marks to Oregon Territory." He had a satisfied smile, took a sip of coffee, and looked deep into her eyes. "I have something I want to talk to you about, Sarah. Something very special that Travis and I have put together." During the session, he and Travis had their mid-day meals together often, usually somewhere near the docks.

BARBARA AND ANGUS were in one fully loaded hay wagon drawn by four mules. Moose and Clemmie were riding their horses, and Travis and Elaine were in another fully loaded wagon, also drawn by four mules. They were assembled in front of the Salem Trading Post. "We didn't have this much stuff with us when we left Fort Bridger," Moose laughed. "You planned this expedition, Papa, but if we don't get these wagons moving we won't be at Zeke's until tomorrow some time."

Elaine gave Travis a little wink and nudge. "Go on, Travis. Tell them. You and Zeke put this together and kept most of us in the dark. Tell him."

The big mountain man took a second, cleared his throat for effect, and said, "Yup, I did plan this so that we could enjoy a little of what we used to take for granted. Along our journey today we'll find a wilderness camp set up and waiting for us about eight miles up the road. Zeke and his family will have a fire going, we'll circle the wagons, and remember that wonderful trip we had coming from the Green River country.

"Now, on that old trail, making eight miles was a full day's work, but with the fine roads we have now, in this glorious state of Oregon, those eight miles will slip under our wheels in nothing flat. Let's roll 'em, folks. Hyah!" he hollered at his mules, flicking the wheelers with his whip.

V

---

# BOOK FOURTEEN: ALL JOURNEYS HAVE BEGINNINGS AND ENDINGS

---

## 26

"I'VE NEVER HAD A BETTER CHRISTMAS HOLIDAY, ever," Zeke said. He and Sarah were sitting on buffalo robes, wrapped in point blankets, near a hot burning fire, watching a cold winter's night sky. Stars were sparkling as ice crystals and they could hear a slight breeze move through brittle leaves that hadn't fallen yet. "Our entire family, together in a friendly camp, wagons keeping us safe from attack, animals foraging wild grasses, and my beautiful wife nestled in my arms. Nothing could best this."

"For a tough old frontiersman, legislator, and tamer of the land, you're a romantic at heart, Sharp Knife. Your hands are soft as down when you hold me, and strike like iron when you defend me. No more crusades, Zeke. Promise. No more windmills challenging your right-eousness."

"No more crusades, my little Hummingbird, I promise. We even surprised Hiram with this wild adventure, and that's hard to do. We have two boys and two girls. What do you think our new baby will be, boy or girl?"

"Alive and well is all I ever ask for. Tomorrow, and we've been here two days already, is Christmas, and then we have to go back home in two days. We need to build a Shoshone wigwam, Zeke, where we can run away from the world from time to time, like this. Sit under the stars, eat fire-cooked meat, and make love anytime we feel like it."

"And you call me a romantic?" He wrapped the blankets a little tighter and held her close, smelling her lustrous hair, nibbling a little at her neck, and enjoying her warmth.

TRAVIS and his group pulled off the main road, two days earlier, and came onto a seldom-used trail that led east across the valley, slowly climbing into the mountains. "Feels like coming out of Oregon City, doesn't it?" he hollered at Moose.

"As long as we don't get hit by a blizzard, it's okay with me," Moose shouted back. The trail went into the foothills a solid five miles, skirted a bluff that led them into the deep forest for another mile and came up on two wagons and four canvas tents set around a large central fire pit. Smaller pits were off to the sides of the large one.

"Hello, the camp," Travis bellowed, leading his group in.

"Welcome to the Travis-Hawthorne holiday camp," Zeke howled back at the man. "Circle 'em up, Travis, and light a spell."

"What a wonderful thing you've done, Papa," Barbara

said, dancing off the wagon. "These huge trees, the frosty air, I'm back home at Green River. Listen to me, I sound like Moose, saying back home like that. This is my home now. I'm in the Oregon mountains, and I'm in love."

"Does she ever slow down?" Gloria asked Hiram as they walked up to the Travis wagons. "Such a beautiful girl, and so full of life. This is the girl you told me about? That you vowed to marry before you met me?" She was teasing and enjoying the camaraderie of this wonderful family she was becoming part of.

"I fell in love with Barbara the first minute I met her. And, then dear girl, I met you. We all came here in one group several years ago, and every night on the Oregon Trail, it was like this. The difference being, we were attacked more than once on our stops."

Travis, Moose, and Angus set up the Travis tents and got the animals moved onto good grass. Hiram and Zeke cut wood for the fires when they arrived, so that chore was already done. The sun was easing its way into the far mountains to the west, the chill was felt immediately, and Elaine and Sarah built up the fires and started on the camp's first supper.

"I propose that we eat buffalo," Sarah said.

"I agree," Elaine said. "Have our warrior husbands provided buffalo for their women?"

"Shoshone women are never satisfied, Angus. Remember that," Barbara squealed. She strode over to stand with her mother and sister, pretending to glare at the men. Moose walked over to Travis's wagon and climbed into the seat.

"You didn't tell them, Papa? For your information, ladies, my good friend Slick Snyder just got back from a trip to Fort Boise and brought me fifty pounds of smoke cured buffalo straight out of the Bitterroots." He reached under the seat and hefted three packages and handed them down to Travis.

"And, you might remember, Clemmie and I came back with packs loaded with smoked buffalo. So, the warriors of the Travis Clan honor their women with good meat."

Hiram looked into Gloria's face. "Remember this, lovely lady. A Shoshone warrior will always provide for his woman."

"So, Moose, was your trip into the Rockies a good one?" Zeke had the fire built up and the family gathered around to hear the story.

"Broken Hand wasn't there, but he sent notes for me, and Buck O'Keefe was there. We had some fine discussions and I remembered what you said, Zeke. I warned them about how the army could not speak for congress, that a treaty wasn't the word of the United States until congress ratified it.

"It was strange to the people, but I think I made the point. The letters from Fitsgerald all said about the same thing, and Buck agreed with what I was saying, so the points were made."

"Was anything completed? Is there a treaty of some kind?" Travis knew just how little a treaty really meant.

"The tribe will work closely with the army to protect the Oregon Trail through that section. Will keep the Crow, Flatheads, Blackfeet, and Sioux out as much as possible. The government wants the Shoshone to be moved to near the Yellowstone, and that would be a disaster.

"Broken Hand promised to fight that proposal as hard

as possible. That is very much up in the air. I'm glad I made the trip, Zeke. I'm also glad I made the decision to remain in Oregon, run my mill, love my wife, and raise many children."

There was laughter and gaiety way into the dark night, a warm fire, good blankets and robes, and love in ample quantity. Travis and Elaine were the first to make their way from the fire, then Barbara and Angus. Moose and Clemmie wandered off a little later, and Zeke took Sarah by the hand, urging her to her feet.

"I think the young ones want to stay up just a little longer," he said. She giggled some, tweaked Zeke's ear, and they headed for their tent. "When Travis came to me with this idea, I wasn't sure it would really work, but he does know how to throw a party."

"I HAVEN'T HAD a family since my parents were killed in that fire, Hi. And even then, it was just the three of us. My folks didn't have any close relatives and I don't have any brothers or sisters. Suzanne and Joanne are already calling me Aunt Gloria, and little Travis wants to crawl in my lap and hug me.

"It's all so new and I love it. I was really scared coming across the plains, and those huge mountains and horrible rivers. I knew I was going to die that night the outlaws attacked us. You and your family came in from Fort Bridger and you weren't afraid?"

"I got scared more than once on that trip," Hiram said. "We were attacked several times, and crossing the Snake River got really scary. With Moose, Travis, and most of all, my Papa, we fought our way here. Suzanne and Joanne were born on the trail, did you know that?"

"My God," Gloria said. "That must have been horrible for your mother."

"If you ask mama she'll tell you it was wonderful. Tomorrow's Christmas, Gloria. I was going to wait until then to give you this, but I can't." He got up and walked to his tent and brought out a small package. "I started on this right after the outlaw attack and finished it last week."

"My goodness, Hiram. Wrapped in buckskin and tied with leather strings? This is impressive by itself." She untied the bow and slowly unwrapped the buckskin. "Oh, my. You did this? Yourself? Oh, my," she said again. "It's beautiful, Hiram."

She held up the drawing, set in an intricate and finely carved frame, of herself, dressed as a frontier lady with a farmstead background. "It's so real. I feel like I could reach out and touch myself or have a conversation. You're an amazing man, Hi. I love you more than I've ever loved anyone."

They sat by the fire, wanted to share a tent and knew they couldn't, and finally Hiram walked her to her tent. "Merry Christmas," he said, and they held each other, kissed so softly, and he skedaddled back to his tent before anything could happen.

CHRISTMAS MORNING WAS utter chaos with everyone singing carols, trading gifts, playing with children, and more than anything, telling stories. Moose told about Zeke and his battle with the Crows. Travis reminded the group that he was alive because of Sharp Knife and his killing of the Crow about to take Travis's head off.

Elaine told stories of meeting this bear of a man with his huge voice and wild attitude, and how he put aside his fur trapping days to open a trading post. "He thought that would impress me. He didn't know I was already impressed," she giggled. "He shot an elk one time, more than a mile from our little camp, and brought it in complete, all by himself."

"Yeah," Travis laughed. "And I didn't move for two days after. Look at our children, Elaine. Sarah, Barbara, Moose." He paused and Sarah was sure she saw him wipe away a tear. "Just look what you've done, Elaine. I've just been having a wonderful life running my trading posts, and you've raised three extraordinary children." This time, Sarah did see a tear on his face.

"You Zeke, just look at you. You came stumbling into our little Fort Bridger, tired and hungry, with that madman Johnson, and brought us here to Oregon country. This has been a wonderful life I've had. All our parties on the Green River, the tribe coming to our feasts and dancing, our hunts for winter meat with the Shoshone warriors, and the most wonderful family any man could ever have."

It was very quiet around that camp, even the little children seemed to understand that this was the time for remembering, for understanding just how their many lives have progressed over these many years. In 1851 some were a happy wilderness family, nestled in the Rocky Mountains. By 1852 they were a frontier family in Oregon Territory.

Here it was, the end of 1858 and they were about to be

an American family living in the state of Oregon. "It's just amazing what this life of mine has become," Zeke whispered softly to Sarah. "I haven't heard this kind of quiet from this family, ever," he chuckled. She gave him a gentle poke in the ribs and he gave her a gentle kiss.

"I gave up the fur business because I wasn't very good at it," Travis said, breaking the reverie. "It was far easier to be a trader, with the trappers and with the Indians, than it was slogging through the mud and ice, chasing beaver. I made the right decision," he said. He was lulled by a sound he loved.

Hiram, sitting quietly by the fire, using a log and a heavy stick, was drumming. It was a slow, almost quiet thump, thump, thump at first, but when Travis stopped talking, he raised the volume some and increased the cadence. Elaine was first on her feet, followed immediately by Moose. The dancing quickened when Sarah and Barbara joined in, and then the chanting started.

It didn't take any beckoning and Suzanne and Joanne stepped into the ring, dancing right along with the family. Sarah had taught them well, and they were in perfect harmony with the rest as they joined the chanting.

Travis threw more wood on the fire, getting it blazing high, the drumming got faster and louder, the chanting turned to howls when Moose started, and Hiram, still drumming, howled right along. The pageant lasted well over an hour.

"That felt so good," Elaine said, almost falling onto her buffalo robes. "We'll rest a bit and then dance some more," she panted.

Moose sat down next to Clemmie and slipped his arm around her. "The immigrants coming across the country call this savage," he said. "Look at my mother, absolutely beautiful, and far, far from being a savage. Those people should open their hearts, their ugly minds, to the beauty of the Indian way."

"I am Indian by birth, Moose, but raised as a white American. I feared all Indians, because the white people have been taught to fear them. From the time we made plans to come west, all we talked about were Indian attacks, savages stealing white women, brutal terror.

"Then, I met you. Sumbitch, Moose, you've taught me to be savage," and they laughed, rolled around on the buffalo robes, and watched the rest of the family who seemed to be intent on watching them. "Maybe we should be a little less savage," Clemmie joshed, sitting up straight, and smiling at them all.

"IF SOMEONE HAD ASKED me what my life was going to be, that day back in Missouri while I was packing my mule, I would never in a million years told this story, Sarah. There was no doubt, as I look back on it, that I knew I would die before reaching Oregon Territory. Die crossing that broad plain of which I knew nothing."

"I can't imagine the loss you must have felt. Maybe you wanted to die, Sharp Knife, but you're too brave, too smart, and survived. For that, dear husband, I'm most grateful."

"All I could think of was my desperation in wanting a family and a farm, grieving as if mad. And look at us now," he chuckled. The sun was again challenging those mountains to the west and the Christmas feast was about to start.

A hindquarter of elk was turning on a spit operated by Hiram with help from Joanne. Sage grouse were roasting near some coals in a smaller pit, and corn was roasting near coals near another pit. A large Dutch oven was filled with beans and bacon, and another pot was filled with smoke-cured buffalo, corn, potatoes, green beans, and onions.

"If anyone leaves this camp tonight, saying they're hungry, I'll shoot 'em," Travis boomed.

Hundreds of pounds of food disappeared amidst a thousand stories told as the extended family sat around the fires. Angus Whitell told about his years working on ships that roamed the earth, chasing whales, fighting pirates, and visiting exotic lands. He told about being just a boy when he made his first voyage and how, years later, he jumped ship in Oregon Territory.

"I'm a land-lubber now," he joked. "I'm a Boston-Irisher married to an Oregon Shoshone, and running a lumber mill a hundred miles from the nearest ocean."

The early evening became dark of night, the stories subsided, and gifts were brought out. Most were hand-made, very few store-bought. Dolls and clothing for the girls, wooden horses and tiny moccasins for little Travis, and sweet hard candy for all.

"I spent time away from the fields while you were away, Papa," Hiram said. He handed Zeke a large, twelve-inch long knife. There was a carved bone handle, and it rested in an ornate leather scabbard, beaded and quilled. "For you, Sharp Knife."

"Will you look at that," Travis said. "You've taught that boy right, Zeke. That's one beautiful knife. Elaine lifted the robes a bit and pulled a set of high-laced elk skin moccasins out and handed them to Travis. "Now I know I'm in heaven," he roared.

Barbara walked into her tent and came out with a buckskin jacket, beaded, quilled, and intricately sewn for Angus. "Every well-dressed Boston sailor should have at least one of these," she said. "For your 'going-to-town' days." He handed her a small package and she found a walrus tusk necklace carved with scenes of their growing farm.

It hung on a silver chain and he slipped it around her neck and fastened the clasp. "I learned to do this on a whaling ship when I was just a boy. From whaling ships to hog slop," he laughed. "I have really come up in the world."

"I'm carrying Zeke's present to me and my present to him. Due as summer starts to get hot," she laughed. "What a wonderful Christmas."

"What a wonderful life," Zeke said. "When we left Green River, there were Travis, Elaine, Moose, Barbara, Sarah, Hiram, and I. My goodness, but do we know how to populate a new state. I have nothing but thankfulness for all the powers that be for this wonderful family. Our journey through life is incredible. Merry Christmas to you, and you, and you," he said, pointing to each person still sitting around the fire.

"We wouldn't be here if it weren't for you, Zeke Hawthorne," Travis boomed. "Hiram, do you think some soft chanting and delightful dancing might be in order, about now?"

"I do, grandpa/" He found a good log, some strong sticks, and slowly set a rhythm for the dancing. Elaine was first to her feet, and the others joined, the singing and chanting softly flowing through the deep forest of the state of Oregon.

"What an incredible journey," Zeke whispered.

THE SECOND HALF of the legislative session was underway, following the long break for the holidays. "I don't think any of us really want this session to end," John Bradley quipped. "There will never be another session of the Oregon Territorial Legislature."

They still had work to do, though, waiting for Congress and the president to do their part of the job. The territorial law still had preference, and things like divorce had to be addressed. Only the legislature had the right to grant divorce, and those asking for it had to have an answer before statehood.

It wasn't until the third week of January that the legislature called it a session. "I'm going home to my farm, no longer an assemblyman, and we still don't know if we're really a state in this wonderful union of ours." Zeke was as frustrated as the rest of the legislators, and was having a cold beer with Sullivan.

"What happens now, Zeke? We don't have a legislature, we don't have a governor or judges or lawmen."

"In a way, you're right, Sully, but not completely. Our lawmen will stay in office until the new state government is in office, the same as district judges. But, we no longer have a sitting governor or other territorial officers. When we're officially notified that we really are a state, then we will hold elections for state offices, the counties will have to elect new officials, and we'll have full representation in Congress."

Zeke and Sullivan weren't aware that Oregon was officially admitted to the union on February 14, 1859. Because communications between the east coast and west coast moved at the speed of a mule, it was some months before the word was received. Zeke was sitting at the large kitchen table talking about how the planting had gone when word came.

"Almost everything we planted is well established, Papa," Hiram said, spreading his planting maps across the table. "The corn is doing well as are the beans and hops. Wheat and barley look good, and the potatoes are in." He cocked his head to one side, "Is that a horse I hear?"

They walked quickly to the front porch and watched Roland Sullivan lope up the long trail from River Road. Hiram jogged off the porch and took the reins when he pulled up at the gate. "Morning, Mr. Sullivan. You look to be in a hurry," Hi said.

"I got good news this morning," he said. He got up on the porch quickly and handed Zeke an envelope. It was sent from Washington. "They said every territorial official was getting one of these. I thought it best if I bring this to you, personally."

"Thank you, Sully," Zeke said. He tore the envelope open and read what was inside. "It seems we've been a state since February. Signed, sealed, and delivered," he said. "That is good news, Sullivan. Come on in, the coffee's hot and Mr. Sullivan has supplied some fine Oregon State bourbon straight from his distillery."

"Don't mind if I do, Zeke." Sully was laughing at the way Zeke had put it. "I like that, and yes, I do believe I did supply that fine drink. Wasn't a bribe, though. You were already out of office. Sarah have any of those sweet rolls of hers?"

Hiram came back from putting up Sullivan's horse and joined them at the table. "Just coffee for me," he said, declining the offer of some 'sweetener' for it. "I have barley, oats, wheat, corn, and hops all growing strong, Mr. Sullivan. We'll have your contracts filled and some extra this year, for you."

"That's fine, Hiram. I'm out of a job, you know, so I have to make sure the brewery and distillery are successful." As territorial land commissioner, his job ended with statehood. "With the new constitution, the position is mixed in with other departments, and the elected official will appoint a commissioner.

"Which brings up the second reason I'm here, Mr. Hawthorne, sir."

"Just what would that be, Sully? You're sitting at the table of a fine Oregon farmer, Mr. Sullivan."

Sullivan laughed, sat back in his chair and sipped some well-laced coffee. "Mr. Chapman, Mr. Snyder, Mr. Pritchert, and I would like to discuss the possibility of you making yourself available, that is, to offer yourself up for election to congress. Oregon needs a man like you in Washington."

There was a resounding "No!" but it didn't come from the kitchen table, it came from the nursery where Sarah was attending to little Travis. "Did I make myself clear, Mr. Sullivan? Zeke, tell him."

"The word is no, Sully. That's spelled, capital N, capital O, and pronounced, No!"

"Emphatically taken," Sullivan joshed back. "But you would be good and you know it."

"Virgil Brown won't run for governor but he might jump at being a senator, and Sam Chastain would be a fine representative from this district. There is no way I will take any position that pulls me away from this farm. I may have been a fair to good assemblyman, I'm a journeyman cabinetmaker, I'm a journeyman blacksmith, and first and foremost, I'm a farmer with a wonderful family to take care of.

"That's all I've ever wanted to be, and I'm very satisfied, sir. Thank you for the kind offer, but no."

Skinny Saunders came bursting into the kitchen. "Hurry, Hiram. We've got a problem with one of the dikes."

Hiram followed Skinny out the door quickly, and Zeke stood up. "Don't want to be rude, Sullivan, old man, but as you can see, my farm needs me a lot more than Oregon does. Until next time," and he headed out the door to help with the broken dike.

"He's all yours, Sarah," Sullivan said with a grand smile on his face. "We won't ask again, but I will stop by often, for his observations on life and your wonderful sweet rolls. Take good care of that man."

"He's all mine, Mr. Sullivan, and I plan to take the best care any man has ever had."

# END NOTE

OREGON'S CONSTITUTION from 1858 carried the exclusion law and that wasn't revoked for one hundred years, not until 1958. The Willamette Valley is one of the most productive and richest little areas in the west. Portland is still one of the finest deepwater ports in the west.

# A LOOK AT: NAME'S CORCORAN, TERRENCE CORCORAN

## BY JOHNNY GUNN

Terrence Corcoran carried a badge in Virginia City, Nevada until one day, in a drunken stupor, he shot the sheriff. Now he's returning to the Comstock looking to get his badge back and stumbles into a conspiracy that might put the sheriff, district attorney, and others in jail for a long time. A lovely working girl is brutally murdered, a Hungarian duke wants a Wells Fargo gold shipment, and the sheriff rehires him after first kicking him in a most tender spot. Corcoran was born on the ship bringing his family to this country, ran away to the frontier at an early age and brings his ideas of the old country and knowledge learned of the west to whatever mess he finds himself in. He's carried a badge, found himself in jail, and stands four-square for right, honor, and truth. You gotta love the guy.

*AVAILABLE NOW FROM JOHNNY GUNN AND WOLFPACK PUBLISHING*

## ABOUT THE AUTHOR

Reno, Nevada novelist, Johnny Gunn, is retired from a long career in journalism. He has worked in print, broadcast, and Internet, including a stint as publisher and editor of the Virginia City Legend. These days, Gunn spends most of his time writing novel length fiction, concentrating on the western genre. Or, you can find him down by the Truckee River with a fly rod in hand.

Gunn and his wife, Patty, live on a small hobby farm about twenty miles north of Reno, sharing space with a couple of horses, some meat rabbits, a flock of chickens, and one crazy goat.